The Icarus Diaries

KATE HOYLAND

Published by Cinnamon Press
Meirion House
Glan yr afon
Tanygrisiau
Blaenau Ffestiniog
Gwynedd LL41 3SU
www.cinnamonpress.com

The right of Kate Hoyland to be identified as author of this work has been asserted by her in accordance with the Copyright, Designs and Patent Act, 1988. © 2010 Kate Hoyland. ISBN 978-1-907090-20-2

British Library Cataloguing in Publication Data. A CIP record for this book can be obtained from the British Library

Designed and typeset in Palatino by Cinnamon Press. Cover design by Cottia Fortune-Wood from original artwork, 'Everything frees me' by Elena Ray ©, Agency: dreamstime.com
Printed in Poland
Cinnamon Press is represented in the UK by Inpress Ltd www.inpressbooks.co.uk and in Wales by the Welsh Books Council www.cllc.org.uk.

The Icarus Diaries

Prologue

The whine of a mosquito cuts the thick air. There are other sounds: sighs and whispers, screeches and throaty cries. The sun is gone, and Venus shines alone in a cloud-smudged sky. The day's heat rises from the earth. To replace it, someone has lit a fire.

The fire marks a point in the middle of a clearing around thirty metres across, circled by clumps of creaking bamboo, and palm leaves as broad as umbrellas. Beyond the clearing the vegetation is thick; it traps the weakening light. The whispers come from within.

Two men and a young woman sit close to the flames. Their arms are bare and dirty, their skin burnt by the sun. Humidity settles on them like sweat. A child sleeps, his head resting on the younger man's lap. The second man sits with his head bowed, his white hair falling in disordered curls. Smoke coils around him.

The whine of the mosquito reaches its highest pitch, levels, fades.

A third man, brown skinned, sits with his back to the others. He is chewing on the stump of a dead cigarette. He is facing a low barn raised on stilts, its walls made from a lattice of bamboo, which filters the last of the evening's light, making a pattern of repeating triangles at the man's bare feet. The building, large enough to house three generations of a family, is empty. The man's eyes are shut, and he breathes through his nostrils. He spits out his cigarette and snorts.

The three behind him make no sign that they notice him. They are talking heatedly, arguing in the manner of old friends. They could be a holiday party resting after a day's trek, and drawn into confidences by the intimacy of the fire. But their smiles are fixed and there is a suggestion of strain on their faces.

Crickets start to sing. The air closes in, warm and soupy.

The woman lowers her face, letting her hair – black, severely cut – fall in front of it to mask the tears. The younger man reaches out a hand to her. She does not take it.

7

He spreads his long fingers and observes his fingernails. They are wide and flat, like spatulas, with a line of dirt trapped under each.

He flexes his hand and strikes a piano chord in the dust. Pauses, strikes another.

There is a glimpse of something in the faces of all three. Fear.

They begin to talk, all at once.

'Go on.'

'No. You.'

The younger man draws something in the dirt. His words spill out.

'A circle, with a line through it. Get it? Circle line. Central line. Genius. So simple. Did you know London Underground has its own typeface? Right? Think about it. So, they wanted to make it easy to read, as easy as possible. No distractions. No serifs. I heard it was revolutionary when they did it – a design classic.' He hesitates. His voice loses its tinny excitement. 'Yeah. A classic, when you think about it.'

A pulse beats in his temple.

The woman murmurs, 'Have you ever been lost on the subway?' Her voice is throaty, American.

'Which one?' The man has green eyes. He raises them to her face, studies her.

'Any of them. Doesn't matter.'

He taps his forehead. 'No. I don't think so.'

She sighs. 'See, my theory is, it isn't possible. Once you get one, you get all of them. Whatever the language. Russian or Chinese. Always the same principle.'

'Universal subway systems.'

'Something like that.' She turns away.

The white-haired man clears his throat. He is thin and rangy, with narrow shoulders that creep up to his ears. His eyes are deep set, and he has a thick line scored between his eyebrows.

He coughs. The smoke has made his eyes water. He looks down, and presses two fingers to his forehead just at the point where the line is at its deepest.

He looks at the others. It is visible, the fear bearing down on their shoulders. A line of sweat runs from his forehead to his chin. He wipes it dry with the back of his hand.

A monkey woops. Leaves shiver.

The white-haired man sighs, gathers himself, and throws a question into the waiting air.

'Well. Would you like to know something about me?'

The younger man swallows. Of course,' he says, softly. 'Please.'

'Yeah,' says the woman, looking up sharply. 'We need a story.'

'A story. Yes.'

'All right.' The older man frowns. 'Maybe it will help. I don't know.'

He says this, and then says nothing.

His audience waits. They watch him anxiously; tense lest the moment – the chance of distraction from other thoughts – be lost. They understand that the white-haired man is shy, and that self-disclosure might not come easily to him; but they are tired, and less willing than they might be to accommodate his peculiarities.

The woman groans. 'Speak. Please. I don't know anything about you.'

'Nor I you.'

The green-eyed man says, 'Why should he do anything for you?'

She mutters, 'We need a story. That's all.' She flings a handful of leaves into the fire. They crackle and fizz, sending up a shower of orange sparks. The last of the daylight has gone, and the sparks are vivid against the inky sky. Each of the three inches closer to the fire.

The child stirs and cries out. He clutches at something in the air, his hand opening and closing like an ineffectual claw.

9

The woman hisses. The child breathes raggedly. The adults sit in silence, watching his small chest rise and fall.

The jungle has receded. The fire has expanded. The fourth man has faded from sight.

The older man clears his throat. He wants to speak. He wants to tell the others – something, it hardly matters what, though the thing that hovers most in his mind is a text message he once sent with a recklessness that surprises him still. He wants to tell the others what he wrote, and why he wrote it; and why it still gnaws at him though many months have past. He wants to ask them why – though they cannot possibly know – he didn't receive a reply.

Before he can say anything the woman speaks. Her voice is hushed, barely audible.

She says, 'It's sad, don't you think, how no-one gets letters these days?'

I

April

April McGee received her father's letter on an airless day in June.

The concierge, a languorous woman with beady eyes and thinning hair, squawked at her as she left her apartment block. 'You have letter!'

April stopped. Nobody sent her letters unless they were bills. One glance at the cramped, childish handwriting, and she knew who it was from. She snatched the letter from the concierge's hand and scuttled across the shiny marble floor to the exit, her shadow following her.

She didn't head straight for the main road but turned into an alley, a refuge for mangy dogs and the occasional drunk. One of the security guards from her building loitered there with a cigarette. He wore a pressed white jacket and trousers with sharp creases ironed in. He smirked at her. She met his eyes, and he looked away.

She tore open the letter.

April,

Surprised? I called around and got your address. Not so easy, but I found it.

Bangkok, well how about that. You could have knocked me down. Didn't I always tell you, you would come good? The Lord will provide, they say – and God knows it is true.

So, how are you April? I'm doing good. I retired last year – getting old – but I keep busy. You know how it is.

Why don't you write once in a while? It wouldn't cost you. Except a stamp, ha ha. The truth is – I miss you. I'm not expecting anything – just hoping.

Well, that's about it.

Your Daddy

She felt pressure rising in her throat and swallowed. Rage, violent and sudden, at the thought of her father: his mild eyes and his bogus easy charm. The muscles in her neck hardened. Without thinking, she began to walk.

April liked to walk. This made her rare in Bangkok, a city of high rises and sky trains but no sidewalk. April's office – a law firm – was twenty minutes from the block where she lived, and although the walk left her out of breath and her clothes sticky, she didn't care. She loved the heat, the shock of it, its stink of rain and rotten fruit.

She walked faster than usual, trying to outpace her rage. She walked past traders selling food cooked on makeshift braziers, skewers of meat or fried seafood laced with spices, fruit cut into delicate shapes (pineapple flowers, mango stars). Smoke stung her eyes. She passed a row of seated beggars with stumps for legs, cigarette lighters and cheap flashing toys laid out on mats in front of them. A little further, two white marble elephants stood guard outside a luxury hotel.

An old woman with no hair nudged April's arm. She held up a garland of orange chrysanthemums close to April's face.

'Lucky'.

April ground her teeth. 'No'.

She brushed past the woman, though on other days she might have been tempted. She liked the idea that luck could be bought.

Ahead of her was an escalator that led up to an overpass for pedestrians, an elevated walkway that branched into air-conditioned department stores and office towers. A blast of chilly air conditioning hit her face. This was the business end of town. Tiny women trotted by, shiny hair neat, tight skirts crippling. Most days April ignored these office girls, but she noticed them today. Did that woman look sad? What was that one smiling about? She shook her head, trying to shake away strange thoughts. Her father's letter, crumpled in her handbag, had acted on her senses, and she was not sure they could be trusted.

She walked on, faster.

She walked past her office block, a silvery finger pointing to the light. Once it was behind her she stopped and glanced back, surprised at what she had done. She squinted to see her window. From up there she hardly noticed the traffic: up there Bangkok was what it aspired to be, shiny and modern, a city of high-rises and advertising billboards, a city gazed down upon by pale goddesses with pearly teeth. At street level things were different.

Not wanting to retrace her steps, she took another escalator down and walked by the side of the main road – *Sukhumvit* – that crawled through the centre of the city. Car exhausts belched at her. Drivers leaned out of their windows and stared. Her lungs thickened. The narrow strip of sidewalk dwindled into nothing.

She took a side road.

She walked for hours. It was stiflingly hot. She bought a bottle of water and a star of pineapple from a roadside cart. Her heels were pinching; her suit clammy with sweat. Her bag – too large – cut into her shoulder. Pollution, rising in an orange fog, obscured faces two blocks ahead. She was lost. This didn't bother her: she knew she only had to wave down a taxi and be home, but she didn't want to go home. She didn't know what she wanted.

She saw a ragged crowd around a baby elephant brought into the suburbs to beg. She noticed other things. A man with a withered hand. A woman selling fake Rolex watches. Smart young couples sat on benches in the road, their shirts ironed and shiny white. A lone youth crouched over a bowl of noodles, listening to a portable radio smashing out local hits.

Her eyes blurred. The light dimmed. Neon signs made vague splashes across her vision.

She walked through a street market; cheap cloth – nylon, rough with sequins – hung down and scratched her face. A tradesman grinned, showed all his crooked teeth, and held up a red shirt. She walked through it, brushing it aside so that the cloth snapped back at him.

She felt faint. She bought another bottle of water and sat down on a low wall. She slumped forwards, and her dark hair fell over her face. She wanted to cry. The thought made her nauseous.

April drank her water, wondering what to do.

She noticed an alley leading off the main road, one of the many tiny streets that burrowed through Bangkok like termite tunnels. On impulse, she turned into it.

The alley was narrow and close, bordered by small apartments stacked matchbox fashion on top of one another. Humming air conditioning units dripped from balconies, spattering April's hair and shoulders. Dirty washing drooped down. Few of the windows were lit. April lowered her eyes and saw a rat flick its tail. She smelt the sweet rising smell of garbage. Concrete split under her heels. She heard a low thudding. A small sign announced a bar. She went inside.

Loud music thumped against her chest. She was the only foreigner in the room, but no heads turned. She liked that discretion, and it occurred to her that maybe it was that – the circumspection – more than her job, which attracted her to living in Asia.

That and the heat.

The bar was small and full, stank of smoke and stale beer. It should have been rank with sweat, but, April reflected, Asian men hardly sweat. She smiled, mirthlessly: they keep their body fluids to themselves too. She liked that.

She ordered a beer and drank it quickly, sitting at the bar. She ordered another. Nobody looked at her. Conversation and music continued; rattle, bang. She lit a cigarette and decided to get drunk.

A group of young men sitting in a circle near her were drunk already. She watched them. They were playing some sort of game, complicated apart from the obvious purpose of intoxication. They were boisterous, and on the edge of a quarrel. Through the corner of her eye she saw a man stand up, his finger jabbing. He left the table. There was a second's pause. The other men at the table laughed.

She relaxed a little. The two drinks were having an effect: the atmosphere in the bar seemed softer than it had when she'd entered, her day of wandering more of a joke, less pointless. She raised her glass.

'Here's to you, you old bastard.'

Behind her someone said, 'You drink to a friend? That is very kind.'

She spun round. A man from the boisterous table had sidled up to the bar and was leaning against it, pressing his stomach to the Formica and looking at her with a puppy-like gaze. He was youngish – twenties, though it was hard to tell – and skinny. He wore a tight green jacket, and round John Lennon spectacles. April's heart sank.

'No friend,' she muttered. 'My father.'

'Oh.' The man's face lit up. 'I am very happy.'

'I'm not.' She shuddered, involuntarily.

The man stared at her.

She said, 'He's no good. You understand? My father. A *no good man.*'

He said 'Oh,' again.

April grimaced. The man had evidently approached her in order to pick her up. That was bad enough, worse that he wasn't doing a better job of it. To punish him, she said: 'He's a creep. My father. You know what that is? Someone who picks up girls.'

'But he is your father, so you love him.'

April snorted and stubbed out her cigarette. She regretted getting drawn into the conversation, but something – the alcohol maybe – meant she couldn't leave it. She said, 'So what if you're right? What if I did love him? Everyone makes mistakes.'

'He betrayed you?' The man asked, quizzically, with a dry little toss of his head.

She stared at him, surprised by the choice of word. He had serious eyes behind his moon glasses; his body was as thin as a pretzel. 'Look, actually it's none of your business. End of story. And end of conversation.' She turned away.

The puppyish man pressed his stomach against the bar again. Maddeningly, he had not taken the hint to go. He shook himself and regarded her.

'Tell me. Your father. What did he do to make you angry?' His round glasses caught the light.

'What didn't he do?' She murmured. 'He was crazy.'

'Tell me.'

'Tell you. Why should I tell you? Jesus.'

The man cocked his head.

April gulped her beer. 'You want to know about my father?'

Another nod.

'Okay. All right.' She fumbled in her bag, lit another cigarette, drew on it. 'All right. I'll tell you about Daddy.'

The man waited, expectant.

'You don't give up, do you?'

He shook his head.

'Ever seen a grown man cry?' She asked, raising her thin eyebrows. She felt angry, wanted a place to put her rage.

'Yes.'

'Then you'll know it's not pretty.'

The young man did not blink.

She said, 'Dear old Daddy. He used to cry like he was broken in two. You know? I would've done anything I could to fix him. There was this one time: he was broken, Okay? So I had to fix him. I put my arms round him. Held him tight. I was so sad. I didn't want my daddy to cry. It was – oh, I don't know why. And you know what? He hit me. Wump.'

The man flinched. April flicked her eyes at him.

'It wasn't the only time, God no, but the first time – the first is the worst don't you think?'

Her words were becoming compressed. 'He slapped me like I was a piece of meat. Again and again. Wump. I thought my eyes would pop. I thought my ears would burst. I thought I was going to die. And you know? I was four years old.'

The man removed his glasses, breathed on them, replaced them again.

He said, 'That is a very terrible thing.'

'Yes. Yes, it is a very terrible thing.' April's hand, holding her cigarette, was trembling.

The little man sucked in his cheeks.

She watched him for a moment. She continued,

'He asked me not to tell, so I didn't. It was our secret. He made me swear on the Bible, and I swore. I never told. Never. Not even when I *knew* he was fraud – that there is no God and there are no angels and everything he ever told me was a lie. I never told.' She stopped, her face red. She slugged her drink and placed it back down on the bar.

'So. You asked me if Daddy betrayed me. You hit it right there. Because he did. He betrayed me.'

'How did he betray you?'

She opened her mouth, and shut it again. 'Enough.'

The little man said, 'You are sad.'

'You think so? No. You're wrong. I don't want your pity.'

'You are right.' He nodded. 'Sometimes it is better not to pity yourself, but to fight instead.'

April grimaced. He was delicate, this pretzel boy, younger-looking, she guessed, than his real age. Solemn. She couldn't imagine him fighting anything. She tried to trace the steps that had led her to this point, but could not.

She raised her empty glass.

'Well. I'll drink to that. To fighting.'

'Cheers!' He grinned and refilled his drink from the can. Diet coke. He said, 'You will come outside with me? I have something to tell you.'

'You want me to come outside with you?' She guffawed, throwing her head back.

'Yes.' He looked puzzled.

'So is that what this is all about?'

'All about what?'

'Never mind. This is crazy, you know?'

'We will speak outside, Okay?' His voice was hushed.

'Sure.' She shrugged. 'Why not? It's been a weird day.'

'I go out first. You follow.' He took a quick, anxious look around the bar, straightened, and left the room. She clicked open the gold fastenings of her handbag and threw enough *baht* on the counter to pay for the drinks. Then, to humour him, she counted to twenty and staggered out.

As soon as she crossed the line beyond which the air conditioning stopped, wet heat pounded her. She took off her jacket and looked around for the man. She felt dizzy. She shut her eyes and tried to clear her head.

'Hello?' She said. And then again, 'Hello?'

She heard a few seconds of silence. Not enough to make her nervous.

The man appeared, out of breath and smiling. 'My name is Mo.'

'Sure. Great. You asked me out here to tell me that?'

'Your name is what?'

'It's April.'

'You will come with me now.'

'Where?'

'Not far. The place where I live. Come quickly.'

'What's the rush?'

He looked at her seriously, his eyes candid. 'I am very sorry. But please, it is better to talk there.'

'You want me to go back to your place?'

He stared at her. Shook himself. 'No – it is very safe. You must not think –'

'It's okay, Mo. I don't.'

'I am very, very sorry. April, if you consider –'

'Don't be sorry. I don't flatter myself.'

Mo pressed his hands together neatly. 'I swear by my life that I will not harm you.'

She snorted. 'I'd knock you down if you tried.'

Mo's shoulders slumped. 'So, you will come.'

'I didn't say that.'

'But you will.'

She shrugged. 'What the hell. I'm curious. You can give me a drink, tell me your life story, and we'll go our separate ways, okay? We're not going to be lifelong buddies or anything.'

He grinned eagerly. 'Of course not.' He began to speed down the alley, till something made him stop short. He turned back.

'We shall take taxi.'

'Is it far?'

'No, not at all.' He pointed. 'Over there. The next block.'

April smiled. 'Then we'll walk.'

'You can walk?' He stared.

'I have legs.' She was beginning – bizarrely – to enjoy herself. 'What do you think I use them for?'

'I have never met a foreign woman who walked before.'

She smiled. 'Actually we're incredibly robust.' She set off in the direction he had pointed and he trotted after her, shaking his head.

His home – if it was that – was a mean room on the third floor of a ramshackle apartment building. The staircase flickered with strip lighting: too light then too dark. It had a thick smell of rotten food. April's heels left pitted holes in the linoleum as she climbed. On each floor she heard sounds of life: a man arguing with his wife, a TV set on too loud. Mo walked backwards ahead of her.

'It is very horrible. So so horrible. I am very sorry.'

'Forget it.'

He reached his room and fumbled with his keys. Once he had opened the door he stood in the doorway, his back to the open room.

'I cannot.'

'What?'

'I cannot. It is too horrible.'

April choked on her laugh. 'Come on sweetheart. You've brought me all this way. Fess up. Show me your room.' She swept towards him, smiling at his panic. She had judged him correctly rather than endure her touch, he stepped aside and let her in.

There were no chairs inside the room, just a single bed pushed against the left hand wall. She sat down on it. Mo removed his ill-fitting jacket and placed it carefully on the bed, before filling an electric kettle from a basin in the far corner. He made strong black tea. April took it gratefully. The room had no air conditioning, and in the heat the tea was thirst quenching.

Mo squatted on the plastic-tiled floor at her feet. Apart from the basin and the bed, the room contained a small desk piled with books, writing paper, and a portable radio in acid pink. A few clothes were heaped on the floor. Like the building – like the rest of Bangkok – the room smelled syrupy sweet. She wiped a hand across her forehead, flicked away drops of sweat.

'So,' she said. She placed her cup down on the floor carefully. 'Will you tell me why I am here?'

'You are here because you are good,' said Mo.

She laughed. 'I don't know what gave you that impression. Nothing deliberate, I'm sure. So what's the story?'

He crossed his legs. 'What do you mean?'

She took a deep breath, trying to be patient. 'Okay. What do you do when you're at home, Mo?'

'I am not at home.'

'It's an expression. I mean, what do you *do*?'

'At home, I am a school teacher. I teach English and mathematics.'

'Very good. And where is home? Not here, I guess.'

'No.' Mo shook his head. 'Mingoria,' he said. 'Have you heard of it?'

'Barely.' April frowned. Mo had used an old fashioned name for a country which, she felt pretty sure, had since reinvented itself. 'But yes, I've heard of it. Some foreigners have. Like some women can walk.' She wrinkled her nose, trying to remember what she knew of the place. Not much, except that it was tiny and closed and had nothing for tourists. Nobody she knew ever went there. She asked, uninterested, 'So how did you wind up in Thailand, Mo?'

'I used to be a sailor,' he said.

'What, you sailed here?'

'No,' said Mo seriously. 'Mingoria is landlocked.'

'Right.' She laughed. 'That would make things hard.'

'Although I could have sailed down river.'

'But you didn't, right?' April smiled.

'No. I came in the back of a big truck. I paid the driver a lot of money and it was very hot. When we stopped at the border I was frightened. Luckily I had paid enough money, so nobody checked to see if I was there. The truck driver had been delivering fish oil, and I smelt very bad for a long time.' Mo wrinkled his nose. 'I washed my clothes many times.'

'So you're an illegal worker.'

'That is correct.' Mo smiled modestly. 'Now I fit air conditioning systems. Here is my company card.' He handed it to April with some ceremony. It bore the legend, *Kleenair Systems.* 'A very good job,' said Mo proudly. 'But not as good as being a schoolteacher. Or a sailor.'

'So why did you leave?' She asked.

Mo uncrossed his legs and crossed them again. 'Is the tea good? Would you like some more?'

'It's fine. And yes I would. So answer my question. I've told you some of my life story already, right?'

'Yes. Yes you have,' said Mo eagerly. 'And I feel, April, although we have not known each other for very long, I feel we can trust one another.'

'Sure. Everyone trusts April.'

Mo nodded. 'You are good. So I can speak to you. I want to tell you, April, that there are many problems in my country. Do you understand? My government is bad.'

'You were in trouble with the government?'

'In a way, yes. Everybody is in trouble with the government.'

'Did you break a law Mo? Is that it?'

Mo looked evasive. 'In fact,' he said, 'My father himself – you have told me about your father, so I shall tell you about mine – my father himself is a member of the SPNSP, that is our ruling Party. He believes in the Party and he drinks alcohol. But my mother is very religious. She believes in Buddhism and she does not drink alcohol. This causes problems in my family.'

'I imagine it would.'

'I love my father. But I believe in my mother.'

'Quite a problem, huh?'

'Are you a Christian?' asked Mo, catching April off guard.

'No. I used to be, but it wore off. Long story.'

Mo nodded, seriously, and spread his hands. 'May I now tell *you* a story, April?'

She made an expansive gesture. 'Please do.'

'It is about when I was a sailor.'

'Right. In a country without any ocean.'

'We had a very small navy.'

'It would be.'

'A merchant navy,' said Mo, as if this explained things. 'When I joined the navy,' he continued, 'my father was very happy. I went to a special college – very good – and my whole family was proud. I was well educated there, not only

24

in naval matters, but also in other things. It was an excellent all-round education. Although,' he added proudly, 'I taught myself English.'

'Your English is very good,' responded April on cue.

'I am just a beginner,' replied Mo, splaying his hands modestly. 'But this is not my story. My story is this. It was my first time ever at sea, and I was young, eighteen years of age. We were a mixed crew, mainly Filipino, some Chinese, and I. We were sailing under a flag of convenience. And there was a storm. Have you ever encountered a storm at sea, April?' He did not pause for her answer. 'It is beyond imagining. This was a force ten gale. The sea rose up many times higher than the sides of the boat, like a wall made only of water. And darkness, nothing but darkness for three days. Impossible to go above deck. All of us were below. Even the old sailors were afraid. For myself, I was sure, April, that I would die. I have never been so frightened, never before nor since. Even now, I am not so frightened, though I also have good reason to be afraid.'

He paused.

'For three days I held on to the edges of my bunk as the sea tossed our boat like a little piece of wood. I tried to block my ears to the roaring. And I prayed, April. I made a bargain: if the Lord Buddha let me live, from then onwards I would be good like my mother. If he let me live. And you see –' He spread his hands – 'I am alive.'

'So you're a good man now?' She asked, curiously. His story, his black eyes behind the moon glasses, his hushed voice: all of these gripped her.

'Of course. I believe everything. My father has never forgiven me.'

'That's too bad.' She yawned suddenly, covering her mouth with her hand.

'You find my story boring?'

'No. Lord, no. Far from it.' She shook herself. 'You know, Mo, I'm tired. I've walked a long way today. And the truth is

I'm not myself.' She looked at the tiny room and the little man perched eagerly at her feet. 'I can't explain.' She stood up. 'I think maybe I'd better go.'

Mo jumped up too. 'I have kept you too long.'

'No. It isn't that, it's just –' She didn't know what it was. She shivered, cold despite the steamy night. Claustrophobic, too: these things they were saying to one other struck too close, were too intimate for her liking. 'Thanks for your hospitality, Mo.' She backed towards the door.

'There are more things that I want to tell you.' Mo frowned. 'But I see you must rest.'

'You know Mo, you're a nice man.' She wanted to say more. She held out her hand.

He shook her fingers uncertainly. His hand was cold, his grip delicate. 'You will come back tomorrow?' He asked. Hopeful. Eager.

'I don't know.' She smiled. 'Maybe.'

But she knew she would.

Hardwick

Duncan Hardwick lurched through Oxford, his long coat billowing behind him. Curious High Street shoppers paused as he passed, stared at him furtively before looking away. He was behaving unusually. Maybe they thought he was drunk? He held out an arm in front of him, stepped backwards, stumbled into a woman. She hit him in the ribs, hard enough to wind him.

'Hey.' Her face was red. 'Get out of the way. Get out. There should be a law.'

He pushed past her, his head down, a detached part of his mind thinking all the while: who would frame such a law? Who would apply it?

The road widened and the crowd thinned. He ducked down a quiet footpath and reached a wide meadow scattered with daisies. Beyond it was the Cherwell, shimmering in the sunlight.

He walked along the river, not caring in which direction or for how long. The unthinkable had happened. Now he must square it with the fact that this luminous June day, this shimmering river, all continued as before.

He was not aware of the girl until he was upon her.

She was sitting square in the middle of the earthy path, blocking his way. A coarse tangle of brambles grew behind her.

He drew up short. 'I'm sorry.'

She was looking down, staring not at the river but the small patch of muddy ground in front of her. He cleared his throat and said again, a little louder, 'I'm sorry.'

She looked up. He realised, with confusion, that this was Lorraine, one of his students. Her hair was loose around her shoulders. She looked miserable, as if she, like him, had been crying. Her skin, always pallid, was drained of colour, and the tip of her nose was red. Her eyes – dark brown and puffy around the lids – met his.

She said, 'What are you sorry about?'

He frowned. 'What I meant was, excuse me.'

'Why didn't you say so?'

'I want to continue my walk. Please would you let me pass. I can hardly step over you.'

She smiled, a brief curling of her lips. 'No, I don't suppose you could.' She stood up slowly, glancing at him as she did so. Her expression changed. 'Are you all right?'

'I'm fine.'

She peered closer. 'But you're not, are you? You've been crying. Haven't you?'

He touched his finger to his cheek, as if to confirm her observation. For some reason he did not feel embarrassed. He said, 'Yes, I have. I think you have too.'

She nodded. 'You're right.'

'Well then.'

'We've both been crying.'

'Yes.'

'Life's a bitch, isn't it?'

'That's one way of putting it.' He wanted to laugh. He brushed aside a tangle of white hair that had fallen into his eyes. He felt a pang of anxiety. 'You won't say anything, will you?'

'No. If you don't.'

'On my honour.' He pressed his fingers to his heart.

'So it's our secret. And I won't ask you why if you don't. All right?' She thrust out her hand. He shook it.

'Thanks. It's Lorraine, isn't it?'

'A year, you've been teaching me.'

'Well.' He coughed. 'I'm not very good with names.'

'No.' She lowered her eyes. 'I suppose there's not much room left. What with all the dates.'

'History isn't just –'

'I know.' She looked up and smiled. 'History isn't just dates. I know. Joking.'

'Right.' Hardwick stood on one leg, shifted to the other. 'Well then. Lorraine. I should continue.'

'Okay.'

'And –' He paused. 'I mean – I mean, thank you. That's all.' He put his hands in his pockets and nodded at the girl. She nodded back, her hair showering over her shoulders. She stepped aside, and he walked on.

He did not look, but he was sure – was as aware as if he could really see – that she stared after him as he walked away.

The second time they met she was sitting cross-legged by the water as before. The sun picked out golden tints in her hair. It seemed to him, caught off guard as he stumbled upon her, that she was glowing with light.

He felt shy and wanted to turn back. She saw him and waved, her face alive with friendliness.

'Hey! Fancy meeting you again!'

He walked towards her uncertainly. He had been thinking of her, but faced with the reality of her he found himself tongue-tied. Did she guess he had come here deliberately? 'I often walk this way,' he said, to head off that supposition.

'That's funny,' she said. 'So do I, but I only ever saw you once before.'

'I usually come much earlier.'

'I don't get up early.'

'I suppose you're out dancing the night before,' he said, imagining her life with difficulty.

'Not dancing. Drinking.' She smiled coyly. 'Doesn't mean I don't work.'

'No. Your work is always on time.'

'But it's shit, isn't it? You think I'm useless.'

'Sometimes I think the subject isn't for you. You do have an insight, but –'

'But not the right sort.'

She stood up, and they began to walk together. She seemed always to be in a hurry, Hardwick noticed. He quickened his pace to keep up with hers.

He said, 'Of course there will always be room for originality. History isn't simply about what happened, the *why* is equally important, as you well know. And infinitely open to interpretation, because it is infinitely subjective, filtered through the eyes of the actors and layers of time. That is the excitement of history, the fact that we take our own subjectivity to it. The meaning of each age is different to each age. It is not simply a puzzle to be unravelled.' He paused, breathless.

Lorraine was silent for a while. Then she said, 'I always saw you as a bit of a puzzle man myself.'

They walked on, Hardwick's shoulders sagging. Did she deliberately set out to tease him? He took a sidelong glance at her. Her face was serene. He slowed down, fearful that his company was irksome to her. He asked, 'Would you prefer to be alone?'

'Oh no.' She turned to him in surprise. 'You don't want to be alone, do you?'

'No. I don't.'

'That's fine then. Unless you're embarrassed?'

The question was designed perfectly to embarrass him. He stammered, 'Why should I be?'

'Oh, I don't know.' She shrugged. 'Nothing.' They continued for a while, until Lorraine asked, 'Is everything all right?'

'Fine,' said Hardwick automatically. He drew his brows together. He had an innate sense of honesty, and for all his shyness was not satisfied with his answer. 'Although I am worried about Felicity, my wife,' he added. 'She isn't well.'

'What's wrong with her?'

'She has cancer,' he answered, briefly.

'Is it curable?' asked Lorraine, her tone equally matter of fact.

'No.' He stopped walking. 'I believe there's absolutely no hope at all.'

'Wow.'

Hardwick resumed his pace. Their footsteps marched along together. Being young, he guessed, the idea of death was exotic to her. She seemed – if anything – impressed by its intrusion into the conversation. He shut his eyes.

She said, 'I don't know how you manage that. I would be a mess.'

'I'm good at putting things to one side.'

'You shouldn't. It'll get to you some time and when it does it'll be worse.'

'Old habits die hard.'

Lorraine did not reply to this directly. Instead she looked thoughtful. 'When do you think we start getting those habits?' She asked. 'When did you? Because, I want to watch out for when it happens.'

'Oh, I don't know.' Hardwick sighed, and made another attempt to settle down his hair. 'I think I was set in my ways a long time ago. Like an old arthritic joint.'

She laughed. 'You shouldn't make fun of yourself. You don't like yourself much, do you?'

'Well,' he said. 'I don't know. I suppose I haven't thought about it.'

She laughed again. Her expression changed quickly. 'I'm really sorry about your wife.' She hesitated. 'I have to go now.'

Hardwick started. 'Oh,' he said. 'Oh. Yes I see you must.'

'Got to work. I really am sorry, you know.'

She was gone before he could frame a reply.

'I'm sorry too,' he was going to say. 'Felicity is my best friend.'

She was sitting in their window seat, holding a cushion decorated with an appliquéd design of a red-skirted dancer. She was pulling at loose threads on the red skirt, pecking at them with her fingertips. The sun shone directly on her face. Her dark eyes were narrowed. Her hair was short and iron grey. She gave the appearance of picking apart some thought, just as her fingers picked apart the cushion. Hardwick shuffled towards her. She narrowed her eyes further. Hardwick stood still on the wool rug, a pool of sunlight at his feet.

'Warm?'

'Very. Unusually.'

Felicity's fingers stopped their pecking. Hardwick found he didn't know what to say. He looked at her and felt that he loved her. He went into the kitchen.

'The sun's in your eyes,' he shouted through to her.

'I know that. I'm a sunflower.'

'I'm making tea. Will you have any?'

'No.'

Hardwick thought he wouldn't have any either. Nevertheless he boiled a kettle, and brought two cups, a jug, and a teapot out to Felicity.

'Thank you.' She reached for the jug of milk. Her hand shook, the jug slipped, and the liquid slopped onto her trousers.

'Stupid of me. Stupid.' She hissed at herself, clicked her tongue. Hardwick jumped and ran for a cloth, began to rub her trousers.

'Don't.' Felicity put a finger on his shoulder. 'Don't worry at it. Don't cry over it.'

'No. No, I –'

He was kneeling at her feet. Hot drops spilled out of his eyes. They splashed onto her trousers and mingled with the milk.

For a week Lorraine wasn't at the riverbank and he walked home alone, relieved and disappointed. It was not the weather that was putting her off because it had turned glorious, with flat cloudless skies that seemed to belong more to Europe than to his corner of England. The meadow was vivid with flowers, yellow buttercups and daisies, white meadowsweet and blue cornflowers in the hedges along with a few bursts of oilseed rape that he knew he should dislike as a weed but couldn't help admiring. If he hadn't been embarrassed by the word, he would have said the gaudy yellow was sensual. But that thought led him treacherously close to Lorraine, and he was glad, then, that he could not find her.

It wasn't until the weather turned grey that he saw her again. He took the walk more out of habit than anything, not imaging that she would be there. The sunburst of flowers had become muted; the air was damp and chilly. He pulled up the collar of his shirt and wished he had brought a jacket. The red sweater he was wearing was inadequate.

She was standing alone a little further up the path, looking into the water. Something about her suggested loneliness, and he wondered whether he should intrude. She saw him and her face changed. She waved.

'What are you doing here? It's not the day for it, is it?'

'For my health,' said Hardwick. 'Have to keep healthy.' He was panting.

'How is your wife?'

'She does not improve. She doesn't deteriorate either.'

'That's good then,' she said, breezily.

He reached her. 'I haven't seen you here for a long time. I thought perhaps you had gone home for the summer.'

She tilted her head coyly. 'Have you been thinking about me?'

'No. I –'

'I'd rather stay here. It's peaceful. Too mad at home.'

'I see.'

'Do you?' she asked abruptly. 'Do you have a mobile?'

'Yes I do, actually,' he said, sheepish. He had bought one recently in case Felicity should need him, and he'd enjoyed the experience of having the shop girls flutter around him as he pretended to be more baffled by it than he actually was. He pulled his phone out of his pocket to show her.

'Oh, I believe you,' she said. 'You don't have to prove it. What I meant was, what's your number?'

'Right. Of course.' He put the phone back in his pocket and pulled a scrap of paper out of his wallet. 'Can't remember it yet. No pattern.'

Lorraine smiled as she entered the number into her phone. 'They're mad, aren't they?'

'You'll give me yours?'

'I'll text you.'

'Of course,' said Hardwick. 'Of course.'

They reached the point where Lorraine usually turned off the path. She was wearing jeans and a white t-shirt and her arms were goose pimpled. She said, 'I'm freezing. Got to go.'

'Yes.'

'You should get back too. You're nearly blue. You clash with your jumper. Your wife knit that for you?'

'Felicity does not knit. She is not a knitter.'

'Yeah. Well.'

She jogged away, a sudden burst of energy that caught him by surprise. It's because she's young, he thought to himself. But he too had once been young, and he could not remember running like that, or laughing out loud at nothing at all.

He received her message as he was on his way to supper in college. He made a point of eating in hall once a week, not because he enjoyed it – he did not – but because he felt that his colleagues expected it of him. He wore his long black gown over his red sweater, and walking through the mellow streets – the clouds had lifted and the evening sun was bursting through – he felt like a storm crow, some ill-omened creature.

34

His phone gave out an electronic buzz and he jumped, shocked that the sound had come from him. He fumbled inside his gown and found his phone. An envelope symbol was flashing on the screen. He pushed the biggest button, which turned out to be the right one. The message read, *'Hello gorgeous!'*

He stood and stared at it. He guessed – and hoped – that the message must be from Lorraine. Who else it could be from? Certainly not Felicity – the thought was absurd – nor any of their mutual friends. He thought of his PhD student: the man often tinkered with his mobile, studying it as if it might reveal some truth. But he would hardly send him such a message. It was incredible. He continued to stare, expecting at any moment that the words would melt away, but they stayed, black and irrefutable. He hurried on, his red sweater showing through the open wings of his gown.

He was late. The chaos of eating had begun, the conversation a roar that Hardwick usually found the most disagreeable part of the experience. Acoustics, he thought to himself, not for the first time: wooden benches, stone walls, ceramic plates. The acoustics were wrong. Gloomy too: whatever the season the cavernous hall remained a place of shadows and cracked paint.

As he took his place at a young mathematician leaned over him. 'What's your secret?'

'What?' Hardwick jumped.

'Why do you look so happy?'

'Oh.' He made a play at slicing into a piece of chicken breast. 'Do I seem happy to you?'

'More than usually. You practically skipped into hall.'

'I've just had a piece of good news.'

'About Felicity? That's excellent.'

'No, no.' Hardwick blushed, and stopped slicing. He supposed it was common knowledge that his wife was dying. He changed the subject. 'Do you know how to send a text?'

'A what?'

'On a mobile phone. A text.'

'I know what you mean. I just couldn't believe you'd asked.'

'That I had one, or was foolish enough not to be able to use it?'

'Look. No offence. Only that you've never asked me a favour before. Do you have your phone here?'

The young man demonstrated. Hardwick thanked him, made his excuses and stepped outside. He retreated to a carved archway and leaned his cheek against the cool yellow stone. Strange feelings flooded through his body – had been since he'd first seen Lorraine by the river. – or, he reminded himself, since he'd known Felicity was dying. One or the other.

He took out his phone. He typed out a message laboriously and hit *send* before he could have second thoughts.

'You are so beautiful.'

His fourth meeting with Lorraine – the last – came weeks later. He bumped into her at the Ashmolean museum. No, not bumped: followed her there, deep into his madness by then and stalking her with fearful pleasure. She stood in the room dedicated to Southeast Asian art. Her hair hung forwards, brushing one of the display cabinets. She looked – marvelous, indescribable. He lingered in the doorway, taking schoolboy peeks.

'Hello.'

He jumped. 'How did you know I was here?'

'I know things.' She beckoned to him. 'More than you think. Come on. Don't be shy.'

He walked towards her.

'Lovely, isn't it?'

'What?'

She pointed through the dusty glass to a golden Buddha's head. It had curling lips and faraway eyes. He peered at the label. It said, 'Mingoria. Third Dynasty.'

'What do you think?'

He cleared his throat.

'I'm not sure what I think. European antiquity is my field. Not this.'

'But you can tell if something is lovely.' She took his hand.

He shut his eyes, sick with desire. He stammered, 'Lovely? No, I don't believe that's the word. He looks – too self satisfied, perhaps? And yet – I don't know. – I don't think he means to judge.'

She whispered, her mouth very close to his ear. 'Maybe he's just laughing at some big joke.'

Hardwick made his excuses and fled.

For days afterwards he returned to the spot, compelled to replay the scene and lose himself in the erotic thrill of remembering: her fingers, touching his skin so lightly; the room spinning uncertainly around that one fact. His body tingled as he remembered. His chest shuddered.

Later, when all was over and Felicity was gone, he returned not only to think of Lorraine but also to squat in front of the Buddha who smiled and witnessed all, but had not judged.

Martin

Martin Morley woke, gasped, and decided to kidnap his son. He looked at his alarm clock. It was twenty past four.

Sam had been conceived five years earlier on a chilly evening in December after Martin and Jen had spent the day fighting. Martin hadn't wanted children. The fight was worse than usual and Jen had cried so hard that Martin, feeling wretched, had put his arm around her with guilty tenderness.

'Is it because you don't want me? Is that it?'

He'd sighed. 'Of course I want you.' What else could he say? 'You don't have to ask me that.'

She raised her eyes to him, teary and red. 'I can't live without you, that's all. I just can't.' She managed a smile.

'Jen.' He held her hard, feeling grateful though he couldn't quite work out why. Her neediness frightened him, but he felt a baffled compassion for her, and a desire to be needed. He began to rock her. 'Jen, Jen.'

'Martin.'

'That's me.'

'I love you, Martin.'

'I know.'

'I mean I really do.'

'Shush.'

A pause.

'Can't you say it?'

'I love you.' The voice he heard lacked conviction. To make up for it, he kissed her eyelids and the curve of her neck. He felt a tiny stirring of desire.

She whispered, 'Come to bed Martin.' Her breath tickled his ear.

'Well…' Martin drew back.

'Come on.' Jen giggled. 'You know you want to.' She began to run her fingers over his chest, pulling up his sweater. She seemed a little tipsy suddenly, as if the fight and the tears had had an intoxicating effect. He tried to keep up with her moods but it was difficult.

'Jen, it wouldn't be –'

'Shush. Come on Martin.' She took him by the hand and led him to the bed. He hopped after her, feeling an anxious need to please, hoping that his anxiety wouldn't stop his body doing the rest. She lay on her back and looked up at him expectantly. He lowered himself over her, supporting his body weight with his arms.

'You know, this wouldn't be a good idea.'

'Poor Martin. So sensible.' She stroked his cheek with the tip of her forefinger – lightly, barely touching him. 'Poor Martin.'

He closed his eyes and kissed her. She kissed him back hard, with a desire that unnerved him. She was breathing heavily. He forced his eyes tighter shut and tried to concentrate. She unzipped his jeans and pulled him down onto her body. To his relief this began to have an effect. He wanted to want her. He pushed his hips to her hips. He pushed harder. He heard a hiss of air escape from his mouth. He wanted everything to be all right.

Her arms gripped his shoulders, pulled him hard against her. She lifted his shirt; pulled up her own. He felt her skin. There was excitement in this, something dangerous, as if they were fighting still. He didn't use a condom. After all, he figured (a brief lucid moment before desire took over) it's not so easy to get pregnant. It takes some couples years, Jen had told him. He hoped it would be true of them.

He groaned, gripped the back of her head, sank down onto her body. Silence. His heart rattled against hers.

Jen murmured, 'You're lovely. Just lovely.'

He smiled at her, shaken, not able to find the words. He put his arms around her. He felt hollowed out. His anger, the way he had expressed it, shocked him. He shut his eyes. His heartbeat slowed down. He held her closer, trying to convey some kind of contrition. She smiled at him. He liked the warm fragile feeling of her body, her easy contentment. He began to feel relief that his trial had been, temporarily, adjourned. He kissed the hair behind her ears, stroked her head. His fingers were trembling.

He said, 'Cold. Want to get under the sheets?'

'Mm.' She nodded and got in beside him, turning her back to him.

'Are you alright?'

'Course. Why shouldn't I be?'

'No reason.'

He shut his eyes. Although it was only late afternoon, it was already dark. He wanted to sink into a tired oblivion where he wouldn't have to think. He could smell Jen's familiar musky smell. Soon he felt her slow breathing. He shouldn't be surprised: whatever the circumstances, Jen could always sleep. He felt his arm under her becoming numb, and wanted to move it, but didn't for fear of disturbing her.

Much later his clearest memory of that evening was this: lying deadly still as his arm numbed, prickled, and finally throbbed with pain. It was one of those things that he did for Jen. One of those things that she would never know about, and could never possibly remember.

He sat upright. The memory had aroused him. The night was close, and the weight of London's air bore down on him. He looked at his alarm clock again. Quarter past five. He kicked his sheets into a tangle at his feet and sat exposed and panting, sweat standing out on his pale skin.

He tried to calm down. He frowned at his rebellious body, knowing he didn't want Jen, annoyed that his body didn't agree. He began to examine it. He had once been athletic, his body angular and hard. Not any longer. Everywhere, he could see more flesh than there used to be. His stomach folded over itself as he bent forwards to look. His curling black pubic hair was flecked with grey, his penis squatting in the middle of the thicket like an impish toad. Large thighs. He couldn't see his buttocks, but he felt sure that they too were getting bigger. Altogether, he had too much white flesh.

He groaned and fell back on his pillow. His self-examination had succeeded: every drop of desire had drained out of him. He rubbed his eyes. They were pale green, the whites cloudy and sore.

He hadn't slept properly in weeks. Some nights he dreamt of holding Sam in his arms, the two of them reunited in a soft-focus future. Some nights – the worst – he imagined Jen dead: a freak accident would claim her, a car crash, anything. He imagined speaking at her funeral. He would talk about how she'd been a good mother. He would cry. He would hold Sam's small hand in his own.

He heaved in a breath. He knew these fantasies did him no good. He didn't want Jen dead. He wanted Sam. He squeezed his eyes shut, bracing himself for the pain. Easier to lose an arm. Easier to cut out his heart. He held his head in his hands and wept. No good. He bit his lip and admonished himself. Stop. Think. Do something. The idea returned. It was simple. Why hadn't he thought of it before? He jumped up, feverish. He needed Sam. He would take him.

He fumbled for some matches, lit a cigarette, and ruffled his hair. He was, he knew, having crazy thoughts. He flexed his fingers, making piano chords. He was a teacher by trade, a musician by inclination; and musicians, he told himself dryly, do not steal children. No, Jen had done that.

For a year after Sam had been born he hadn't listened to music at all: the tension and elation of the new baby had closed off every other emotion. He'd felt that his heart was sealed over with gristle; until one morning when he'd heard Monteverdi's Vespers on the radio and collapsed in tears. Jen, already a stranger, had only frowned about something – where were her keys? And he had shuddered and not replied.

His stomach tightened. He began to pace his flat, exclaiming at thoughts. He only had to work out how; after all, he knew well enough where his son would be. And then? He was taking time off work; his rented flat was not an unbreakable tie. He could disappear.

He fell back down on his bed and lit another cigarette. He felt light-headed, unburdened. Would it work? He felt sure of it. He would see Sam; he would hold him in his arms. Was it right? The question worried him. He shivered. He swore out loud, angry with the question.

'I need him. Fuck it, Jen. I need him. That's all.'

He sat and smoked. As new light filtered through his bedroom window it seemed obvious: stealing his son was only taking what was his.

At six he showered, scrubbing his skin till it tingled because he didn't want Sam to think he hadn't been looking after himself. He shaved, dragging the razor over his cheeks, and splashed his face and neck in cologne. He looked at himself in the mirror. Not bad for forty. His green eyes were bleary, swollen by too little sleep and the crying he had done that night; but otherwise he looked fresh and clean. His hair was sticking up in clumps, but he decided to leave it. Sam liked it messy.

Sam.

He shut his eyes.

He dressed, made himself some toast and cereal and then realised that he couldn't eat, so drank coffee instead. He allowed himself a final cigarette. He brushed his teeth.

He sat down and tried to read his book to pass the time, and, in the absurd way of these things, fell asleep.

He woke at ten and it was almost too late. He thought, later, that maybe that had been his last chance: he might have slept late, woken chastened, dismissed the whole idea as desperate and pitiable. As it was he woke with a jerk, sprang upright, and did not think further.

He threw a few clothes, some documents – Jen had forgotten to take Sam's passport with her when she'd left – into a small holdall. He scribbled a rent cheque and a note to his landlord, turned off the lights and the gas, and locked his front door.

He stepped outside. He felt liberated and drunk. He reached the corner of the street and, unable to walk further, leant against a wall. He felt sick, and wished he had eaten. He swung his bag onto his shoulder. He was on the edge of something terrible, he knew it clearly: a detached part of himself hovered above him and judged him. Even so, he couldn't turn back.

His local bank was a few minutes away. He chose the counter with the youngest and prettiest woman (the kind he could impress), showed her his passport, and took out all the money he had.

He drove across London. Camberwell to Paddington, crossing the river at Vauxhall Bridge. Jen was a creature of habit, and he knew exactly where she would be. He parked.

Time shifted forwards.

Later he would notice these gaps in his memory, the details of the drive, and the walk across the park, all lost.

The playground was ahead of him, a sudden shift into focus. A red slide, swings, a sandpit. He squatted behind some yellow shrubs for cover. The air was loud with children's voices. He picked out Sam from amongst the throng: a shock of light brown hair and a fierce expression. He was playing in the sandpit. Jen was sitting on a bench with her face in profile. Everything about her was familiar: the extraordinary fire-red hair, the slight tilt of her chin. Martin fought a sudden temptation to go up to her and talk, forget everything, shift time back. A second look at Sam erased the urge.

He hunkered low to the ground, taking care not to be seen.

Jen was deep in conversation with Amanda, a prickly, miserable friend of hers who'd never liked him. She glanced up at Sam sometimes but not often. Her feet were crossed at the ankles; she was frowning, absorbed. Martin knew her look meant she believed Sam to be occupied and safe.

He took his chance.

He whistled, an owl whistle he had once taught Sam. Jen would not pause to think about hearing an owl in the park. To her, birds were birds. He whistled a second time. Sam looked up, puzzled. Martin waved. Sam's face broke into a wide grin. Martin grinned back and signalled urgently to Sam to keep quiet. Sam nodded: he understood. They stood fixed in one another's gaze, conspirators together. A pause, another gap in time.

Martin beckoned wildly. Sam ran towards him, his arms flapping, a delighted grin on his face. Martin scooped him up and put his hand over his mouth to suppress the peal of laughter that threatened to alert Jen. He held his son tight in his arms. He wanted to cry.

'Sam. You've got to be very quiet. Do you understand?'

Sam nodded, his mouth still covered.

'Do you want to go for a ride in my car?'

Sam's eyes widened.

'Listen. I'm going to carry you. We've got to be quick, Okay?'

Gently, Martin removed his hand from Sam's mouth. Sam said, so quietly the word was hardly hinted at, 'Okay.'

Martin bolted across the parched grass, his heart hammering against his son's little body. The distance seemed vast. A mother, two identical blond girls on either side of her, watched him with thin lips. He pushed himself to run faster. *He's mine, don't you get it?* He wanted to say. *Mine.*

Time lengthened, contracted again. At the far entrance to the park he risked putting Sam down. He drank in air, half laughing, half crying. Seeing Sam's anxious look he bent down and tried to quiet his breathing. He didn't want to frighten his son.

He said, 'Do you want to come for a ride now?'

Sam was silent. Uncertain.

'We can go fast.'

'Okay.'

Martin scooped him up and carried him to the car.

'Can we go really fast?'

'Yes. But we won't break the speed limit.'

'Can we go on the motorway?'

'We might do. Yes. It's a good idea.'

'With the roof down?'

'Yes.' Martin laughed, bundled Sam into the child seat, and jumped in. He flicked on the radio: Mozart's clarinet concerto, the notes pure and soaring. He began to drive, the music on loud, tears rolling down his cheeks. He felt no doubt. He had done the right thing.

He drove through London. Crazy, directionless, snatching glances at his son whenever the road allowed. The boy, he saw, was watching him. At first Sam seemed excited, but soon his expression shifted into worry. Martin tightened his grip on the wheel. He had Sam. Now what did he want?

He said, 'Do you want a story?'

Sam nodded. 'A story about me.'

'What kind of story?'

'Me and Mr. Icarus.'

'Okay'. Martin smiled. He'd found the story in a dog-eared library book: it had become one of Sam's favourites. He shifted gear and tried to concentrate.

'Right. So there was this crazy man called Mr. Icarus.'

'He was STUPID,' shouted Sam, and Martin smiled.

'Yeah, really stupid. He thought he could fly – '

'But he couldn't –'

'No, not until he made some wings.'

'Why did he want to fly?' asked Sam.

'I don't know.' Martin frowned. 'I suppose he wanted to get away from the ground.'

Sam snorted in derision.

'Mm. And everyone laughed at him. Thing is though, his wings actually worked. He made them out of feathers and wax. And so he actually flew –'

'But it didn't work –' added Sam.

'No, because he flew too close to the sun, and the wax melted, and he crashed down to the ground.'

'So, I turned into a Power Ranger,' interrupted Sam.

'Yes, you turned into a Power Ranger. And you flew up to him. And –'

'– and I caught him. And everything was okay.'

'That's it. Everything was okay.'

Sam frowned. 'Tell me another story.'

'Not now, Sam. We're nearly there.'

'One more.'

'I can't –'

'PLEASE. I said please.'

'Sam,' Martin spoke softly. 'Not now.'

His arm ached. He loosened his grip on the wheel. He was on the Westway. Heathrow. Now he was in the airport, Sam's hand in his, the only man in the place who seemed not to know where to go. He walked to the BA desk and asked for a ticket. The woman at the counter was bad tempered and sleepy, two wisps of hair escaping from her tightly pinned coiffure. She watched him with suspicious eyes. Sam tugged at his hand and whimpered: 'I want to go home.'

'Where exactly do you want a ticket *for*, sir?' The woman asked in a nasal voice. 'It's usual to state a destination.'

'What flights do you have in the next few hours?' Martin chewed a fingernail. Everything had been sharp and clear to him that morning. During the drive rising panic had clouded his mind.

'We have plenty of flights.' The woman's eyes flicked up and down, taking in the nervous man, the exhausted child. Martin felt the situation slipping out of his control. He straightened his shoulders. Forced a smile.

'Taking him on holiday. Bit of a last minute thing.'

'I see.' The woman pursed her lips.

Martin grinned, his expression easy, open. He knew his forearms, resting on the counter, were well-moulded. He pushed a hand through his hair, ruffled it, conscious of the effect he could have.

'He needs a treat. I've been working too much – makes you forget what's important, doesn't it?' The lie contained a half-truth. Work of late had exhausted him; the kids – tone deaf and sullen – were driving him crazy.

He saw the woman's nostrils flicker, her face soften a touch. 'Hmm.'

'Does you good to be spontaneous.' He was leaning close, his lies conveying intimacy. 'Don't you think?'

'And the destination?' The woman, he saw, was fighting a smile.

Martin struggled, his mind blank until some obscure memory surfaced: his father whispering stories to him of a distant place he had once sailed through. Stories of a vast river, of overpowering heat, of a comrade shaking with malaria. His father no longer a little man who lost his socks, but mysterious, heroic. Mingoria, the name was. A lost place, his father had told him. A place to disappear.

'Bangkok?' Martin asked, tentatively. The woman nodded. She looked back at her keyboard with a yielding expression. Martin waited, tightening and releasing his fists. Surely, there would be flights to Bangkok? And from there he would find a way of travelling on. It sounded like a plan – or the nearest he had to one.

The woman typed, gave him a time and a flight number. He sighed, thanking her with his eyes. As she gave him the tickets he touched her hand, briefly, lightly, with his forefinger. The smile she had been struggling against broke out.

II

1

Martin guessed most of the passengers aboard the twin-prop plane were used to the journey. They slumped in their seats, bored, showing no fear as the tiny craft strained towards the yellow-stained night. Martin gripped the sides of his seat with sweating hands, as if he could still the plane's crazy juddering. The aircraft bounced, whined, gradually righted itself. Cabin lights blinked on. Twenty seatbelts clicked open. The breath of twenty sighs filled the flat air. Martin sighed too.

A stewardess in a long wrap-around skirt swayed down the aisle with practiced poise, her face young and hard in her make up. She handed out orange squash in paper cups decorated with party balloons. Martin held his cup delicately in long fingers, fearing it would crumple. He gulped at the drink; the childhood taste was calming. He put the cup down and drummed at his armrest. The back of his neck was cold. He swallowed again, trying to shift the popping in his ears. The stewardess returned, carrying a stack of cardboard boxes filled with rice and a slop of meat stew. Around him, Martin's fellow passengers settled down to guzzle. All but two of them. The only other westerners on board fidgeted and picked at their stew, jumping, like Martin, at any sudden rattle or roar of the engine. One of them – a gangly man with a mass of white hair – sat directly across the aisle from Martin. He had been leaning with his nose pressed hard against the cold window since take off, though the lights of the sprawling city below soon became fuzzy, and had now disappeared altogether. A young woman – twenties, Martin thought, with a face that would have been pretty had it not been so severe – sat beside the old man. She was dressed in a tailored suit, an odd contrast, thought Martin, to the comfortable tracksuits and pyjama bottoms most of the local passengers wore. He wondered if she regretted her choice: the stiff fabric of the suit must have made her skin itch. Its formal cut emphasised, rather than concealed, the youthfulness of her face. She had painted her lips a bright red that shaded into orange, an unsettling colour. Her dark hair was cut to fall forward; it hid her features when she bent her head. The old man and the young woman sat in silence, each avoiding the others' eyes.

Sam wriggled in his seat. 'Daddy, what's that noise mean? What does it *mean*?'

Martin answered quietly, leaning close to his son. 'It doesn't mean anything.'

He stared at the child. He admired the way his son's long eyelashes curled against his cheek, and, distracted by this detail, lost the thread of the boy's next question. It was astonishing to him that Sam sat beside him; miraculous that he, a tired, disillusioned man, could have produced such a lovely child. He reached out and flipped a lock of light brown hair from Sam's forehead. He wanted to kiss his son's cheek. He jammed his head against the headrest and resisted the urge.

Across the aisle the woman with the sullen expression fished for her handbag. She began to fiddle with its gold fastenings. The man with the mass of hair glanced at her. His eyes lingered on her restless hands, and he gave a deep and exaggerated sigh. The woman, ignoring him, continued to fasten and unfasten her bag.

Click. Click.

Martin, watching the scene through the corner of his eye, smiled to himself.

The white-haired man felt in the pocket of the seat in front of him and pulled out an in-flight magazine: '*Mingoria Airlines – Come Let us Fly!*' He began to rustle the pages, turning them with an emphatic snap. If his action was intended to irritate the woman, it had no effect: she continued to fiddle with her handbag with the same agitation. Eventually, an article seemed to draw the man's attention. He leaned back, adjusted the page until he had it in his field of vision, and gave a low, rumbling chuckle.

Martin, noticing this, recognised an opportunity to quiet his restive son. He pulled out the magazine too, opened a page at random, and pointed.

'Look. Dolphins.'

'Where?' Sam twisted in his seat.

'I think I can see one there.'

Sam craned over the picture. It was grainy and badly printed; what might have been a dolphin could just as easily have been a smudge of yellow weed in the water. Sam, however, took it on trust. He stared, captivated.

Martin skimmed the article. It ended with a poem:

> *What a beautiful Khonphang water current!*
> *After falling down your foams were launched up to the heaven*
> *When the sun shines to you, you looked so nice*
>
> *You are famously by the nature creating,*
> *I astoundingly see you under the moonlight.*
> *What a beautify god place for the mankind!*
> *See, everything lovely integrated.*

Martin chuckled.

'What?' snapped Sam. 'Why are you laughing?'

'It says things in a funny way. The English isn't right.'

'What? Tell me.'

Martin sighed, and wondered how to explain. Before he could formulate an answer the plane banked and dipped, the cabin lights dimmed, and the pilot began a rapid and noisy descent. Martin's stomach lurched. He winced, trying to block out the plane's high-pitched screams. The young woman opposite him drew in a sharp breath. Martin saw a flash of panic in his son's eyes, and he placed his arm around him. Sam squirmed away, too grown-up to accept such comfort. Instead, he pressed his nose against the window.

'Everything's black. No – I can see a town. Some lights in the houses. Can't see much.'

'Maybe they don't have street lights.'

'No.' Sam nodded sagely. 'They can't afford them.'

Martin peered over his son's head. He saw dense trees rushing past, low roofed houses, the curve of a great river. A skinny man, lit for a second by the plane's landing lights, gazed up at them.

The plane shuddered, there was a tearing noise, and they were down.

In the silence that followed he gripped Sam's hand. He was further away from home than he had ever been, and the thick night outside did not look welcoming.

'Welcome to Viensong Airport, thank you for flying Mingoria National Airlines, I hope you enjoy your flight,' sang the stewardess.

Hard light flooded the cabin. Martin winced. He felt weary. The last few days had been disturbing, and he had not had time, in the rush of it all, to question what he had done. He did not want to now. He and Sam had spent the previous night in a scabrous guest house is Bangkok, and had bought their Mingoria tickets and visas from a bucket shop tout with lazy eyes, her head flopping from too many nights awake. The woman had misspelled the names on their tickets, and Martin hoped that this fact, coupled with the inefficiency of Mingorian bureaucracy, might mean that after Bangkok their trail would go cold. Beyond that, he could not think.

He leant over and undid Sam's seat belt. The boy turned to him, his eyes wide with excitement.

'I can do it.'

'Let me help you.'

'Where are we?'

'Somewhere far away.'

'Oh.' The boy fell silent, his hands lolling over the belt.

'Come on, Sam.'

Sam slipped from the seat and stood up. He was unsteady. Martin reached forward to help him. Sam shook his head and drew away. The other passengers were already pulling at their overhead luggage and scrambling to get out of the exit. Martin put a protective hand on Sam's shoulders. He waited till the rush had passed before retrieving his modest rucksack from the locker. Beside him, he noticed that the other two foreigners were also holding back. He indulged himself, briefly, with the thought that the young woman was attractive. He wondered if the older man was her companion. The man reached up and fumbled for his luggage. Martin considered helping him, but quickly changed his mind. Foolish to attract attention.

He nudged Sam forwards. 'Okay,' he muttered. 'We can go now.'

The boy tottered ahead, his back straight. Martin followed in his son's footsteps, hoping not to betray any of the doubt that could make him falter.

They stepped outside. The heat and the intensity of the darkness hit Martin like a wall. He felt dizzy. He could hear something – insects – singing in the night. The noise echoed around the barren airstrip.

Sam was already walking down the steps, quite prepared to stride across the open tarmac alone. Martin dashed forwards and took his arm.

'Be careful. Don't fall.'

'I won't.' Sam shook the arm away.

'But *I* might.'

Sam looked at his father, not trusting his seriousness. He broke into a grin. 'If you do, I'll catch you.'

Martin squeezed his son's hand. They walked towards the distant arrivals hall together, holding fast to one another.

Inside, everything was bright and modern and Martin felt his expectations momentarily confounded. From what his father had told him of Mingoria he had anticipated something colourfully primitive: men on wooden benches fanning themselves in the heat perhaps, a clamour of voices from locals hoping for his custom. Instead the arrivals hall was clean and quiet, the only sound coming from the hushed tread of the passengers. Martin's feet echoed on white marble shiny enough for him to see his own reflection.

He stopped walking. The local passengers had already melted through passport control, and he and Sam were alone. No, not quite alone: he saw the sullen young woman waiting a little further back. Near her – though not with her – was the tall foreigner with the cloud of white hair. Not her companion then.

Martin smiled, pulled his and Sam's passports from his jeans pocket, and placed them on the nearest counter with a snap. For the first time since the day of the kidnap, a jolt of excitement ran through him.

Three steps away, Duncan Hardwick fought his disappointment. It was all so much smarter than he had expected, so echoing and empty, with the same soulless brightness of airports everywhere. He wanted strangeness, not this. Heat deadened the air; the tap of his feet on marble became a soft thud. The officials in the cavernous immigration hall wore clean white uniforms, with peaked caps that seemed comically too big for them.

Hardwick stepped up to one of the white plastic desks that served as passport control. A young soldier with grave eyes gave a start. No, the soldier told him, shaking his head, he could not go through yet. Yes, he had to fill out these forms. Three times. Did he have photo? Pay fifty dollars.

Hardwick withdrew, feeling shaky and confused. He retreated to fill out the forms, returned, and handed them over with the money in clean new bills. The soldier took his papers from him and studied them for a long time, his eyes flicking from the passport photo to Hardwick's face, and back. Humidity soaked through the linen of Hardwick's jacket. His shirt clung to him. He shut his eyes and willed himself elsewhere. His fingers throbbed, swollen by heat and too many hours of flying. He felt the room sway.

The young soldier gave a bark of alarm. Hardwick opened his eyes, saw the anxiety on the young man's face, and made a dismissive gesture. He felt sick, true, but the feeling in his stomach did not have a physical cause.

It was longing.

He straightened, and banished thoughts of Lorraine from his mind.

The soldier sniffed, and waved him through.

He drifted through the empty building. In the far corner, near the exit, he saw a small pile of neatly packed luggage. He retrieved his suitcase, newly labeled in precise, hand-written English. He felt a movement in the dead air near him. The sharp-faced American passenger brushed past. She had a lost look, and his heart twisted in sympathy. He felt, for the first time, a sense of kinship with her: her tapping fingers, her imperious demeanor, had irked him until now. He glanced at her shyly. The woman fetched up her suitcase smartly and walked past him without a word.

A short distance beyond her Hardwick noticed the father and small boy, who had sat near him on the flight. They were standing by the exit door and performing, as Hardwick watched, a droll little dance, first approaching and then hesitating before the door, backwards and forwards; no decision made.

Hardwick frowned. His suitcase slipped from his damp palm and fell to the ground with a crash, sending ripples of sound through the yawning airport. He apologised to no one in particular, crouched down, and put his head in his hands. It was ridiculous that he should be here, in this over-bright airport in the middle of nowhere at all. Why had he convinced himself to do it?

He screwed up the muscles in his face, trying to recollect the steps that had led him to this point.

After Felicity's funeral he'd visited the smirking Buddha in the Ashmolean daily. Slowly, the idea of travelling to Mingoria had taken hold. He had lost himself in research. It was soothing, to lose himself in such a way. He had asked for, and got, a sabbatical. After that, his trip took on a momentum of its own. He studied maps, intrigued by their lack of accuracy. He read fragments of history, and tried to grasp what had been included, and what deliberately missed out. A colleague at the School of Oriental and African Studies in London suggested he take a local guide. Hardwick refused, discovering that the thought of spending so many hours with a stranger bothered him more than the thought of being lost or alone.

He raised his head. The young man with the child had noticed him.

The man smiled and approached, offering his hand. 'Hi. I'm Martin. Let me guess: you're new here.'

Hardwick got to his feet. 'Professor Duncan Hardwick. I suppose we are all new.' He hesitated, then shook the proffered hand.

'Yes, I suppose so.' The man released his grip and, with an odd, nervous movement, ran his hand through his hair. It was black and tousled, making the man look somewhat rakish. His smile, though, was candid, and Hardwick warmed to it.

Martin asked, 'Don't 'spose you've booked anywhere to stay?'

'I haven't,' said Hardwick; trying to inject a firmness into his voice he didn't feel.

'Want to look for somewhere? Maybe she'd like to too.'

The two of them turned to the woman in the black suit. A dark expression crossed her face. She shook her head briefly, before heading towards the exit.

Hardwick exchanged glances with Martin. They stepped after her together.

A heartbeat later Hardwick – surrendering to an impulse he could not clearly explain – looked back. He noticed – and saw that the others had not – the young soldier from passport control following quietly behind.

April McGee glared in frustration at the single taxi waiting outside the now deserted airport. She felt angry with herself, and with the whole world. In particular she felt angry with the two men – the clown with the little boy, the old guy with the superior expression – who were hovering so anxiously close by, as if she – of all people – could help them.

She swore under her breath. It was vital she was alone. She fished inside her handbag and pulled out a scrap of paper with the name of a guesthouse scribbled on it in her own frazzled scrawl. At least she had made some preparations. Was it her fault if they hadn't? What did they expect of her? She tensed her shoulders. Her suit was too tight, and she felt hot. She needed to move.

Even so, she hesitated. Against her will she felt the same tug that the two men must also, she guessed, be feeling: the need for some companionship, a small buffer against isolation. It amounted to an instinct for self-preservation, did it not?

The little boy, clinging tight to his father, said in a piping voice: 'Where are we going?'

April shut her bag. Click.

'I suppose you two have a place fixed up?'

'Well, no.' The father turned to her, a little too quickly for her liking. 'We left in a bit of a rush. Didn't have time to sort anything.' His British accent was clipped, a barely perceptible hesitation fluttering in it. He added, his face hopeful, 'Did you?'

'Of course. I'm always prepared.' April turned her attention to the other. 'What about you? Nothing arranged? Just waiting for someone to rescue you?'

'Well, I —' The older man straightened himself. 'I can make my own arrangements.'

She shook her head impatiently. 'It's dark. It's late. There isn't time. You may as well stay at this place I booked. Figure things out in the morning, if you have to.' She didn't wait for his response. She picked up her luggage and marched towards the taxi. Glancing back, she saw the two men follow. The child trailed along behind, touching the sweat that was forming on his upper lip.

The taxi was tiny and decrepit. The driver craned his head out of the window, eager and twinkling.

'Where you go?'

'This place.' April thrust the scrap of paper at him.

The driver read April's squiggles. He nodded brightly. 'My Friend Guest House. Very good. Very expensive. I find you cheaper place.'

'No.' April wanted to scream. Instead she matched the man's smile and said through, gritted teeth, 'This place. Nowhere else. Okay?'

'Okay.' The driver nodded, unperturbed. He skipped out and opened the back door; the two men and the child squeezed in. April slid into the front seat. The driver tried to take her bag; but she hugged it protectively to herself.

'Ten dollars,' he said, not looking at her.

'You're kidding. Come on.'

Behind her the father said anxiously, 'Don't worry. I'll pay. It's not so much.'

'It's a scam.' April sighed. The man was naïve, but if he wanted to pay then so be it. She leaned back in the car seat. She was tense, and it was showing. She shut her eyes and let the breeze blow over her face.

The road was quiet. A few scattered houses had lights burning inside, beacons in the warm darkness. Beyond them the landscape was flat and featureless.

Minutes of silence.

She turned back to look at her fellow passengers and saw that they, like her, were transfixed by the empty road and the strange hush. They stared out of the open windows and did not speak.

The driver passed an open truck, with women in white dresses squashed together in the back. The taxi's headlamps lit up their dresses like torches.

The road widened. Ahead was a tall building lit in bright green neon, a sickly colour that leaked into the indigo air. The building was incongruous, a space-age mirage rising from the sleeping highway. A clean swept drive bordered by flowers led from the dirt road towards a pair of great iron gates. Security guards in pressed uniforms stroked unholstered guns. Looming above them was a madman's vision of luxury, chrome and glass and ejaculating fountains. A sign said, 'Lucky Palace Casino.'

'For gambling,' said the driver, quietly. 'Lots of gambling.' April stared at the building. Her fists were clenched. She swore under her breath. The Casino's lights blurred, became a mark on her retina as it passed out of sight.

The town began, although the transition was difficult for April to judge. Hard to believe that this was a capital city. It was true then, what Mo had told her: that this was a dream place, a lost place. So silent. She was used to Bangkok's mindless jangle, a background roar that clogged her skin and gave her headaches, but without it she was on edge. She strained forward, looking for something to fill the emptiness.

The streets were barely lit, the houses low rise and crumbling. She spotted a few French colonial buildings with closed shutters and ornate, battered facades. Peering over a low wall she saw the sensuously curved roof of a temple, its pointed tiles reaching out like fingers into the night. Further on, a grimacing statue – a temple guard, she guessed – loomed towards her. It had bulging eyes and snaky, wild hair. As April watched the fierce scowl softened. She twisted in her seat. Had it moved? Had she?

Her skin prickled. She swallowed back her fear.

The taxi chugged along, the driver veering to avoid cracks and potholes. April peered. The light was too dim to see much now. What she could see seemed uncared for and forlorn: two-storey houses with washing hanging from open windows, silent alleyways planted with a few scrubby trees.

The taxi turned into one of them. It bumped along over cobbles. Ahead was a large nineteenth century house, with a wide veranda crammed with trailing pot plants. Two chickens ran out of it into the road. The driver screeched on his brakes.

'You are here. This is it.' He sat back. April guessed they would be his only ride of the day. For the week, perhaps.

'So we owe you ten dollars,' she said.

Behind her, the father snapped out of whatever reverie he was in. He fished for his wallet.

'Here. And a tip.'

The driver grinned and shoved the money into the neck of his shirt. He got out of the taxi, pulled the bags from the trunk and dumped them on the ground before jumping back inside to drive away, his wheels juddering on the cobbles.

April listened till the rattle died and the night was still again. A chicken squawked. Insects sang.

Someone whispered hello.

April spun. A young woman was standing on the porch of the house, her hands folded in front of her. April hissed out a breath. The woman wore a long, richly patterned skirt of russet silk. A bunch of keys was looped round a knot at her hip. Her round face was expressionless.

'Hello,' the woman whispered again.

'April McGee. I called you from Bangkok. I booked a room tonight.' April thrust out her hand.

'Yes.' The woman nodded. She did not take the proffered hand.

'Do you have two others? For these men?'

'Yes.'

'Good then.' April lowered her hand and caught it in the other, feeling clumsy and ill at ease.

The woman turned abruptly. She slipped inside the big shuttered house.

The place was large and silent, with flaking wooden floors and wilting pot plants crowded into every space. There was no light on inside, so the party had to follow the woman closely to find their rooms. April matched her step for step as she padded softly upstairs, the key chain jangling as her hips moved. She reached a low corridor with four doors leading off it, nodded to April, and whispered, 'Passport.'

April handed the woman her documents.

'How long you stay?'

'Not long. Till Thursday.'

The woman gave her head a slight tilt. 'No.'

'What do you mean, no? I reserved for two days.'

'Two days, yes. But no Thursday.'

April narrowed her eyes. She said, articulating the words precisely, 'And two days from now is Thursday. Jesus. I'm too tired for this.'

The woman smiled, nodded, and handed back April's passport.

April stepped inside the nearest room. It contained a basin and a single bed. A wire mesh window kept out mosquitoes but not the heat nor the squawking blend of chickens and insects outside. April switched on the electric fan suspended from the ceiling. Its blades turned in great slow swoops, ruffling the air but not cooling it.

She fell onto the bed, her hair moving with the air from the fan and shut her eyes.

Pictures rose in her consciousness, flash frames playing through her head. Fast and violent. She saw a crowd surge forwards, and heard Mo shout. She saw him make desperate gestures as she walked away. Screams. Faces. Mo's blood spilling thickly on the sidewalk.

She sat up on the edge of her bed, her breath coming in gulps.

'Jesus.'

She touched her throat. Impossible to sleep. She stood up.

A cracked mirror stood next to the washbasin. She shuffled towards it and peered. Without lipstick her face was smudgy and ill-defined. This did not please her: she liked things to be definite. She pulled off her clothes and stood naked in front of the mirror.

She stared without wincing. Her flesh was white and gleaming. She believed in sun protection, and the usual leathery yellow of expatriate skin revolted her. Her dark hair, reaching to her shoulders, proved a striking frame to this pale picture. Striking: April said the word to herself. She did not consider herself striking, much less beautiful. She imagined beauty to be something soft and amenable, while she was all angles and hard lines.

She looked downwards. Brown scar tissue started just below her waist. It covered her pelvis and travelled all the way down her left thigh. It was shiny; stretched and wrinkled in odd places. She was barely conscious of it when clothed, though in hot weather it itched. It had been itching today. She shivered, and covered her thin body with a t-shirt.

At dawn she pulled on her suit and re-applied her make-up. Appearance is everything, she muttered. One of the many things she had learnt over the years.

She opened her shutters and peered out. Sunlight was boiling off the last of a pale mist. She retrieved her large black handbag and opened it. It was stuffed with dollar bills. She touched them and sighed. She withdrew her hand and her fingers brushed against a letter, dog-eared and fragile. She plucked it out, her eyes lingering on her father's handwriting. She dropped the letter back into the bag, left the room and walked downstairs, heels tapping on the wooden floor.

Outside, she strode down the lane to the main road, confident of finding transport. She had researched the place well: a pedicab driver was waiting already, tipped off by the guesthouse perhaps and hopeful, even in early dawn, for a fare from the foreign arrivals.

'Where you go?'

April stepped on board. 'Just go.' She hugged her bag to her chest. 'Go quickly.'

2

Martin began to chew on a few indigestible crumbs of a dream. Beside him, Sam squirmed and muttered. Martin sank deeper into unconsciousness, turned onto his back, leaving his stomach soft and exposed.

A sudden, jabbing pain cut through his sleep.

He cried out.

Where was he? What had attacked him? The room revolved about him in a fug of jetlag. He tossed his head. His eyes found Sam's small white body. He saw a sharp, flexed heel. The drunken spinning slowed. He reached out a tentative hand, and, with great gentleness, patted the boy's foot.

His son.

His heart rate decelerated. His body relaxed. He shut his eyes; opened them again to be sure the boy was still there. Sam's eyelids fluttered. He was there. Martin turned to one side and stared at him.

Sam's hair flopped carelessly over a pale forehead. His mouth was slightly open, taking soft breaths. He wore a small frown, as if his dream puzzled him. Beyond that his face showed no sign of fear or anxiety. Martin fought an urge to hold him. It was odd: the boy was so much a part of him, every curve of his features imprinted on his brain. Yet he was separate, locked in a private world which Martin could not reach. Martin shrugged this thought away.

He let his eyes focus on the rest of the room. Gradually, he pieced together where he was and how he had got there. He remembered the taxi ride through the secret town, the chickens in the secluded courtyard, the grumpy American woman. He smiled. It would be no loss to be parted from her quickly but at least she had got them here. He shook his head, baffled by his lack of preparation. He had needed to run, so he'd run to the furthest place he could imagine. What to do now was beyond him.

He looked back at Sam, his nervousness returning. What had he been thinking of? What on earth should he do next? The skin on his son's face had taken on a golden cast in the early morning sun. He looked beautiful. Martin shuddered, caught off guard. Sam is here, he told himself. We are together. For now, that is enough.

He sat up, walked across the room, and splashed his face and naked body with brackish water from the small basin. A filmy swirl settled in the pan and would not drain away. Martin pulled on shorts and moved over to the window, opened the shutters, and filled the room with light.

Sam let out a moan. 'Oh no.'

'What's the matter?'

'The lightness. Stop it.'

'It's morning now. Actually it's foggy.'

'Oh no.' The boy wriggled and turned his face away.

'Don't you want breakfast?'

'No. Yes.'

'Yes or no?'

'I want toast.'

'I don't know if they have toast. I'll try and find out. Let's get up.'

Sam sat up, looking as crumpled and confused as Martin had felt earlier. Martin watched his son anxiously.

'Are you all right?'

'Yes.' Sam stuck out his lip.

'Do you want to get up?'

Sam nodded. Martin hesitated, then began to hunt around in his rucksack. He had bought one change of clothes for Sam at a concession stall in Heathrow. The things were so tiny that they had sunk under the tangle of his own wretched, grown-up belongings. After much digging he pulled out a small pair of shorts. He held them out in front of him for Sam to take. Without warning, his hands shook. The vulnerability of the little shorts hurt him. He winced and turned his face away.

Sam, unperturbed, climbed from the bed, snatched the shorts from him and pulled them on. Martin knelt down, and helped Sam with his t-shirt and sandals. His hands, trembling still, fumbled with the straps.

'I'm hungry,' said Sam, his voice a whine.

'We'll try and find something to eat, Sam,' Martin whispered. 'I don't know. It's early. We'll just try. Okay?'

Sam nodded. 'Okay.' He held out his hand. Martin took it. They walked out together to face the day.

The rest of the guesthouse was silent as they tiptoed through it. Martin peered outside and saw the young woman who had ushered them in the night before sitting on the porch steps. She looked up and smiled at them. Martin said,

'Good morning.'

She nodded.

'Is it too early to get breakfast? My little boy is hungry.'

The woman's smile widened. Martin realised she was older than he had previously thought, in her thirties perhaps, with a few delicate creases round her eyes. He was about to repeat his question when she said,

'Not early. You can buy bread. Across the road and turn left, walk quite far. By the fountain. They sell you bread.'

Martin nodded. 'And here?' He pointed to the ground. 'Do you make breakfast here?'

'Not today.'

'I see.' There was no obvious answer to this, though Martin was intrigued to know which day they *did* serve breakfast. 'Tomorrow?' He asked. 'Thursday?'

She drew in a sharp breath. 'No Thursday.'

He blinked at the woman for a while. She stared back. He felt awkward and turned away.

He pulled Sam up the cobbled track that led from the secluded courtyard. He stepped gingerly. The humidity was thick and soft around him. Sam kept looking back at the silent woman. A tiny bantam chicken ran past, squawking. Sam, skittish, let go of Martin's hand and ran after it.

'Don't.' Martin sighed, and followed. The chicken vanished in a cloud of dust. Sam squatted, captivated by something else: a nursing dog and three puppies, tiny runtish things with blind eyes suckling by the side of the track. Sam stared at them. He held out a finger to poke them. Martin snatched his hand away.

'Don't.'

Sam flinched. 'Don't HURT me!'

'They're dirty, that's all.' Martin tried to soften his voice. 'They might bite you. You've got to be careful.'

Sam pulled his hand from Martin's. His face was red. 'I HATE you. You hurt me, you – MAN.'

'No. Listen. No.' Martin tried to put his arm around him. Sam twisted away.

'Go away.'

'Listen. Hey. We can watch the puppies, Okay? It's only because I don't want you to get hurt.' He gestured helplessly. 'Please, Sam.'

The boy shook his head, his lips a thin line.

'Don't you want to get breakfast? I'm hungry, are you? We can go to the bakery and explore the town. We can be explorers.'

Sam let out a sharp breath and shrugged; an exasperated gesture that Martin recognised as one of his own. He tried not to smile.

Sam said, 'Yes but we've got to have breakfast first. Or we'll be tired.'

'That's right.' Martin stood up and held out his hand again. Sam trotted beside him.

The track disgorged them onto a main road. A couple of bicycles drifted past. Martin could see no cars, and he wondered if this was because of the hour, or because there never would be any traffic. An old man sat in the dust and picked his nose. His bare knees pointed at the sky.

The pavement was cracked and broken, with many potholes opening up unexpectedly to reveal a skeleton of pipes beneath the road. Martin stared at them, and up at the low houses with half open windows exposing glimpses of the shadowy rooms within. He thought, the town is showing itself to me in layers: skin, and then the bones underneath.

He picked his way over the pipes, lifting Sam in the air to avoid the potholes.

'You couldn't play sleeping lions, could you?' He said, offhandedly. 'Too many cracks. Too easy to get caught.'

'No.' Sam shook his head. After a pause he said, 'You could, though.' He began avoiding the cracks with studied concentration, taking giant steps or tiny wobbly ones to reach the next island of unbroken paving. He started to mutter to himself as they walked: 'They are not getting me. We are hiding. The lions can't see me in this street. They will NOT roar.'

Their pace slowed. Martin's mind drifted.

A wall opened out into what he guessed must be a temple complex to their left, a cluster of low buildings with gracefully curved roofs set in an acre or two of yellow grass. The roofs were covered with dark green tiles, and dipped and sloped like the curved hands of a dancer. Silver mosaic tiles on some of the walls flashed coded signals. The sun picked out an elaborate swirling design – a tree, with animals sitting underneath – in flaking gold leaf. The parched grass in front of the temple was strewn with litter, thin bits of paper and plastic that fluttered in the low breeze. Martin frowned: the contrast disappointed him. He looked further into the complex and saw a flash of orange. Robes on a washing line were drying in the sun. He supposed monks must do laundry too. He paused and watched the robes swaying in the breeze for a moment. He was about to turn away when a loud, angry bell pierced the air. The sound made Martin start. Sam swiveled his head.

'What is it?'

'A bell.' Martin tugged at Sam's arm, but the child was immovable. 'Come on, Sam. Breakfast.'

Sam pointed in the direction of the temple. 'There,' he said, fiercely. 'There.' He was staring at a young boy monk. The barefoot child – eleven or twelve, Martin guessed – was dressed in dirty yellow and had a roughly shaven head. This was not what had attracted Sam's attention: it was the fact that the monk was standing on a podium and tugging at a rope to chime the bell.

Sam was transfixed. Martin knew what he was thinking without having to ask: he wanted to be that boy, and he wanted to ring that bell. He pulled at Sam's arm a second time, but to no effect. Sam was not going to move till the matter had been investigated. Martin took a few uncertain steps into the temple complex. Sam, needing no encouragement, towed him further inside.

Martin whispered, 'Hush. Slow down. We might not be allowed.'

By now the boy monk had seen them. He left off his ringing, hopped from the podium and approached, grinning.

'Hello.'

'Hello,' said Martin, surprised that the monk spoke English.

'Where you from?' The monk asked.

Sam said, 'Camberwell.' and hid behind Martin's legs.

The monk looked at them both quizzically. 'Camberwell?'

'England. London,' said Martin.

'Oh.' The monk nodded and smiled. He pulled out a packet of cigarettes. 'Want one?'

'Oh? Oh, sure.' It occurred to Martin that a cigarette was exactly what he wanted. He nodded gratefully, with only a small twinge of guilt. The boy sparked up a lighter with a rough fingernail, and lit a cigarette in his mouth. He passed it to Martin.

'Thanks.'

'From England, London.' The boy smiled, showing very white teeth. 'I am from here.' He pointed to the ground. He said, formally as if reading a quotation, 'The joyful land of Mingoria.'

'And um, how long have you been a monk?' Asked Martin, wondering if this was appropriate small talk.

'Very long time. I have no mom and dad,' said the boy, cheerfully. 'So here is better. I go to school.'

'I see. So it's for your education.'

'Mmm, yes.' The boy nodded. 'I like to learn English.'

'Your English is very good.'

'Thank you very much.'

'You ring the bell,' said Sam, emerging from behind Martin's legs.

'Yes.' The monk nodded. 'Every day, I ring it.' Sam nodded back, seeing that this was important. The monk's eyes fixed on Martin. 'Why you here now?'

'Why?' Martin struggled, discomfited. He cast around for reasons. 'I'm on holiday.'

The boy smiled broadly. 'It's not good, you here.'

'Oh.' Martin was taken aback. 'I'm sorry. I mean, don't you like tourists?'

'I like foreigners. I like learning English.'

'Then –'

'Do you know Mr Karasin?'

'Mr–?'

'Mr Karasin. Okay, it's better. You talk to him now. Thank you very much.'

Martin took a drag on his cigarette. The nicotine was doing excellent things to his brain, sharpening his eyes and bringing the temple, the morning and the smiling boy into bright focus. Maybe Mr Karasin was inside the temple. The chief monk or something. Martin took a step forward. The monk put a gentle restraining hand on his arm.

'Not this way, the other way. Outside at the bakery. You know the bakery?'

'No. Well, yes. We were going there – for breakfast.' Martin remembered. His stomach rumbled.

'Okay, it's good. Mr Karasin is having breakfast. So you go and talk to him now.'

'Who is Mr Karasin?'

'Very good guy, Russian guy, knows a lot of things. He will tell you that you must go away and go back home to England. Camberwell.'

'But I don't want to go back home to England, Camberwell.'

Sam asked lightly, looking up, 'When are we going home?'

Martin grimaced. 'Later, Sam.' He said to the monk, 'I don't think I want to meet this Mr Karasin.'

'But you want breakfast.' The boy smiled.

Martin nodded, conceding the point. He scattered ash, and put the cigarette out under his foot, screwing it into the ground. He glanced at the monk to see if he disapproved of this addition to the temple litter. The boy hadn't registered.

'Okay. I guess we'll bump into your friend.'

'Yes. Bump into him.' The boy clapped his hands together to indicate bumping.

'And you, ah – you want to come? Have breakfast? Or do you have – ah – monk things to do?'

'Monk things. Yes.' The boy nodded.

'Fine.' Martin winked, liking the knowing little fellow. He pulled at Sam's hand. 'Come on then. Breakfast.' He nodded to the monk, wanting to offer him something in return for the cigarette and the broad smile. The boy nodded and retreated swiftly from them, smiling still.

Martin and Sam walked on, hand in hand. Martin felt he was beginning to get a sense of the town. Their guesthouse was down an alley running off a central boulevard, which was intersected by a network of smaller side streets. These led to another wide boulevard, which ran parallel to the road he was on. He passed a sign: 'Street Seven.' He smiled, amused. Whoever had named the roads was pragmatic rather than romantic. The numbering might be helpful, except that they'd passed 'Lane Seven' earlier, and the monk's home was 'Temple Seven'. The road was lined with two-storey houses, some of which had ironwork balconies with plants curling through them. Most had peeling shutters painted in faded party colours: pink, white, pale blue. Their walls were fissured and crumbling. Martin smelt a faint sweetness or rottenness in the air. He passed a bush heavy with white blossom. Clouds of flowers had fallen to the ground and were clogging up an open drain below. Jasmine? Frangipani? He squinted through the sun, trying to name the blooms. Nearby, a dog with half its fur missing lay panting on the ground, its grey tongue swelling wetly on the road. Martin stepped gingerly round it. Heat beat down on his bare head.

From what he'd seen from the taxi the night before he guessed the entire city was no bigger than an English market town, and a good deal quieter. The bakery, therefore, was easy to find. It advertised itself as 'Genuine French,' and was the only place in the whole town that seemed busy, Martin noticed with relief. He was beginning to find the unruffled silence eerie.

The bakery was situated in the middle of a crescent of buildings, in the centre of which was a dried-up fountain full of bits of plastic and discarded bottles. Rattan chairs and tables were set out on the broken pavements, and the occupants – most of them old men – were deep in conversation. None of them looked up when Martin and Sam walked past them into the building.

It was shady and cool inside. Rectangles of light filtered through the window. Martin sank into a chair, realising, now that he was cool, how intense the outside heat had been. His shirt stuck to his back. He ran his hand through his hair. It stood up in clumps. Sam was flushed. He looked at Martin's hair and laughed. Martin pulled a face.

There were two other customers inside: a young local woman who was staring into space and seemed not at all interested in her food, and a grizzled white man with thinning hair, who was stirring a cup of thick black coffee.

A waitress approached. She was wearing a red headscarf knotted at the back and a gaudy green checked apron. Humiliating attire, thought Martin, but what must pass as 'genuine French' around here. The girl smiled sweetly.

'Que desirez-vous boire?'

'Um…'

'What you like?'

'A coffee please,' said Martin. 'And toast?'

'Croissant and egg?'

Martin glanced at Sam, who nodded energetically. 'Yes. An egg. Thanks. And juice for the boy.'

She disappeared silently. Martin was struck by how little noise the people he had met so far made: his landlady, the monk, this girl. They came and went like ghosts, making him feel clumsy and too corporeal. The silence from the other two customers thickened in the air, broken only by the chink, chink of the grizzled man's coffee spoon. Martin's own coffee came and it was good, thick and bitter. He found that he too was inclined to dribble it over his spoon. Sam ate his egg happily, humming to himself.

The other foreigner seemed to be feeling the heat. He groaned, and wiped a handkerchief over his head.

'Terrible,' he said. 'Terrible country.' Martin shrugged at the man, not wanting to talk.

'The heat, you know,' continued the foreigner. 'And then we wonder why everyone is crazy.' The man laughed softly, regarding Martin with watery blue eyes. 'All crazy. Every one of them. And we are the craziest of all for coming here. To the *Joyful* Land.' He dabbed his handkerchief over his mouth as he leaned forwards. 'American?'

'English.'

'Ah yes. My apologies.'

'There's no need.'

'I haven't offended you? Strange. I would be offended.' He took another slurp of his drink. His eyes had large bags under them. Despite his wheezy laughter, everything about him – his saggy eyes, his dirty suit – was wilting and melancholic.

Martin turned to Sam, absorbed in his egg. 'Do you want to make soldiers?'

'No,' said the boy, firmly.

'Are you sure? I can cut them up for you?'

'Oh no.' Sam shivered at the thought.

Martin tried to think of another ruse, but it was too late. The sagging foreigner had eased himself out of his chair and wandered over to join them, bringing with him his half-drunk coffee.

'You don't mind, of course?' He indicated the seat next to Martin.

'Please.'

'Good.' The creases of the man's face lifted into a smile. 'I am Karasin.' He held out his hand.

'Martin Morley. I've heard of you.'

'Yes. I knew you were coming.'

'You did?'

'Please.' The man made a gesture. 'No need to look so concerned. The boy at the temple ran ahead, that's all. I have been looking out for you. You are, I think, quite conspicuous. As we all are. We strangers.' He wiped his forehead again, then folded his handkerchief and placed it neatly on the table in front of him, to the left of his coffee.

'So,' said Martin. 'What do you do here? You're not a tourist, obviously.'

'What? No.' The man grimaced. His eyes wandered over to the girl, lingered on her body.

'I see.'

'Yes, yes. I am not a tourist. In fact I am a government official. Please, not *this* government. I am the official Trade Commissioner for the government of Russia. Which is an amusing position to be in, because this country has nothing to trade, and Russia has nothing it wishes to buy. So you see, I have an easy life.'

'I see.'

'Hmm.' The man unfolded his handkerchief and wiped his face again. He inclined his head at Sam. 'Charming boy.'

Martin drew Sam closer. 'Yes. Thank you. My son.'

'Hmm.' Karasin's eyes drifted away, losing interest. He gulped the last of his coffee, and pulled out a wilted cigarette from one of his deep pockets. He lit it fussily and took a long drag. He said, looking into the distance, 'I would like to suggest something to you. I would like to suggest, Mr Morley, that you leave now. Things are happening here that you cannot understand. And it would be much better – for you and your sweet boy – that you left very soon and did not think about coming back. This place is not as it seems. The silence you hear conceals unpleasant things. There is a great deal of – unpleasantness. I say this–' His eyebrows beetled up, 'as a disinterested observer. I think that you are stupid to come here in the first place, but that is only because I abhor travel. I would not have come. And now I advise you to leave.'

He took another long drag of the cigarette, looked at in disappointment, and tipped ash over the floor.

Martin stared. 'What are you talking about?'

'Yes. I see. You don't believe me.'

'What is there to believe? You haven't told me anything.'

'You seek knowledge?'

'Knowledge? I'd like to know your reasons. It all seems fine to me.'

'Appearances can be deceptive. My appearance, for example, is deceptive. You take me to be an eccentric?'

Martin shrugged. 'No. Not particularly. I don't know who you are.'

'I am the official Trade Commissioner of the country of Russia.' He added, as if an afterthought: 'And I am very tired.'

Martin felt a rush of hostility. 'So you're saying we should leave, for no apparent reason?'

'Yes,' sighed Karasin. 'That's what I think. And no, I can't tell you why because I am not sure myself. Nobody is. I may be wrong. I hope so. All I can say with certainty is that arrangements here are becoming – unstable. Things are – how shall I describe it – tipping a little...' he illustrated by making a cradle with his arms, 'and they may tip in a certain direction, or another, or they may settle in some other equilibrium altogether. Who can tell? Rock-a-bye, baby, yes? And perhaps we shall all be rocked to sleep, in this place that is always sleeping. Or perhaps we shall fall. I can't tell. I can only say that you should leave this lovely sleepy place. This crazy place, this kleptocracy, whose chief thief is getting fatter even than me and has only recently, in a fit of pique, banned Thursdays. It would be easy to arrange a flight.' He waved his hand lightly. 'You can believe me or not, as you choose.'

'I choose not,' muttered Martin. 'Everything seems fine. I can't just leave.'

'Well. Well.' The man sighed. He stood up abruptly, scraping his chair. 'I am sorry. Perhaps there is nothing more to say.' He held out his hand. Martin rose to take it. Karasin shook the hand briefly, and left, dragging his feet.

Martin sat down. His anger had risen to his face, and he felt it burning. He sipped his coffee.

'Who was that man?' Sam asked.

'No-one,' growled Martin. 'An idiot.' He got up, tugged Sam by the arm, and propelled him outside.

3

A little further up the road Duncan Hardwick, open guidebook in hand, Panama hat on his head, was drifting through the heat. He was barely awake. His night had been disturbed by the dreams that had haunted him since Felicity's death: dreams of decay, of flesh melting from bones. His disquiet had not left him on waking; it had if anything been intensified by the strangeness of the place. Here, everything was dreamlike, and the movement in and out of consciousness that had afflicted him through the night seemed hardly different from walking, now, through this peculiar mid-morning quiet.

He took off his hat and scratched his head. He felt – difficult to describe it – disconnected, but at the same time as if this reality was more intense and present than any he was used to. It had a dream's eerie clarity, a dream's unease. He replaced his hat and shuffled on, blinking. He had never in his life worn sunglasses. He wondered now if they would help him, and removed a pair that he had bought in Heathrow from his jacket pocket. He squinted through them against the glare. He stepped into some shade, and it blinded him by contrast.

He drank in the crumbling colonial facades, the goggle-eyed temple idols with their leers and upraised fists, the gaping cracks in the pavement. All astonished him. He lingered over small details: a door with a rough iron handle painted in bright blue, a shutter carved with an intricate Fleur-de-Lys design. He ignored the curious glance of an old woman who fanned herself in the heat.

A group of small boys ran by, pointing and laughing. Hardwick tipped his hat at them and they ran from him, screaming with terror and glee. He chuckled. He felt suddenly, unaccountably, happy. Happy. He stopped to take this in.

His guidebook was old and battered. He'd picked it up from an antique bookseller in Banbury before he'd left, and although it was roughly one hundred years out of print the map of the town still seemed accurate. The town was built on a grid pattern, with two wide boulevards running in parallel towards the banks of a swollen river. Several smaller roads intersected these two thoroughfares, and were themselves criss-crossed by a bewildering network of small alleys that looked, on his map, like a child's scribble. Before he left England Hardwick had underlined passages in his book about various temples, and memorised pieces on different architectural styles and their symbolism. He was gratified to find little examples here and there which illustrated things he had learnt. The book also contained quotes from early travellers and French colonists. One, from an official newly arrived from Paris, was not altogether complimentary about his fellows:

> *They have abandoned dignity and allowed themselves to sink into a life of voluptuous torpor beloved of the native* Min. *Few rise before mid morning. Those that do sit at their desks, listless, idling away their hours in gossip or meaningless speculation. Their greatest preoccupation is their bellies. Many have taken native wives and dress them in outlandish costumes, seeming to take pride in the tawdry show. Some wear native dress themselves. A few smoke opium, and call their indolence happiness. There is little help for these fellows. Their work is neglected or seen to half-heartedly at best. Half measures, indeed, are the highest standard to be expected here.*

Hardwick bent down the corner of the page and closed his book. The picture painted by the shocked official sounded rather attractive to him. Torpor. Listlessness. Did that not describe his state of mind these last few months? Might there be a certain relief in sinking into such a state without guilt or regret, swaddled by heat and knowing that others had been there before him?

Through an open doorway he noticed a group of men hunched over cups of liquid. He noticed his dry mouth and wandered inside, stooping low under the lintel to pass through the door. The hum of talk subsided. He sat down stiffly. A plump woman bustled up to him, batting her hands as if swatting flies. Hardwick took off his hat.

'Can I have something to drink?'

She gaped.

'Drink,' said Hardwick. 'Tea. Oh dear.' He pointed at one of the cups, and mimed the act of drinking. The woman's face brightened; she nodded and hurried away. The men smiled. All of them were old, and Hardwick wondered about this. The young, he presumed, were working, though he had seen little evidence of work being done so far. In fact he had seen little evidence of people at all. He remembered the children who had laughed at him, but otherwise the streets had been empty. Perhaps today was a holiday.

He tried to smile at the old men, but they did not respond. Shyness overcame him and he looked away. Once his tea arrived (pale and bitter, without milk) he drank it hastily, unhappy at the continuing silence and feeling as though he had intruded. At length the conversation picked up around him, in whispers – absurd, he thought, as he couldn't understand the language.

Whatever the men were discussing seemed a topic of some importance to them. The whispers – though they stayed whispers – soon became animated. One man spat on the floor. Another, his face red, banged his fist on a table. A third calmed them both with a gesture. The silence that followed was dense and uncomfortable. Hardwick tried to concentrate on his drink. It was shady inside. Even so, heat prowled in through the doorway and open windows.

He stood up and left some notes on the table. Far too many, probably: the few dollars he had exchanged at the airport had been returned to him as a grubby brick of fading red *Khuap*, calculated by weight rather than numerals and held together with an elastic band. He did not wait to check the amount. He left without tipping his hat.

He walked to a wide thoroughfare, more smoothly paved than the rest of the streets but equally lacking in traffic. He was disconcerted to notice – having just made this observation – two sleek Mercedes with blacked out windows crawl by. He peered at them, trying to make out passengers. The windows reflected back his face. The cars slowed, giving him the alarming impression that their occupants were studying him in return. They revved up and sped away.

Hardwick walked a little further. He came to a three storey building constructed in a heavy utilitarian style, adorned with flowing red banners. Over the door was a large seal – a hammer and sickle above an ox and plough – that he recognised as the symbol of the governing party. He halted, arrested by the sight. Seeing that there were no guards outside the building (he had suspected at first that it was government offices; perhaps even the parliament) he approached, ascending wide steps leading to an open doorway. He saw a small sign by the door advertising the building as the Mingoria National Museum. His curiosity aroused, he stepped inside.

The place was poorly lit, and (as far as he could tell) empty apart from himself and one shrivelled attendant who sat hunched over a desk. The man motioned to him wordlessly to buy a ticket. Hardwick gave him a sweaty note, fingered by many hands before him. The shrivelled man made a great show of tearing off a piece of paper from a book of what looked to Hardwick like raffle tickets. Hardwick made a quick calculation: the ticket had cost him around three pence. He passed through the open doors of two consecutive rooms, walking swiftly till he escaped the suspicious eye of the attendant. Then, delighted by his new environment, he set out to explore at his leisure.

He found the lower floors disappointing. The history they contained was fractured and partial, and related in a mixture of French – a language he was not fluent in – and broken English. He read of the tyranny of five ancient Kingdoms, of the oppression of the people by a succession of despots, of wealth counted in elephants and gold. It was a child's history, written with naive simplicity. Little mention was made of the ethnic make up of the country, or the long-standing enmity he had read about between the plains people – the *Min*, who formed the majority of the population – and the ethnically diverse groups who lived in the mountains and northern hinterland. In the accounts he'd read, the five main Kingdoms had coalesced two hundred years ago to form a loose nation, but this had been at the expense of tribal minorities scattered throughout the country. These had at best been ignored, at worst subjugated. He pulled out his guidebook to find a quote:

> *The* Khia a*re a milk cow to be taxed and kicked or otherwise – if they are lucky – ignored by the* Min. *The French in this are as guilty as any, seeing the* Khia *as incidental to their* mission civilatrice *and thus fair game to any petty official wishing to make a supplement to his meagre income.*

Where the minority people were mentioned at all in the museum, it was in sugary references to random curios; fine silverware necklaces, woven bags, or indigo dyed clothing. Hardwick shook his head and moved on.

He found the upper floors of the museum more interesting. They dealt with modern history. This was not usually a field that excited him, and he was particularly uninterested in the grubby dictatorship which apparently ran the country today. However, while the accounts were partial to the point of absurdity, the objects on display compelled him with their authenticity. Of most interest to him was a small photograph, faded at the edges, of the first National

Party Congress in 1952, a ramshackle affair by the look of it. Fifteen young men sat at a long wooden table in an otherwise bare room. They posed stiffly for the photograph, their plain western-style suits conveying hard work and utility but at the same time marking them out as intellectuals, a cut above the common people they purported to serve. Vien Song – later self-styled president for life – was, Hardwick knew, merely a minor figure in the struggle against French rule. Despite this, the inscription drew attention to him, rather than the sad looking man in the centre of the photograph, although the sad man was Sisavong, the country's first Prime Minister. Looking more like an awe-struck provincial than a dictator in waiting, Vien Song smiled affably to the left of the shot, sweetly delighted to be posing for a photograph at all. To his right the Chinese delegate sat watchful, the only one of the group not smiling.

The room contained several other curious objects. Hardwick ticked off a list in his mind to keep and show Felicity later, a habit he had not yet been able to break. There was the pitted table on which Vien Song had composed his political strategy and later, in the sixties, his battle plan during the long and painful civil war which had finally brought him to power. Beside it, absurdly, sat Vien Song's exercise braces. The museum's *piece de resistance* was a full size anti-aircraft gun. It had been used, the inscription proudly announced, to shoot down an American B52 bomber before it discharged its load. Hardwick bowed his head, made queasy by the triumphalism of the display. He returned downstairs, mildly depressed.

The central stairway was dusty and echoing, and the tantalising strangeness of this – and the sight of fingers of sunlight creeping down from a high window and picking out dust motes scuttling through the air – revived him.

Back on the street, he met a wall of heat. It was past midday. This time the silence could be accounted for: anyone with any sense would be taking a siesta. Hardwick, however, walked on. There was a certain feature in the middle of town that he wanted to reach: an archway over a crossroads, intricately carved in a soft swirling design, possibly of Khmer origin according to his book. He had been vaguely heading that way all morning. He consulted his map, and set out.

The road widened. He kicked up dry dust as he walked, and it clouded in front of his eyes. Earlier, he had seen one or two palm fronds peeking over walls enclosing small gardens. Here there was no greenery, just a patch of yellow grass a little to the left of the road. He crossed over. Ahead of him, hazy in the hot air, was a great, murky river.

The riverbank was low, a strip of caked mud. There was a small island in the middle of the river, overgrown with long weeds that trailed into the water like hair. On the far bank – just visible in the haze – was another country, one almost as poor and forgotten as Mingoria.

Hardwick walked to the river's edge. Someone had set out a few tables and chairs there in a vain attempt to give the place a jaunty, resort-like atmosphere. Hardwick ignored the hopeful glance of a man standing alert by a far table. He walked till he reached the place where the muddy water lapped the dry earth, leaving shadowy, mysterious stains.

It was perhaps the heat, or perhaps the brittle light reflected on the water, but when he heard a scream his senses were too dull to react.

The scream came again, and a crack, like thunder. Hardwick froze. The sound had come from behind him, and the river was in front. He was no swimmer. His back felt horribly exposed.

Echoes from the crack rippled out across the water. Hardwick spun round.

The scene was as quiet and still as before. The proprietor of the little attempt at a café was standing by the far table twisting his hands. Hardwick glanced at him. The man looked down, avoiding his eyes.

Hardwick stumbled up the riverbank to the road.

He stood under the heavy heat. The road rippled in front of him. For a second everything was still.

He heard another scream, a shrill and desperate sound.

A man staggered out of a doorway onto the road, his white shirt stained scarlet. A woman supported his arm. She saw Hardwick and screamed again. Two other men ran to her, shouting and flailing their arms. One of them grabbed the wounded man's shoulders, supporting him just as his knees buckled. He fell. A child ran to him, sobbing. He sat in the road at Hardwick's feet.

Hardwick shouted, 'What's happened? Has he been shot?'

The screaming woman began to gesticulate violently. Hardwick held out his hands to her.

'I'm sorry. I don't understand. I'm so sorry.'

She batted his hands away and began to point, jabbing her finger at something beyond him. Her wide mouth revealed gaps between her teeth; her tongue was a thick worm.

'I'm sorry. Can I help? Can I take him to a hospital?' Hardwick tried to step towards the wounded man, but more people gathered and barred his way. A young man with bloodshot eyes wagged a finger at him. Hardwick hesitated, distressed. A blur of faces surrounded him, questioning, accusing, threatening.

He stumbled backwards.

He fled.

He ran through the streets, ignoring the heat and the tearing of his lungs. He did not think to consult his map, wanting only to get as far from the scene as possible. Soon he was lost in a maze of back alleys and blind corners.

A dead end brought him up short. He stopped, panting. His chest hurt. He leaned against a wall and became aware of his shirt clinging to his clammy flesh. Trembling, he opened his guidebook and unfolded the map. He looked about him for clues, saw the shining green roof of a temple, and realised he was only a few streets from the guesthouse. He set off towards it with relief. By the time he reached it his sweat – though not his fear – had evaporated.

He shut and locked the door to his small room, stripped off his shirt and splashed himself with the lukewarm water that came juddering from the tap. He lay on his bed.

Insects began buzzing against the shutters. Hardwick's eyelids drew down.

He slept.

He woke and felt cold. His bed was soaking. Though the night was warm and cradling, the damp, and some chilly residue of fear, made him shiver. He retrieved a towel from his suitcase, dried himself, and put on a crumpled but clean shirt. He sat on the edge of his bed, feeling disoriented. He had no idea what time it was, and the darkness felt unnatural. He was hungry. Everything was wrong.

He stood up and switched on a light. An insect fluttering on the edge of his hearing retreated into a shadowy corner. Better. He stumbled out in search of food.

Downstairs he heard voices. In the shaded lobby, a small group of *Min* was gathered around a flickering television screen. Hardwick approached. The screen was filled with the orange and pudgy face of President Vien Song. The president's words were inter-cut with martial music and what appeared to be archive footage of a military parade. The group around the TV listened, straining forwards. Hardwick watched for a while, biting his lip. Learning nothing, he crept away.

Stepping outside, he was relieved to see the dim silhouette of the other foreigner – Martin, he recalled – sitting on the veranda.

Hardwick was not a sociable man, and ordinarily would have been too shy to thrust himself upon the other. Tonight, though, was a night to seek out human company. He shuffled onto the veranda and asked if he could pull up a chair.

'Sure.' Martin's smile was warm. 'Have a beer too. Actually it's not bad.' The younger man pulled open a can with a fizz, and thrust it into Hardwick's hand.

'Thank you. I don't usually drink beer.' Hardwick looked at the can.

Martin shrugged. 'Suit yourself. It's cold though.'

Hardwick took an experimental sip. 'Yes. It is cold,' he reflected. 'Perhaps I shall have it.'

'After all, you're on holiday.'

'Indeed. Yes, I am.'

Martin pushed a plate of rice and fish towards him. 'She made me loads. Have some.'

'Thank you.' Hardwick smiled gratefully, took the plate, and began to eat. The man, it appeared, was kind. Hardwick felt subdued at this thought.

Martin said, his voice polite, 'Nice place. The guesthouse I mean.'

'Yes. Very peaceful.' Hardwick agreed.

A pause. Hardwick listened to the evening's unknowable sounds. Martin hummed, rocking in his rattan chair.

'Yes. Peaceful.' Hardwick's words trailed into the night. He clicked his tongue. 'So. Your son is asleep?'

'Like a babe.' The man nodded towards an upstairs balcony. 'I'd hear him if he woke.'

'And what brought you here?'

'What?' Martin seemed surprised by the question. He mumbled, 'Oh, a holiday. You know.'

'Of course.' Hardwick looked at the ground.

'You?'

'The same.' Hardwick coughed, his throat catching.

'I'm a teacher,' offered Martin. 'Music. We get long breaks. It's true what they say – bloody lazy, the lot of us. Still, school kills sometimes. The kids – wild. It's nice to get away.'

Hardwick nodded eagerly. 'I'm a teacher too, of sorts. An historian. I teach, sometimes.'

Another silence. The younger man drummed his fingers on the table. He seemed as nervous as himself. Though Hardwick wondered about this, his natural sensitivity did not allow him to inquire further. His own agitation was deep, and had not been assuaged by the beer or the polite chitchat. He took a breath.

'Something happened earlier, you know,' he said. 'In the town. I feel troubled by it. May I talk to you?'

Martin's eyes searched him. Green eyes, Hardwick noticed. 'Of course,' he said, softly. 'What happened?'

Hardwick blushed. 'A man. A man was shot, I believe.'

Martin spluttered, spilling beer onto his shirt. 'What? Christ. Why didn't you say so before?'

Hardwick shrank back. 'I wasn't sure – I may be wrong, you know.'

'Wrong? What do you mean? Was he shot or not?' Martin began to stand up.

'I don't know.' Hardwick waved him down. 'I heard a bang. A loud crack in the air. I went to have a look, and – well, this man was covered in blood.'

'Jesus Christ.' Martin was white. 'Did you ask what had happened?'

'Nobody spoke English. There was a crowd. I didn't want to interfere.'

'Christ. Christ.' Martin sank back in his chair.

'Perhaps it was nothing. A quarrel. I can't even be sure it was a gunshot I heard.'

'No. I suppose not. Good God.'

Hardwick wanted, now, to find a rational explanation. 'It really may have been nothing, you know. This place – it truly is peaceful. And the people – they seem so gentle and untroubled. Perhaps it was simply an accident or some such.'

'Maybe.' Martin hesitated. 'The Joyful Land, isn't it? Except that, today, first thing, someone told me I should get out of here as soon as I could.'

He told Hardwick, briefly, about Karasin.

Hardwick considered, flicking his forefinger over his chin. 'Some of what he said was true. I read about the banning of Thursdays, and other little eccentricities, before I came. But nothing to suggest danger. If anything, they are beginning to encourage tourists, in a small way. Your friend, he was just a little odd, perhaps?'

Martin raised his eyebrows. 'Oh, no doubt. He was weird. Been out in the sun too long maybe – he looked sort of leathery. He probably has the same story for everyone. But – I don't know. He gave me the creeps. Frightened Sam, too.'

'Did you tell anyone else about this?'

'In the guesthouse? Yes. The landlady.' Martin laughed. 'Butter wouldn't melt in her mouth, would it? She just smiled. I think I like her.'

Hardwick smiled. 'You've charmed her, no doubt.'

'No doubt.' Martin looked embarrassed.

'Well.' Hardwick took another sip of beer. He felt it melting through his limbs, softening them. 'It's nothing. Obviously nothing.' He looked out beyond the veranda. His night vision had adjusted during their conversation, and shapes that had been hidden or threatening to him before revealed themselves now: hanging baskets dripping with water, succulent leaves, palm fronds. To his left, a crowd of dark purple bougainvillea. The bodies of four nursing puppies lay side by side on the ground near his foot, their hearts beating through their ribs. He wanted to laugh. He felt full of sudden immense good will towards Martin, his fellow traveller, his companion in the night.

He raised his beer. 'Listen now. A toast. To peace and quiet.'

Martin returned the salute. 'Yeah. Cheers. To peace and quiet. And the hope that we don't ever meet that bloody American again.'

'Oh yes. My goodness, yes.' Hardwick snickered.

'I mean, Christ. What a bitch.'

Hardwick tried to take a gulp of beer but spat it out, spluttering. Martin doubled over. Hardwick leaned across the table and patted the man's shoulder. Their laughter drifted away from them like curls of cigarette smoke.

April heard the laughter from her room. She had been sitting in the guesthouse for an hour, smoking too much, trying to calm down. She'd run most of the way back into the city from the casino. By the time she'd reached the guesthouse she was limping and disoriented. Even so, she had walked through the lobby with her head held high, so as not to meet the gaze of the creepy girl at the desk. She had gone straight to her room, showered and changed. Once she had put on a fresh suit and a new coat of lipstick she felt a little more like herself.

She had been sitting by the open window ever since, waiting for her hands to stop shaking. She drew one cigarette after another to her lips. She listened to the laughter, watched the easy companionship of the men. She shut her eyes, and shivered despite the heat.

4

Earlier that day, low morning sunlight fell across April's shoulders as she rode her pedicab through town. She watched as her driver strove to push harder on his bicycle peddles, the muscles bunching out on his back like knotted ropes. He wore his hair cropped close, shaved around the neck. His neck was brown, thin, and had two deep wrinkles running across it like a mouth. He asked, without turning round to her or pausing in his movement, 'Where you go now. Around?'

'Yes. Around. Show me your town.'

'My town?'

'Here.' She gestured impatiently, scowled at his neck. 'Show me here.'

'I take you stupa.'

'What? What's stupid?'

'Stupa.'

April growled. 'Take me anywhere. I don't care.' She raised her voice. 'I pay all day. Okay? You stay with me.'

'Okay'. The man nodded.

April sat back on the small wooden seat and tried to relax. It was too early to do anything – she may as well play tourist. She regretted leaving the guest house, but having left it, there was little else she could do. Despite her lack of sleep, she did not feel tired. Adrenalin, she supposed. She fidgeted, digging her fingers into the leather of her bag. Annoyed by her own agitation she swore and halted her movement. She tried to think of something practical to do. She made a list in her mind. She pulled a piece of paper from her suit pocket with an address on it, frowned, and put it back. She glanced around her, fixing her eyes on landmarks she might plot her route home by: the white house with the red roof on the street corner; the stone arch across the road. Her thoughts wandered.

She surprised herself by thinking of the two men who had shared her flight. What, she wondered, were they doing here? Her mind, suspicious and sharp, lingered on them. Was there something odd in their presence, in the fact that they had arrived together? Vague fears, worse for being unformed, preyed on her. She bit her lip. The older man seemed amiable enough; the younger was arrogant, a buffoon. They were tourists. Nothing. She put them from her mind.

She looked up, and noticed they were leaving the town. The road had widened, and the gaps between the squat houses had become more distinct. She leaned forward and tapped the driver on the shoulder, a series of sharp jabs.

'Hey. Hey. What are you doing?'

'To stupa.'

'You stay in town, Okay?'

The man cycled on, unperturbed. She jabbed him on the shoulder again. 'You stop. Now. Stop.'

He stopped, immediately, in the middle of the road. Behind her, a cyclist she hadn't noticed before stopped too.

April looked back at him. In her swift glance she took in a round face, large flat sunglasses, an open necked white shirt. She whispered, 'Go on.'

'Eh?'

'Go on.' She said it louder, would have screamed it if she dared. 'Move.'

The driver began to peddle. The cyclist did the same. April stared ahead. There were far fewer houses now. The surface of the road had become yellow, dusty. It rose around her vehicle in a cloud. The wheels of the pedicab squeaked. She heard the whir of bicycle gears behind her. A hut with two white tables outside it caught her attention. A blond man – European or American – was lounging at one of them, stretching out long bare legs.

'Stop. Right here, stop.'

Her driver stopped. She got out, signaled to him to wait, and watched as the round-faced cyclist rode slowly past. Her shoulders sagged.

'Hey.' She nodded at the blond man sitting at the table. He removed a pair of mirrored sunglasses.

'Hi.' He was wearing a purple, close fitting t-shirt, and had perfect white teeth. He thrust out an arm. 'Mike.'

'April.' She stepped towards him.

'Hi.'

'Hi.'

The blond man grinned. 'So, April, how are you? Want a beer? They're slow, but they serve good beer.'

'Early for a beer.' After a moment's hesitation she touched fingers with the man.

'Relax,' he said. 'You can do anything here.'

April sat down slowly, watching until the cyclist disappeared out of sight. 'Okay. A beer.' She eyed the tourist. Bare arms, bleached hairs crawling up them. He was unshaven, tanned, handsome. 'So where are you from, Mike?'

'USA. Boston.'

'Kentucky.'

'How about that?'

'How about it.'

He laughed and clapped his hands together, twisting his body towards the house as he did so. 'Whoa. You inside. Two more beers. Hurry this time.' He smiled back at April, flashing his teeth. 'So slow. This country is *slow*, man. You know they spend most of their lives sleeping?' He laughed. 'Don't even need a bed. Just sleep while they walk.'

A bent woman shuffled out of the hut, placed two glasses on the table beside two other empty glasses. Mike patted the woman's backside. She didn't flinch. 'See that?' laughed Mike. 'Fast asleep. All of them.'

April asked – watching the road, making small talk because it filled time – 'You here alone, Mike?'

'Nope. Richie's asleep inside. Caught the national disease. He's not alone either – know what I mean?' Mike smirked, waiting for April to share the joke.

She murmured, 'He got lucky.'

'Oh yeah. Everyone's lucky here. It's a lucky place.'

'I guess it is.' She sipped her beer. 'So. Is that what you came for, Mike?'

He shrugged, unabashed. 'What did you come for, April?'

She narrowed her eyes. 'I came to see a stupa.'

'What?' He laughed.

'A monument,' she said. 'They say the shape represents an enlightened mind.'

'Right.' Mike nodded, and slurped his beer. 'So that's what you're into.'

'It must be.'

'Everyone's here for something,' said Mike, his manner becoming more jovial as hers became frostier.

'Is that right?'

'Uh ha. And the cool thing is – everyone finds it.'

'I suppose so.' April sipped her beer. It fizzed up her nose.

'Man, I love this place,' continued Mike, unperturbed by her lack of response. He was, she realised, drunker than she'd at first thought. The skin on his cheeks had a waxy sheen; his sweat smelt of beer. He leaned closer. 'Trust me, April. It's gotta stay our secret, right?' He lowered his voice. 'Right now, it's great. No-one knows. Too many people know about it, and the girls get cynical. You know what I mean? Then it's like anywhere. Any fucking shit hole. As it is, right now they're fresh. They just want company. They'll do anything for a little company – believe me – anything. Oh man.' He winked at her.

'So how much do you pay them?' asked April, deadpan.

'Pay them?' Mike drew back, offended. 'It's not like that. They *like* me. They should be paying me. Yeah.' He laughed to himself, enjoying this thought. 'Paying me for the experience.'

April compressed her mouth. 'Yeah. I guess that's right.'

Mike grinned, too drunk to notice. 'You're a sport.'

She drank up her beer. 'Got to go, Mike.'

He smiled, amiably. 'Sure. You got to go. Find what you're looking for. Fucking enlightenment. Fucking whatever.' He flashed his teeth.

She wiped her hands down the front of her skirt as she stood up. The pedicab driver, who had been crouching in the shade, straightened his back. April asked him, 'You want water? Something, before we go?' She made a gesture of drinking. The man shook his head. He said, 'Stupa.'

'Sure. Stupa.' She climbed into the vehicle.

Behind her she heard Mike laugh. He called out as they rode on, 'Stupa, stupa, stupa. Hey dog, good dog. Stupa, stupa, stupa.'

The stupa blazed gold, and April shielded her eyes. The pedicab driver had parked in some scanty shade nearby, and she had left him squatting by his vehicle, having thrust a few oily notes in his hand to be sure he waited till her return. The monument was bigger than she had expected. It rose, tall as a three storey house, from a square base to a fine curved point. It was covered with gold leaf, and the reflected light from it was too bright to look at head on. April passed through an outer courtyard and sat down with her back to the main building. Her ankles were swollen, her body was heavy. She shut her eyes to the blaze of light.

She was here. What now? Her head pounded. A miscalculation: although she was used to heat, she rarely stayed out in it for such a length of time. The sun was directly ahead, and there was no air conditioned mall close at hand in which to gain respite from it. The conversation with Mike had angered her to a degree that she no longer felt fearful, but her mind was sluggish, gluey. A memory of her father broke through the surface of her consciousness. She pushed it back. The scar on her leg began to itch.

She hadn't eaten. Spots of red light danced across the film of her closed eyelids. Beer bubbled in her empty stomach. She stood up. Blood rushed to her head. She sat down again, groaning as she did so. She raked her nails across her scar, not because it itched but in order that the sensation might sharpen her mind. She counted to ten, and stood up once again. Resolved, she strode back to her driver.

'Can you buy me bread?'

He looked at her blankly.

'Food.' She pointed to her mouth. 'Bread.' She gave him some money, more than enough.

He nodded and scurried off. She sat down in the scanty grass. Hard shafts of it prickled her leg. Light from the stupa crashed down on her. She fastened and unfastened her bag. The driver returned with a piece of cake in his hand. She thanked him. The cake was sweet and dry and she choked as she ate it. She washed it down with a bottle of water the driver had brought her, and stepped back into the pedicab.

'Casino,' She said, her heart pounding. 'Hurry.'

She hadn't expected it to be open, but business apparently started early. She recognised the building from the night before, though in daylight the gushing fountains springing from the arid ground seemed less surreal than at night. The gates in front of the wide straight drive were closed, and a pack of dirty children thronged outside them. April stepped out of the pedicab and paid the driver; as she did so the children surged towards her. Small hands tugged at her skirt, probing fingers pulled her arm. She strode forwards, holding her bag tight. A security guard moved towards her and shoved the children aside. April inclined her head towards the gate. Impassive, the guard opened it and let her through, shutting the children out.

She trod on soft carpets. The air was dry and cool. Piped music wafted around pot plants. Their leaves quivered as she passed: shiny, succulent. A girl in a tight green dress smiled and bowed. Another girl behind her did the same. Their blood red lips hovered in the air.

April blinked. 'Where can I get a drink?'

The first girl gestured, smiling fixedly.

April walked in the direction the woman had pointed until she reached a plush bar. A small, bright eyed man sat behind a mahogany slab. Dark velvet walls sucked up the light. There were no windows. The bar might have existed in any time or place.

She said, 'I just want water.'

The man nodded. 'Still or sparkle.'

'Sparkle.'

He made a performance of pouring her drink. He set out a mat for it, then opened a bag of peanuts and placed them in a white bowl beside it.

'Where can I play?'

'Cards, chips, roulette?'

'I don't know. Cards. Anything.'

'This way ma'am.' He opened a door to the side of the bar, and April stepped out on to a wide gaming floor.

The casino's patrons were richly dressed, mostly Chinese and Thai at a guess. Fifty people – maybe more – were losing and winning their money without a backwards glance. A few looked up to regard the newcomer, and finding her without interest, looked down again. They appeared to be enjoying themselves. Occasional bursts of shrill laughter filled the room. Bracelets flashed on delicate wrists; men unpeeled wads of dollar bills. The room was airless, thickly carpeted. April sat down.

The patrons settled into a manic state of concentration. The rattle of tokens hovered above the incessant piped music, gave it a feverish, discordant backbeat. April waited. She was crazily conspicuous, but that was what she wanted, because she wanted someone to notice her. Who, she wasn't sure. Someone. She searched faces, hoping for a flicker of recognition in answer to her gaze. None came.

She waited till evening. She ate nothing and drank only enough to give her a reason to be there. She watched. Her eyes glazed over. She lost concentration. She stared for hours at a card game she didn't understand. She had no interest in gambling – did not believe in luck – but the game was hypnotic: the spreading of the cards, the shuffling and reshuffling of the deck. She got lost in it. Her thoughts floated from her.

She thought about her father, retired with an easy conscience in Kentucky. She pictured his mild eyes gazing down on her. She thought about Mo. Her father. Mo. She felt her eyelids close.

A hand gripped her arm. A breathy voice had tickled her ear. 'You go. Now.'

The face was young, as she had expected it to be. Beyond that it revealed nothing. She whispered back, 'Who are you?' Her hands clawed the sides of her chair.

A smile. 'I am a friend.'

'What kind of a friend?'

'Good friend.'

'And you want me to leave so soon? You upset me.'

'Go. Now.' The voice was urgent.

'Now? Before we've got acquainted?'

'Now, lady,' the young man whispered, leaning very close. A pause. 'You want to die?'

April didn't. She got up and walked to the door, controlling each step she took on the thick, silent carpet. The guard snapped to attention. He opened the gate for her.

Warm air hit her. The throng of children swarmed towards her. They plucked her clothes, pulled her hair.

She hissed at them, pushed them away. She ran.

5

At midnight, Martin lay naked and awake on his bed. Sam slept beside him, a little breath of air fluting through his nose. Martin squinted at his son. He tried to control his anxiety. Hardwick's story had disturbed him. But it was not, surely, reason to turn back? People get hurt in London, do they not? He chewed his lip, trying to justify his desire to stay. He wanted to be with Sam more than anything. He would protect him. Yes. Together they would be safe. He sighed. His temples throbbed. He stared at the ceiling, trying to distinguish something in the shadows.

He was relieved to have met the professor. Having another foreigner to talk to gave the place a taste of familiarity, and he felt less lonely now than he had done that morning. He and Hardwick had agreed, before parting, to spend tomorrow together. Martin chewed his nails. That was something. He had company. That was progress.

He sighed and turned his back on Sam, embarrassed to perform his nightly examination of himself in front of his sleeping son. It had become a habit, since Jen had left him. He felt anxious about his own attractiveness. It was not something he had ever doubted before, and the more he doubted, the more he found himself examining. He had once been proud of Jen's striking beauty: her long red hair, her catlike eyes. The fact that she had chosen him had flattered his already healthy vanity. The two of them – so his friends told him – made a handsome couple. Women considered him unattainable (he was with somebody, she was beautiful). This made him desirable to them. He recognised this, and it made him feel good. He was well built, charming if he needed to be, and had a certain manner (a slow hand on the shoulder, an easy smile), which women responded to. He knew it, and flirted lightly with Jen's friends, enjoying the frisson of imagined danger, secure that it was not real.

Before Jen – it was hard to remember anything before Jen. He supposed he had been sure of himself. Cocky, perhaps. More than likely he would hate his former self if he ever met him now: hate his youth, his confidence. No, not hate – hate is too strong – he would be resentful, feel jealous of his self-assurance. Crave it.

He touched his face. He felt a couple of day's stubble around his chin. That was Okay – he considered it gave him a raffish air. More than three days growth, though, and raffish became tramp-like. Besides, Sam didn't like the scratchiness when they kissed. He resolved to shave tomorrow. He ruffled his hair. Better. It was greying at the edges – that had better stop – but it was still thick and quite black in parts. It needed a wash – it stuck firmly in place when his hand left it. Maybe it needed a cut. He sighed. Bad haircuts had a tendency to make his hair sit too firmly round his skull, making him look like an aging Mr Spock.

He felt his chest. His nipples seemed, to him, full and lumpy. The thought that they were growing was beginning to prey on him, and he touched them often. He moved his hand down, through a thicket of hair, to his belly. Martin had no doubt this was getting bigger. He pinched it. The soft flesh came away easily between his finger and thumb. He couldn't understand it – he wasn't eating any more, and though he hadn't exercised for a long time, he believed he wasn't unfit. Drinking, maybe? He rubbed his tummy, feeling miserable. How many pints of beer made this? How could he claw it back? He pinched hard, enough to hurt. He deserved it, silly fool, for not looking after himself more.

His hand crept further down, through thick pubic hair. He let out a breath. He wanted that pleasure. What else to relieve the anxiety? His blood pumped harder. His shoulders tightened. He was aware of Sam sleeping behind him. He moved a little further away, so that the boy's back was no longer in contact with his own. Quietly. He would have to be very quiet. He rubbed, furtively, shutting his eyes tight.

101

Pleasure and guilt combined, until pleasure took over and he gave himself up to it.

Sam, weary and hot, slept without dreaming. Once, deep in the night, he sat up and opened his eyes. Sleep loosened its grip, but not entirely. Something troubled him. He pulled off the sheet that was covering him. He needed to work out what was different. He had it. There was a muffled shape beside him. He knew what it was without looking. There was a whale in the bed. He wondered how it had got there. Had it swam across the ocean, and in through his open window?

He said, out loud, 'I don't know. Do you know, Whale?'

He shivered, fell back on the bed, and slept until morning.

Martin's mood lifted with each step as he, Hardwick and Sam walked into town together. Last night Hardwick had spoken knowledgeably about places of interest in the town, and Martin had agreed, eagerly, to the professor's proposed itinerary. Walking with him now felt promisingly normal, as if today was the beginning of a genuine holiday. He looked down at Sam, wanting to smile. The boy buried his face in his leg.

'Say hello to Professor Hardwick, Sam'

Sam grunted.

Hardwick bent towards him.

'You are a very big boy, aren't you?'

Sam blinked.

'How old are you?'

Sam turned away. Martin said, 'He's four. And a bit.'

Sam whispered, 'Tell him four and a half.'

'Four and a half.'

'Yes. Very old.' Hardwick nodded. 'Can you guess how old I am?'

Sam shook his head.

'As old as the hills, that's how old.'

Martin felt Sam cling tighter.

Hardwick sighed. 'I know a game. Do you want to know a game?' He glanced at Martin.

Martin said, 'You'd love to know a game, wouldn't you Sam? Professor Hardwick is going to show you.'

Sam shrugged, though his eyes showed a flicker of interest.

'Well then. Well.' Hardwick stopped, and fished inside his pocket. 'Yes, I have them. Two-pence coins. These are the only ones large enough, you see.'

Sam began to look. Hardwick went on, 'I'm not sure, you know, that I can do this still. It's a game of skill, and I'm not as quick as I used to be. But let's try. I balance the coins on my elbow, thus –' he balanced them, in a pile, on his upturned elbow – 'Give a flick, and –' he jerked his arm and the coins flew into the air and disappeared.

Sam gasped.

Hardwick smiled, opened his hands, and showed Sam the stack of coins he had caught. 'Here. Take one.'

Sam, incredulous, took a coin and looked at it. Martin said,

'That was pretty good, wasn't it?'

Sam nodded.

Martin nudged him. 'Say thank you to Professor Hardwick.'

'Thank you.' He paused. 'Do it *again*.'

Hardwick blushed. 'Well. Thank *you*. But I think it's one of those tricks that can only be done once a day. The elbow you see. Too stiff. I'm glad you liked it.'

Martin smiled. 'Let's get breakfast. That bakery I was telling you about? It's just a couple of streets away. I don't know about you, but I'm famished. Makes me hungry, all this tourism.'

'Indeed.'

They continued together in silence. Martin grasped Sam's hand affectionately. If nothing else, he thought, he was showing his son the world. It would do. He smiled to himself. For now, it would do.

They crossed the street and reached the dried up fountain in front of the French bakery. Hardwick strolled forwards, but Martin, sensing that something was wrong, grasped his arm to prevent him.

Hardwick said, 'What is it?'

'I don't know. No people.' There were upturned chairs and tables outside the bakery. Some lay scattered on the road. A policeman, dressed in black, was standing outside the door. He carried a rifle.

Martin took a step forward. The policeman saw them and waved them on with a gloved hand. They retreated.

Hardwick whispered, 'What's going on, do you think?'

'I don't know.' Martin held Sam's hand tighter. 'Actually, I think we should go back to the guesthouse.'

'A local dispute? A bar brawl perhaps?' Hardwick's voice was tremulous.

'This doesn't seem the sort of place where people would stage bar brawls. Maybe I'm wrong.'

'Foreigners then. Your Russian chap?'

'Maybe.'

Hardwick insisted, 'I don't think we should be discouraged. It may be nothing. Why don't we simply find somewhere else to eat? I found a little café of sorts yesterday, and I think I could find it again. We could eat there, and then take a pedicab out of town. I'm sure it will be quite all right.'

Martin glanced at him, and smiled as cheerfully as he could muster. 'Okay. You're the boss. Lead on.'

Hardwick veered left, and began to guide them through the warren of little streets that he told Martin he could recall from the day before. He began boldly enough, pointing out details as they walked: a carved head over a doorway, a certain latticed window with sky blue paint peeling from it.

After a while, though, he slowed. They walked on. The streets were tiny, and looked, to Martin, bafflingly similar. He gave Hardwick a questioning glance. Hardwick shook his head.

Martin peered through open doors, searching for a clue to their location. Some of the houses were open to the street, wide front rooms crowded with sewing machines or crates of washing. In one, boxes of nails were stacked to the ceiling.

No people. No noise. Martin's foreboding grew.

Sam began to whine. 'I'm tired. Let's stop now.'

'Okay. Come and ride with me.' Martin hitched the boy into his arms. They walked on through the empty streets. A skeletal cat upturned a bucket, and the sound made Martin jump.

He swallowed, and asked Hardwick, 'Are you sure you know where you're going?'

Hardwick hesitated. 'I think so. The town isn't big. If I remember, the river should be –'

The street sloped downwards, and they saw the wide boulevard and the murky river straight ahead. By the side of the road was a cart full of ripe watermelons the size of beach balls. Martin sprang forwards. A moment later he stopped, arrested by a noise.

It was a whisper of voices, a tinkling of bells. The whisper swelled, became fuller. It was not a loud sound, but it was a broad one: the sound of a crowd. Martin began to hear footsteps. Sam's body tensed in his arms.

He edged forwards. Hardwick followed. The crowd came upon them suddenly, to their right as it emerged from behind a bend in the river. A line of old men led the procession, holding tinkling bells in their hands. Behind them, men, women and children walked purposefully, their shoulders squared, their eyes fixed ahead. The sun beat down on them; light bleached into the edges of the scene. A hundred people, maybe more. Martin had seen so few people in the town that he was fascinated, at first, by the numbers alone.

Then he noticed the crowd's solemnity. He guessed at some religious procession: a festival might explain the general silence in the streets. Heat sent a ripple through the air above. The whole scene appeared unreal, as if viewed through a veil. He held Sam close.

Without warning, the marchers started to run. Something was happening behind them, hidden by the curve of the river. Many were making droll, cartoon gestures, knocking into one another in their haste. Martin laughed. Some comic performance? A woman ducked into a bush, and Martin snorted and slapped his thigh.

The crowd gave another ripple, and Martin's laughter died. He heard a scatter of shots, unmistakable from a thousand news reports.

No one fell, and Martin hoped the shots had been fired into the air. The crowd surged forwards. He heard more shots, rapid gunfire. His heart began to thump.

Somebody gasped, and crumpled inwards. More than one person.

In an instant, everyone was screaming. Martin held Sam hard, the muscles in his arms rigid. His mind was working very slowly. He saw soldiers approaching from behind the rippled heat. His mind registered, in a disconnected way, that they were firing randomly into the crowd.

Yes, he thought. Yes, it must be so. Things like this happen.

People began to fall. A woman, pretty, staggered to the ground beside him. A boy ran towards her and was shot himself. His body jerked upwards and then slammed onto the floor. Someone upended the cart of watermelons. They rolled into the road, the green skin cracked, the red fruit showing underneath. An old man stumbled, lurched towards Martin, half his head a bloody pulp. There was a split in his skull. Blood oozed from the fissure. Martin watched gouts of it slide down over the man's half-closed eye.

'Oh, God.'

Fear coursed through Martin's body. He began to run, blindly. He ran faster than the day he'd taken Sam from Jen. The fear that day had been real, but nothing like this. He saw black spots in front of his eyes.

Hardwick was beside him. They reached the river, swerved left and continued to run. Martin's arms ached with Sam's weight. He held him tighter. He felt the soft earth of the riverbank pounding underneath him; at the same time he felt apart from it, as if he were being propelled forward without touching the ground at all. His breath grated against his throat. He realised, after a disconnected time during which he thought nothing, that he and Hardwick were running alone. The rest of the crowd had melted away, into doorways and blind alleys.

'Please. Please.' A voice wheezed behind him.

He turned to look. Hardwick was bent double, clutching his knees. Martin stopped.

'Are you all right?'

'Can't run.'

'Walk then. Don't stop.' Martin approached the older man. He put a tentative hand on his back. 'You sure you're all right?'

Hardwick was taking rasping breaths. 'Yes. Fine.'

'Walk. We'll walk.'

'Please. A moment.'

'All right.' Martin slumped to the ground. He lowered Sam down beside him, and hugged him close. 'It's all right,' he whispered to the boy. 'Everything's all right. It's safe.' He felt his heart knocking against his son's body.

Hardwick sat down in the dust. Martin thought: we are like insects baking on the yellow road.

'My God.' This was Hardwick.

'Yes.'

'Shooting. There was shooting.' Hardwick's voice shook.

'Yes.'

'But at people.'

'Yes.'

'Why on earth…? I mean, at people – '

'I don't know.'

'What shall we do?'

Martin shut his eyes. 'Find somewhere safe. I don't know.'

'Do you suppose people have been killed?'

Martin opened his eyes and looked at Sam. He supposed they had. He put his hands over his son's ears and eyes, as if he could, in retrospect, shield the boy's senses from what had happened. The boy's knees buckled, and he lay in a crumpled heap in his lap. Martin sat in dazed silence.

Hardwick said, presently, 'You see that bridge ahead? Let's go that way. I think perhaps the road on the left runs from there around the outskirts of the town, towards the airport. If we take it, and then make a left again, we will have made a circle, and we can reach the guesthouse.'

Martin nodded. He stood up, taking Sam's hand. The boy was covered in dust. Martin asked him, 'Can you walk?'

Sam nodded, and began to totter ahead. The two men followed.

It was hotter than before, and the silence had menace in it. Martin tried to keep his mind blank. Hardwick, stumbling beside him, was silent. Martin shot a glance at the tall figure. His skin was drawn tight against his face; his white hair was wild. An unexpected thought struck Martin, as he gazed at the shambling professor. He liked him.

The road curved round and took them back into town. Their walk was laboured, every step now a battle against a wall of heat. There were houses on either side of the road, but no sign of people inside. Ahead, Martin saw something that might have been familiar. Approaching, he recognised the dried up fountain in the little square next to the bakery. He walked up to it and touched its hot stone edge.

'What is it?' Asked Hardwick

'The fountain.'

Hardwick looked confusesd. 'But no water.'

Martin gaped. This struck him as funny. He began to laugh, shading his eyes against the sun.

'What is it? What?' Sam jumped up and down, his face red and contorted.

Hardwick frowned. 'Martin.'

Martin spluttered, trying to control himself. 'A fountain, and no bloody water. Bloody funny country. Bloody funny.'

'Please,' said Hardwick.

Martin doubled over, his eyes watering. 'No fucking water.' He kicked the edge of the fountain. 'Fuck. Oh, fuck.' He leaned against it. The stone burnt his hand. He began to sob.

He felt Sam put small tentative arms around his body. A moment later, Hardwick put a bony hand on his shoulder.

'Come on, man,' he heard the professor say. 'Rest for a moment.'

'Yes. Better rest. Yes.' Martin cried quietly, holding Sam close. The boy cried too, his thin arms gripping Martin hard. It was not clear to Martin who was comforting whom.

Behind him, somebody whistled.

Martin snapped upright. 'What was that?'

'I don't know.' Hardwick scanned the horizon, his body alert.

'What is it? Martin shouted. 'Where the fuck are you?' He wheeled about. 'Come on. Where are you, fucker?'

Sam began to wail.

'Please, Martin.' He felt Hardwick's hand dig into his shoulder.

He whirled around. The silence deepened. 'There's nobody here. Let's get out.'

There was another whistle. A voice said, 'Inside. Come on. Inside.'

Martin looked in the direction of the voice and saw a man standing in the window of the bakery, beckoning to them. He hesitated.

The voice spoke again. 'Must I come and drag you in by your hair? Come in, and stop being so frankly idiotic.'

They stumbled inside, blinking as their eyes adjusted to the dimmer light. Standing in front of them was the Russian, Karasin.

He clicked his tongue. 'Well,' he said. 'Well well. Have you been having an interesting Thursday?'

6

Hardwick sipped the iced tea that Karasin had made the three of them. It was cool and good. He drank sluggishly, feeling no desire at all to talk.

He watched as Martin jiggled Sam on his lap. The boy gulped at his tea, making satisfied noises. Hardwick observed him carefully for signs of distress. Sam was clinging more closely to his father than usual, but otherwise the tea, and a place to sit, seemed to have reassured him. Hardwick marvelled at his resilience. He wondered if all children were so. Had he been, once?

The crumpled Russian drew a cigarette from his pocket, smoothed it through his fingers, tapped it on the table and lit it.

'You don't mind?' He asked Martin. 'In front of the child?'

'All right.'

'Yes. I remember, you are not American. Not given to puritanical excesses.'

Martin shrugged. 'It's not the worst thing that's happened today.'

Karasin took another draw on his cigarette and inspected it. 'Well,' he said. 'You did not leave.'

'Clearly.'

'And your friend?'

'Professor Hardwick,' interjected Hardwick, with a polite half nod.

'Ah.' Karasin leaned closer, a gleam of interest in his eyes. 'A professor.'

'Of history,' said Hardwick. 'Nothing contemporary.'

'But the past is the only way we can understand the present.'

'Yes.' Hardwick nodded. 'Yes. I used to tell myself that.'

'You are modest.'

'Perhaps we can learn the lessons of history,' said Hardwick, feeling weary. 'But I doubt it. I never had such grandiose ambitions.' He paused. 'It would help if you told us what is happening, Mr Karasin.'

'Yes. Yes, you are right. It would help. But the assumption that you make is that I know what is happening.'

'Do you?'

'A little. Not everything. I hadn't expected anything so sudden, although there had been rumours.'

'Of what?' asked Hardwick.

'Of this. Anger. Anger deeper than fear. And the reaction you witnessed is to be expected. The only uncertainty is what happens next. What do you think?' Karasin leaned closer. 'You are a professor. You must have a theory.'

'Not about this.' Hardwick leaned away.

'So. Tell me from the beginning,' said Karasin. 'Have you been struck by anything unusual since you arrived?'

'Well.' Hardwick reflected. 'I suppose things have been odd since we got here. We should have noticed that. Everything so quiet. Only one didn't know how things were normally, so it was impossible to tell if there was anything unusual in it. And then – oh yes, then, yesterday, I saw a man shot.'

'You did?' Karasin looked at him with surprise.

'Yes. Or at least, I think I did.' Hardwick knitted his brows. 'I heard what I thought was a gunshot. And I saw a man covered in blood. I didn't know why – I thought a quarrel, perhaps.'

'Where?'

'By the river.'

'Is that all you saw?' Karasin narrowed his eyes.

'Some people milling about. A woman.'

'Yes.'

'Does it happen here?' Hardwick asked. He found he had an urge to make the situation normal.

'That people get shot?' queried Karasin. 'No. It doesn't happen here. Not in the middle of the town. Not in broad daylight. It was broad daylight?'

'Yes. About midday. I think so.' Hardwick realised he had not kept track of time. He frowned, annoyed with himself. Time keeping was something he prided himself on.

'I see.' Karasin tapped his fingers on the table. The wood was sweating.

Hardwick sipped at his drink. The ice had melted, and the drink was warm. Soft light from the window travelled across the back of his hand in stripes. He stared at his hand. He noted a liver spot, protruding veins.

Karasin said, 'You can't recall any more than that?'

'No.'

'So.' Karasin stopped his tapping. 'So. More. What did you notice today?'

'The silence,' said Hardwick, reflecting. 'I noticed the silence today. That, first of all. It seemed peculiar. And then – I didn't know where we were. We were lost. Between the fountain and the river, I think. A maze of streets. When we reached the river, there was a crowd. We heard a lot of shots, and people running and shouting. We ran too.'

'Bodies?' Karasin directed this at Martin.

Hardwick saw Martin flinch, and glance at Sam. He answered, in a low voice, 'Yes. I think so.'

'How many?' Karasin appeared, to Hardwick, unnaturally excited. He took another sharp draw on his cigarette.

Martin shook his head. 'I don't know. A few. I saw three or four. There may have been more.' He turned away.

Hardwick clenched his fists. Cruel, this questioning of Martin in front of the child. He wanted to interject, but was tongue-tied.

Karasin went on, 'I have heard of ten, twenty, in that part of town. Just outside, in a village called Paraseng, many more have been killed. And I heard a story just now from a sailor berthed upriver, of bodies floating down and getting caught in the estuary along with all the other garbage. Yes. Bodies like garbage floating down the river. That is what is happening today. We are throwing out our litter, cleansing ourselves of human waste.' He cleared his throat. 'We will hear of worse by the evening. It is a bad, bad day.'

Martin put his hand around Sam's body. With a rush of impatience, Hardwick said, 'We have to get out of here.'

'As I told your friend.'

'We'll head for the airport.'

Karasin shook his head. 'It is closed. No flights to anywhere. You are too late.'

'My God.' Hardwick stared. 'Then how do we get out?'

Karasin did not answer.

'We should find the British Embassy,' said Martin, his voice low.

'There is none,' cut in Karasin. 'There is a man who enjoys the name of Trade Representative. He is most informed of the best places to buy women. I doubt he will help you much.'

'Then what?' Hardwick asked, trying, for Martin's sake, to quell his panic.

Karasin clicked his tongue. 'I will think. I will help you. I don't, in fact, want you to be killed.'

Hardwick slumped, too exhausted to keep up a pretence of *sang-froid*. He asked, his voice catching, 'Why is this happening, Mr Karasin? Why does anyone have to be killed?'

Karasin touched his lip. 'You wish to know why. So I see you have been too modest. You wish to learn, not of the past, but the lessons of the present. So. I will tell you.' He sat back, lit another cigarette, and stared past Hardwick out of the window.

Hardwick sighed. He saw that Karasin was enjoying his captive audience, and there would be no hurrying him: his explanation, like his offer of help, would take time to materialise. At least the bakery seemed to be quiet and safe. He followed Karasin's line of sight. It was now dark. He observed this without remarking on it, although he was surprised, once again, to find that time had passed so quickly. He moved closer to the window and saw his own face reflected back. The face was startled, a man he hardly recognised: pale, with sunken eyes. He turned back to the room. Sam, he saw, was now asleep in Martin's arms, exhausted by the terrible day. Hardwick felt a rush of relief. He supposed Martin would explain to him later how a man can kill another man, how a woman can be left lying face down and dying in the dirt. He would have to try and understand such things himself.

Karasin drew on his cigarette. 'Yes. It is late,' he acknowledged. He stood up and flicked a switch. Electric light changed the character of the room, making it seem, to Hardwick, hard and cheap. He rubbed his eyes.

Karasin said, sinking back into his chair, 'We should move from here.'

'Where?'

He grinned thickly. 'Separately. Not hastily. I have things I must do.'

'What about us?'

'Wait a little. A friend will come with a car – I am expecting him – and he will take you back to your hotel.'

'Is it safe?' Asked Hardwick.

'Safe?' Karasin raised an eyebrow. 'Nowhere is safe, my friend. But if you stay quiet and don't do anything foolish you may be all right. Do not leave your rooms tonight, that is all. No stupid wandering all around and about.' Karasin made an impatient gesture, batting the air. 'You are not tourists any more. You are stupid bystanders, witnesses to something that you don't understand.' He frowned, as a thought seemed to strike him. 'Though now that you are witnesses, perhaps you are more important than you think.' He put his finger to his lips and stroked them gently.

Hardwick interrupted. 'We still want to know what's happening,' he said. 'You can't simply expect us to go back to the guest house and wait like little lambs till you decide what you can do with us.'

He saw Martin shoot him a look of surprise. It seemed the younger man was a little afraid of Karasin; while he found that he was not. One of the smaller peculiarities of the day.

Karasin laughed.

'Yes. You want to know, professor. I like that. *Intellectual curiosity*. So, I will tell you. It is simple. This place – so quiet and gentle – has reached a point of desperation, and when people are desperate, they do foolish things. Do you understand that?'

Martin muttered, 'I understand it very well.'

'Hmm.' Karasin studied Martin with the beginnings of what might be interest. He shrugged, and turned back to Hardwick. 'All this year it has been gathering. I didn't believe it at first. I have been here long enough – since the *good old* Soviet days – that I myself had come to assume that people here could be pushed a little, and then pushed further, and then pushed further still, and would never push back. A mistake. Don't you think so, Professor Hardwick?'

'I hardly know.'

'But you know history. Therefore you understand cruelty.'

Hardwick coughed. 'Cruelty? An interpretation – someone's cruelty could be another's necessity. I am interested in facts.'

'Then facts. Tell me what facts you know.'

'Well. The early kingdoms, you mean? The Buddhist schools? I know a little…'

Karasin waved his hands impatiently. 'A little more up to date, please.'

'From the French period? Well. Of course, a familiar story. Colonialism.'

'But Mingoria was never formally a colony.'

'No. True. But strategically useful. Central, small, between powerful nations. It still is. Little wealth, of course.'

'And still little. Although the French were pleased with their coffee crop.'

'Only because they liked the taste. It was never profitable.'

'Quite. Go on.'

Heat rose to Hardwick's face: he did not care to be cross-examined. He leaned forward and tried to concentrate. He said, 'There's not too much I can add. The French – from my readings, which are sketchy – seemed to have been both enchanted and a little frustrated by the place. Enchanted by the beauty – of, well, everything, as I recall. The landscape, the art, the – one hesitates to use the word – the exoticism of it. Religion and superstition. The civility of the people.'

'The women,' said Karasin

'Yes. The women. Yes, that too.'

'But frustrated also, you say?'

'Oh, yes. By many things. Heat. Climate. Those who came first seemed instantly struck down by it. Those who followed were at first disgusted by their comrades' lethargy, and then infected by it themselves. Infected, yes. That is the word.'

'The administration was – how do you say it? Notoriously corrupt.'

'Yes, but without any particular natural wealth to *lubricate* the corruption, as it were. These were functionaries, first and foremost. They had small tasks.'

'Running what they pleased to call the administration,' Karasin picked up. 'Overseeing a railway, which never quite got built. Even the Japanese, later, didn't manage to build it. And, meanwhile, gathering what personal wealth they could muster. Taking what was beautiful. Leaving little. You refer to these things.'

'Precisely. My sense is that they simply got bored. Felt themselves to be in a rotting backwater. It was not a place for ambitious men.'

Karasin snickered. 'And this holds true still. I am not an ambitious man.'

Hardwick did not react. 'There were scandals,' he continued. 'A few, amongst the higher ups. Intermarriage with local women. Desperate inefficiency. That sort of thing. People became lost, I think.'

'Many of them became drunks.'

'Yes.'

Karasin lit another cigarette. 'Think of your Trade Representative.'

'I see.'

Karasin was leaning close to him, as if sharing intimate confidences. Beside him Hardwick noticed Martin fidget. Karasin, ignoring this, said, 'Go on.'

'Well.' Hardwick furrowed his brow. His tongue was thick. His words were becoming slurred. 'I'm afraid my reading – you see my interest goes further back. Before the colonial period –'

Karasin waved impatiently. 'We shall make the story quicker. It has been repeated in many places, so we need only the essentials. A small nationalist movement, born amongst the educated elite. A messy little fight, quickly put down. Then the world war of course, and although the Japanese wisely refused to show much interest in the place after a cursory invasion, by the time the war was over the French found themselves compelled to cede independence out of sheer embarrassment. Disastrous. The government was horribly corrupt, and worse, hopelessly inefficient. Without foreign money it would have collapsed immediately. As it is, it did collapse a decade or so later. After another nasty little war a marvelous new government was established in the name of the people. And joy reigned.'

Hardwick frowned. 'You are joking, of course.'

Karasin shook his head. 'Not a joke. Many believed it.' He sighed. 'Once I believed it myself. The reality is a military government that exists for its own good and nobody else's. There is terrible poverty, still. During the Soviet days the ruble replaced the dollar as the currency of choice – hardly ever a good swap. The *khuap*, of course, has been and still is entirely useless. A dictator for life...' He made a dismissive gesture. 'And then, after our *dear* Soviet Union collapsed, no rubles, no dollars, nothing. Nada. Rien. Only birthday greetings to Cuba each year, and a pretence at independence which is bought by arms, and funded by the highest bidder. Only our friend the dictator – Mr Vien Song – only he remains.'

'How bad is he?' Asked Martin, apparently interested at last. 'I mean, the dictator.' He blushed. Hardwick turned to him and smiled.

Karasin said, 'Oh. As these things go, not so bad. Far too inefficient to be a really first class dictator. But mean and petty enough. He has become very fond, recently, of styling himself in the model of one of the old kings. A sort of socialist-Buddhist deity, if you can imagine it. Very, how would you say, *kitsch*. In his portraits he looks rather plump these days, I have noticed. He is extremely superstitious. His lucky number is seven, which is why we have so many Street Number Seven's and so forth. Very confusing. He has a habit of locking up certain venerable old men who disagree with him. Or, of course, *anyone* who disagrees with him. And then they are lost. You see, a place like this is of little interest elsewhere. A tiny pebble in a stream.' Karasin's eyes lost their focus. 'And why not? We have no oil, we are insignificant. The back of beyond: isn't that your phrase? The edge of nowhere. A place in which it is easy to be lost.'

'And that's why people demonstrated?' Asked Martin.

'What? Oh, not at all.' Karasin looked surprised, and shook his head. 'No, no. You need to hurt people far more than that before they act. Especially if they are afraid. You see, we have been the proud recipients of much foreign money. International donors are charmed by us and wish very much to help us. Mr Vien Song is very grateful. He has shown his gratitude by building that very large casino you can see on the way to the airport. It is luxurious and pleasant. I have been there myself, although strictly it is for the *very* rich, and I am not of that number. I believe the customers are finding it convenient, not only for entertainment, but as a means to bury money gained from certain kinds of illegal trades.' Karasin shrugged. 'But that is irrelevant. What is relevant is this nice little picture: the casino – there – and rice, too expensive to buy – here. People became upset.'

'It's easy to see why,' said Hardwick.

'Yes. It is not difficult. There have been rumours all year. And last month some students, just a few, took to the streets. Rounded up of course, and haven't been seen since. I thought that might be the last of it, but I was wrong. And here –' He looked up, his walrus eyes misty – 'here is your ride home.'

Hardwick followed his eyes, and noticed, as he did so, a low humming from outside the window. A spry, old man entered, nodding and grinning. He hopped across the room and addressed Karasin rapidly in *Min*. At Karasin's reply his smile faded. He frowned, anxiously, and said a few hasty words, rubbing his hands together as if suppressing an itch. In the middle of a sentence he broke off, shook himself, and smiled broadly once again. He hopped towards Martin.

'He is boy?' The old man asked in high-pitched English, indicating Sam.

'Yes. Mine.' Sam had woken a few minutes earlier, and was staring at the man.

'He is a good boy. Yes.' The man squatted on the floor at Sam's level and began to chuckle. Sam's hair was glued with sweat; his face was flushed.

Martin said, quietly, 'I think he's good.'

'He is old?'

Martin whispered, 'How old are you, Sam?'

'Four,' said Sam, addressing Martin rather than the stranger. 'Four and a half.'

'Ah.' The man looked serious. 'Four. That is why you are so big. Bigger than me!' He held out his hand. 'I am Van.' He shook Sam's little arm.

Hardwick asked, thinking he had misheard, 'You have a van?'

'Yes.' The man grinned his easy grin. 'Yes. I am Van, and I have a van. My name is Van.' He clapped his hands, delighted at this pun.

'Well, that's easy to remember,' Hardwick murmured.

'It is funny, yes?' The man squeaked. 'My name is Van, and I have a van. Funny!' He laughed, stood up, and took a few small shuffling steps on the spot.

'Hilarious,' muttered Martin. He crouched down. 'Do you think that's funny, Sam?'

Sam nodded, gravely. He opened his mouth to say something, but Karasin interrupted.

'Van will take you home now. Stay there till morning. Do nothing, whatever happens. Do not go outside. Pack your bags and be ready to leave by dawn tomorrow. Van will take you somewhere safer than the place you are staying. Your names are registered there. You need to be elsewhere. That is all.'

They stood up. Hardwick's legs bowed. He clutched the side of the table to steady himself. Martin reached out and put a hand on his arm.

'Thank you,' said Hardwick, softly. 'I can walk. But thank you.'

They followed Van as he danced out into the evening air. Hardwick glanced back at the Russian as he left. Karasin did not stir to look at them.

Van ushered them inside his vehicle and kicked the door shut. He drove for five minutes or so, bumping on the uneven road, before depositing them at the guest house. He grinned at them wordlessly and drove rapidly away.

Hardwick stood in the lobby and listened as the engine's growl faded. He glanced at Martin, awkward for a moment

121

before extending his hand formally. Martin shook it, and returned Hardwick's half bow.

'Well,' Martin said, briskly. 'I guess we'd better follow instructions. I'll wait for you tomorrow by the door.'

'Yes. Yes, I suppose so.' Hardwick hesitated, dissatisfied. 'What is it?'

'No, it's just –' Hardwick's hand wandered to his hair. He patted it, trying, ineffectually, to cure its wildness. 'The American woman. I can't help wondering if she is –'

'God, I hadn't thought about her at all.' Martin shrugged. 'She'll be all right. She was a battleaxe.'

Hardwick said, uncertainly, 'Maybe. Maybe. Even so, I think we should find her. And I think we should take her with us.'

'You think so?' Martin flushed. 'I mean, she's probably long gone by now.'

'You don't like her,' Hardwick said, quietly. 'I don't like her either. But we have a moral duty –'

'Oh God.' Martin frowned. 'A moral duty. If you put it like that, what can I do?' He blew into his cheeks. 'If she's here – and I mean if, because I'm not leaving this place tonight to look for her – then we'll take her with us.' His expression darkened, as he added, 'Wherever it is we are going.'

April sat on the edge of her bed, her shoes off, her bags packed. She blinked at the walls. The day had passed uselessly. She chewed her lip, listless and frustrated, eager to leave. She was about to stir when she heard footsteps pad down the hallway. The footsteps stopped. There was a soft knock at her door.

She frowned. 'Who is it?'

'Me. Martin.'

She recognised the voice: the man with the child. She sighed. A social call.

'Come in.'

Martin entered. She had nothing to say to him. She was about to tell him so, when she caught something odd in his expression. His eyes were bloodshot. She opened her mouth. Before she could speak, Martin exclaimed, 'You're leaving.'

'Yes. Tonight.' She followed his gaze to her packed suitcase.

He hovered in her doorway. 'Do you have a flight?'

'No. I'm going to the airport to get the next one that's going.'

'Oh.'

'Any more questions?'

'Yes.' Martin walked into her room and sat down on the bed beside her. 'Do you know if the airport's open?'

April narrowed her eyes. The man was stocky, and his weight made her bed sag. She inched away from him. 'Why wouldn't the airport be open?'

Martin exhaled, a sudden expression of fatigue. He said, 'I don't think you should leave the hotel tonight. It's dangerous.' He hesitated. 'We saw something terrible today,' he continued, his voice thick. 'Soldiers opened fire on a crowd. People – were killed.' He swallowed. 'Sam saw it.'

'I see.' April fumbled with her lighter. She lit a cigarette, sucked on it.

Martin said, tightly, 'You don't seem surprised.'

'Nothing surprises me.' She tipped ash onto the floor.

'Really? Then I pity you.'

She raised her eyebrows at him. If he was judging her, she resented it.

He said, 'The airport has been closed.'

'How do you know?'

He drew back. 'I was told by someone who knows. It doesn't matter.'

'And why do you believe this man? This somebody?'

Martin hesitated again. April watched him closely, observing his nervousness, his restless hands. He said, 'He's the Russian Consul. He seemed to know what he was talking about.'

'He did. Right.'

'Look, if you don't believe me –'

'I'd like to find out for myself.' She strode over to a table near her bed. She screwed her cigarette into an ashtray. 'The airport. Why don't we call?' She dialled the number. She listened for a while. There was no response. She slammed the phone down. Not wanting to waste any more time, she picked up her bags and strode past Martin into the hallway.

He scampered after her. 'Where are you going?'

'To the airport.'

'Are you crazy?'

'No. You are. For believing everything you hear.'

'Look, it's really dangerous. You shouldn't go out tonight.'

'I didn't say you had to come.' She began to walk downstairs. Martin shouted after her,

'You're right: I don't have to come with you.'

'Good,' she muttered. 'Don't.'

'Go and get killed on your own.'

She stopped and looked back at him. His face was hovering over the banister, flushed, anxious. 'Sure,' she said. 'Fine.'

He groaned. 'Wait. You're right. I'll come with you.'

She sighed, and turned again. As she did so, she was buffeted by the small hurrying figure of their landlady.

'Watch it. Jesus.' April recoiled.

'Sorry. I am sorry.' The woman stared at them both with stricken eyes. She grabbed April's hand. 'Up. Up.'

'What?'

'Get up. You are not here. Up.' She was pushing April back up the stairs, her strength astounding, her panic infectious. She bundled April and Martin back down the hallway and flung them both into April's room. She motioned to them to crouch down, and cut the light. She slammed the door.

April heard it lock.

Silence. Retreating footsteps.

She felt Martin's shoulder against her arm. She heard his hard breathing. They were crouching down together, close, like children playing sardines.

More silence. Then shouting, downstairs. The landlady's voice, pleading, placating. A bang. April jumped. She shut her eyes and tried not to think. She felt Martin's body moving with her breath. She began to feel nauseous. Clammy darkness pressed down on her.

After an age she heard footsteps. She heard the door handle being rattled. She froze. Beside her, she felt Martin stiffen. The door did not open. The footsteps retreated. They kneeled together, unmoving, their shoulders touching, his skin slick against her arm. She watched him stand up. He opened the door an inch, and peered out down the corridor.

'What?' she whispered.

'Nothing there,' he whispered back. He retreated back into the room and sat down on her bed. His face was white. After a moment she joined him. He extended a hand. She felt it cover hers. His hand was heavy, cold. She slipped hers away. She turned her back to him, lit a cigarette. She offered it to him. He took it from her fingers, held it to his lips, inhaled deeply. He blew smoke through his nose. He handed back the cigarette. She sucked it. They smoked together for a while, handing the cigarette back and forth with shaking hands.

She stubbed out the cigarette.

She said, 'I will go with you.'

III

1

Night shaded into morning. Martin rose and tried to make some calls, first to the airport again and then, after some thought, to a friend back home. But either the lines were engaged or the power was down; he couldn't use the landline in his room or get a signal on his mobile. He felt how odd it was to be so cut off from the world.

He sat beside Sam and shivered.

'I'm sorry. What have I done?'

Sam stirred fitfully. He groaned and seemed about to wake, but only turned and slept again, his body shaking from some troublesome reflex.

As dawn broke Martin ventured onto the veranda, holding a sleepy and miserable Sam in his arms. The sky was soft pink and cast a lovely light on the dripping foliage. He leaned against the balcony and gazed at the cool light, the hanging plants. His arms became sticky where they touched Sam's flesh.

A few minutes later Hardwick joined him.

'How are you?'

'I slept a little, thank you.' For all that he had been through the day before, Hardwick remained impeccably courteous – a kind of strength, Martin reflected.

They stood together in companionable silence, watching as the light deepened from pink to orange to blue.

After twenty minutes of waiting, Martin began to wonder if Karasin would keep his word. April, too, was late to make an appearance. Martin was about to stir, intending to look for her, when the rumble of a vehicle broke the morning silence. A grey truck spluttered down the cobbled road, and Van's impish face appeared at the driver's window. He grinned when he saw them, and waved energetically. He had taken care over his appearance, Martin observed: he was wearing a clean white shirt, crisply ironed. His arms stuck out of the bright sleeves like twisted brown rope. He hopped out of the truck and did a curious little caper in the road, as if superfluous energy made it impossible for him to stand still.

'You are ready. Good. Put all things inside.'

He picked up the rucksack at Martin's side and threw it into the truck as April approached. Martin was startled by her appearance. She was not wearing her suit, and looked smaller – much younger – in jeans and a t-shirt. Without make up her face appeared indistinct, her features oddly blurred. She had pushed her hair forwards, as if, Martin thought, she wanted to hide behind it. She was carrying the large black bag she seemed always to have with her, along with her suitcase. She met Martin's stare and pulled her hair back behind her ears.

'Thought I wasn't coming?' She said, tersely.

'I was just about to come and get you.'

'You were?' She peered at him. 'Well. I've saved you the trouble.' She hauled her suitcase inside the truck and placed the black bag gingerly on top of it. Then she stepped inside, squeezing herself into a corner of the vehicle, and turned her face to the wall. After a moment, Martin and Hardwick followed her.

Van slammed the door and began to drive.

The foreigners squashed together, bouncing on top of their luggage. It was hot and dark. Sam whimpered, half asleep still. Martin tried to guess where they were going, but after a few turns his sense of direction left him. He couldn't hear much above the roar of the engine, though at one point he thought he caught a crack of gunfire in the distance. He winced, his ears straining for more, but nothing came.

They drove for an hour, ample time to leave the city behind them. Sam shifted restlessly. Once he had woken, Martin tried to keep him distracted by talking of a football game they had seen last year: Arsenal playing Newcastle at home, an event that had since featured large in Sam's mythology. Martin kept his voice bright, but as he talked his misgivings grew. What was he doing? Was he stupid to put so much faith in strangers? He ran through other options in his head, and could find none.

He banged the dividing wall separating them from Van.

The vehicle stopped. The door swung open and Van appeared. His face was dusty, though his shirt was still shiny bright.

'Yes?' Van looked anxious. 'What is trouble?'

'We need to know where we are going, before we go any further.' Martin peered outside. They were on a flat nondescript road, with parched fields on either side. Van said,

'To the safe place. okay?'

'Will Karasin be there?' Martin squinted, trying to make out more detail through the flat light.

'No. Maybe later. Maybe not.' Van made a vague gesture. 'We go somewhere safe, maybe Karasin comes later.'

'How can we trust you?'

'Yes. You trust.' Van smirked. 'Or you stay here.'

Martin was silent, looking out at the empty landscape.

Sam whined. 'What's happening?'

Van shrugged, passed the child a bottle of water, and slammed the door shut. It echoed like the door of a vault.

The journey continued without incident. After a time Sam fell back into an uneasy sleep. Martin, too, drifted. His head rolled forwards onto his chest. When the vehicle finally came to a halt he started and his head jerked up. Sam gave a yell.

'It's okay,' Martin whispered. 'We're here.'

The truck door swung open once again. Van beckoned them out. Martin's legs were wobbly on firm ground. He blinked, and tried to take in his surroundings.

They were in a scattered hamlet strung out along the banks of the same swollen river that crawled through the city. The road under their feet was packed mud. Four or five houses, with low awnings and closed shutters, were threaded along the riverbank. If anyone was sheltering within, they made no sound. Martin saw bright chili peppers laid out to dry in front of one shady porch; a fishing net, mended in many places, was strung up outside another. Two filthy hens ran across his feet, bedraggled creatures with plucked tails. Martin jumped away from them.

The banks of the river were higher here than in the city. Peering down, he could make out crude steps leading towards the water. On either side of the steps were two stone idols roughly carved in the shape of cats. Their blank eyes stared out across the river. Below them, several narrow wooden boats were moored haphazardly. The largest of these was some ten feet long and five feet across. It had a tarpaulin covering that served to create a cabin, and an outboard motor dripping a slick of black oil into the river. The smell of petrol rose in the air.

'So, we're here then,' said Martin, uneasily. 'We'll stay for a day or so, wait for things to quiet down, then go back to the city. Right.'

Van nodded, and pointed to the largest boat. He scampered down the steps and climbed onboard. He fished up a hooked pole and steadied the boat against the jetty. Once the boat was stable, he waved the others down to him. They joined him swiftly, taking their cue from his nervous haste. He squatted under the tarpaulin, his legs sticking out either side of him like a spider's. He reached up and Martin handed him his rucksack. He placed it neatly underneath the rain cover, and stacked the rest of the luggage alongside it, including a small backpack of his own.

'You come.' He helped them on board one by one, his grip hard and steady. He motioned Martin to sit down on a wooden plank that served as a bench at the prow of the boat. Once the foreigners were settled, he pulled at the engine. It roared into life, spewing a rainbow of petrol into the water.

Martin stared dumbly at the riverbank as it began to slip away.

Sam roused himself before Martin could. Fizzing with excitement, he stood up and moved slowly towards the edge. He leaned over as far as his small frame would allow and trailed his hand into the murky water.

Martin stirred. 'Sam. Stop.'

Sam froze. He raised his hand an inch from the water. He watched Martin carefully. He lowered his hand again.

'Sam.' Martin moved towards him. The boat was cramped, just wide enough for Martin to stand and walk around its edge. Sam pulled his hand out of the water. With a defiant glance he propped himself on his elbows and leaned over the side, staring at the slow whorls that the boat stirred up. Martin wiped his forehead and sat down again.

Van sucked at a cigarette and spat it out. He turned to the three adults, and shouted over the snarl of the engine. 'We go up river, to the north. Three, maybe four days. No roads. Difficult. Okay?'

Martin squinted. Sunlight on the water leapt into the air. 'Three days?'

Van nodded.

Hardwick asked, 'But where are we going?'

'Safe place, lovely place, nice and quiet.'

'Are you sure?'

Van only giggled.

Martin spat into the water. 'Three days?'

Van shrugged. 'Army. Danger – you remember? Bang, bang.'

'But – can the army follow us? Use a boat like this?'

'No.' Van frowned. 'Army not use boats. Airplane maybe sometimes. Or walk.' He used his fingers to demonstrate. 'Walk on feet.'

Martin clutched his head, fighting anger and bewilderment. A three day journey. He had not signed up for this. Van was being evasive, it was clear, and as for Karasin, there was no sign of him at all. What was Van's relationship with the Russian anyway? It seemed to Martin that there were many things he was not being told, and he wondered if they would have followed Van so meekly had it not been for their panic the night before. Then, it had simply seemed imperative that they leave the city, and Karasin had given them what seemed their only means of doing so. But where, exactly, were they headed? There was no way of knowing if they were running from danger or sailing into it.

Martin squinted at the banks of the river. The landscape was alien. Grey mud crumbled into the sluggish water; parched yellow fields trailed off behind. There were few sounds apart from the putter of the outboard motor. Everything seemed half awake. A bird cawed. He blinked, and turned back to Van. He annunciated carefully.

'What is the name of the place we are going to?'

'No name. Mountains there, in north. Far from here.'

'Why are we going there?'

'Because it is safe –'

'I know, you told us that. But why that place in particular?'

Van smiled and tossed his head. He had rolled up the sleeves of his white shirt, and Martin noticed once again how well-muscled his arms were. He wondered how much of Van's air of easy innocence was put on for effect: crouching in the boat, with his body relaxed and his eyes restlessly skimming the horizon, he did not appear innocent at all.

He said, 'We go to that place because it is my home.'

Hardwick stirred. 'It's in the north west? Near the mountains? Does that mean you are a *Khia*?'

Van's eyes settled on him.

'I guessed,' said Hardwick, acknowledging his look with a nod. 'I read a little before I left. And I saw something about your history in the museum in town.'

Van gave a grunt. 'Not very true.'

'No,' said Hardwick, mildly. 'Of course not. I heard about it elsewhere too. You took the wrong side in the civil war. There were refugee camps on the border for years.' Van nodded. Hardwick continued, glancing at the other two,

'From what I believe there is still a little skirmishing every now and again in the remoter areas, though it doesn't amount to much. It is as much banditry as anything else: a few buildings attacked, a few passengers robbed of their money, that sort of thing. The occasional small explosion, minor injuries. Nothing much, in the scale of these things. I mean it's hardly a war. Though some might see it differently.' He made an apologetic noise in his throat. 'I'm no expert of course.'

Once Hardwick had fallen silent, Van grinned. 'You are lucky,' he said. 'Very lucky and happy, live in lovely places. That is good. Very good.' He started to whistle through his white teeth.

April said, 'Right.'

Martin turned to her, surprised. She hadn't spoken since this morning.

'Right,' She repeated. 'Right. So it's just a little skirmish. Not actually a war. Great. That's just great.' She fumbled for her cigarettes. 'You know, I'm getting a little tired of people telling me how lucky I am. You think I have a perfect life? I don't. Who knows —' she gestured impatiently towards Hardwick and Martin — 'maybe these men don't either.' She shook herself. 'That doesn't matter. Never mind. All I want to know is where we're going, and if it's safe. Well?'

'It is safe,' said Van placidly.

'Says who?'

'I say,' he replied.

'And we take your word for it? Who are you, anyway?'

'I am Van,' he said, glancing at Martin and Hardwick as if reproaching them for being remiss in their introductions.

She muttered, 'Wonderful.'

Van said, levelly, 'You want to get out of boat? Okay. You get out.'

She glared at him. After a moment she hissed between her teeth, and moved away to sit with her back to the others. She lit a cigarette and smoked, staring at the water.

Hardwick wiped his brow. The group descended into silence.

Martin, seeing the uselessness of questioning Van further, started to fan Sam with his hands. He began to think about mosquitoes. He had soaked both of them in repellant that morning, but he wasn't sure if the stuff he'd bought in Heathrow was strong enough. He peered uneasily at the murky water, and wondered if flowing rivers, as well as stagnant pools, could serve as breeding grounds for the malignant insects.

Sam looked up. 'Are we there yet?'

Martin did not answer.

An hour upriver Van unwrapped a bundle from his pack and handed each of them a little carton of sticky rice and vegetables, and a can of coke. He also banged at a water tank by his feet, and indicated they could drink from there if they wished. Martin thanked him. Van nodded, expressionless, and moved down the boat to eat alone, one hand resting on the engine lever. He began to hum, his voice surprisingly low and musical. His body had a suppressed nervousness in it which made a curious contrast, Martin thought, to this soft, relaxed singing.

They ate in silence, huddled together at the opposite end of the boat to Van. Martin noticed the divide but did not remark on it. He wolfed his food greedily: he hadn't realised how hungry he had been.

Shortly afterwards they reached a turbulent stretch of water, and Van left off his humming to steer with more attention. He powered up the motor a notch, and its rattle, alongside the increased volume of water, drowned out other voices.

Martin, confident that he could not be heard above the engine, leaned towards Hardwick. 'What do you think? Are we right to trust him?'

Hardwick smiled sadly and did not reply. Martin drummed his fingers on his wooden seat. He was caged. Around them, large currents foamed white.

April lit another cigarette. Martin watched her enviously, wishing he'd brought his own.

Earlier, the surrounding countryside had been flat and sunburnt. Now they were on the edge of rolling landscape. The riverbank was dense with dark green foliage. Twisting creepers hung down into the water. The air was cooler, the heat softened by the misty rain that had begun to roll off the hills. In the distance taller mountains rose up, swaddled in green. Teak, Martin guessed, remembering from somewhere. He inhaled deeply, taking in the moist air sharpened by the acid of April's cigarette smoke. A fresh wind made the skin on his arms prickle and the hairs on his arms stood erect.

He blinked, elated suddenly. He was floating on an ancient river, surrounded by an alien landscape. He remembered Sam and bent his head, ashamed of his brief excitement. To his relief his son was staring at the lively river, and, as Martin listened, began to make a bubbling little commentary: 'The water's going round and then to the other side, and it's fast here and then it gets brown and white all the time. And over there is the jungle. And the trees are messy but there isn't any grass. And that was a monkey. And the river is so big now. And when it gets faster it gets whiter and more yellow and it's getting all white now. And we can go swimming later but there will be sharks so I will get bit.'

Watching Sam, Martin remembered his camera. He clambered to the back of the boat and hauled his rucksack our from under the tarpaulin. He retrieved the camera and began to take pictures, first of Sam, then of the view around him: a water buffalo drinking, knee-deep in water; boys fishing; a young woman washing herself in the flowing currents. It wasn't until he had pressed the shutter on this last that he realised the woman had been naked from the waist up. He lowered the camera, embarrassed.

137

April muttered, looking up, 'Peeping Tom.'

'Oh God. I didn't realise.' Martin's blush rose. 'Do you think she saw me?'

April blew smoke at him. 'I doubt it.' The girl had turned back to look, her black hair falling like a snake across her breasts. 'She probably doesn't even know what a camera is anyway.'

'Do you think so?' Martin squinted at the girl uncertainly. The boat put on a spurt of speed, and soon she was a small dot floating above the water.

He turned back to April, glad at least that she was talking, and asked, tentatively, 'Are you okay?'

'What?' She looked at him with clear disdain. 'Oh sure. I'd like to know who this Van person is. And where we're going. Or if anyone is following us. Apart from that – sure, I'm great.'

Martin eyed Van at the far end of the boat, 'You think we were stupid to go with him.'

She sighed. 'Stupid? I don't know. We were scared. And now we're here.'

Martin nodded, miserably.

April sighed again. 'I just wish I'd been able to call someone. You have a cell phone, right?'

He held up his phone. 'No network. I tried.'

'Does anyone know you're here?'

'No. You?'

She shook her head. 'What about you, Professor?' She shouted to Hardwick.

'Eh?'

'Does anyone know you're here?'

'What? No.' Hardwick blinked. 'No, I suppose they don't. They know I'm on extended sabbatical, but I didn't actually tell the college where I was going. And I have no close relatives.'

'What about friends?'

'No. I mean, no, I didn't tell them.'

138

'So,' mused April. 'Nobody knows where we are or what we are doing. Strange, huh?'

'Doesn't your wife know, at least?' Hardwick asked Martin, his expression anxious.

'I'm not married. We're separated. Me and Sam's mother. So no, she doesn't know.'

April frowned. 'You mean you haven't told her where you've taken her kid?'

'No.' He hunched his shoulders. 'I haven't told her anything.'

'Oh great.' She threw her cigarette into the water. It gave a hiss.

'What's that supposed to mean?'

'It means, don't you think she had a right to know? I mean, just a guess, but if I had a kid – which I don't – I'd kind of like to know where he was. Especially if it turned out to be here.' She looked at Sam. The boy stared back.

Martin muttered, 'But you don't have a kid. As you've said. So you don't know what the fuck you're talking about.'

'Right.'

'Look.' He was taut with irritation. 'I'm sick of this. We asked you along with us, probably saving your life, and you've done nothing to help. Nothing. I'm not asking you to be grateful, but you could at least make an effort. We're all in this situation. We've all fucked up and we've all got to get out of it. We have to live with each other. Okay?'

'Sure,' said April, quietly. 'We're all in the same boat.'

Hardwick laughed at this. Martin stood up, flushed, and promptly slipped and sat down again, grabbing clumsily at the side of the boat.

Hardwick said, mildly, 'It seems that you are rocking it. The boat, I mean.'

April snorted with laughter. Sam, without the least idea of what the joke was, cackled.

Martin stared at them both. 'All right. All right.' He pulled Sam onto his knee and jiggled him up and down. The boy squealed.

After a moment, April offered Martin her hand. 'Look, I apologise, okay?'

'Well. Okay.' He took the hand awkwardly, grabbing at the fingers. They were cool. 'We're kind of stuck together.' He let her hand drop, conscious that his own hand was sweating.

'Good,' said Hardwick. 'Peace is restored. Splendid.'

Van, observing from the far end of the boat, nodded. 'Yes,' he shouted over the engine. 'Be friends. Be friends and stay quiet.'

'Anything to make your life easier,' said April, but if Van noticed her tone he did not show it. He went back to his interrupted meal.

Martin watched him. The old man was deeply involved in his food, hunched over the box and scooping up rice in his hands urgently. Martin thought: he's a clown one minute, a dictator the next. And now look at him, shoveling in his rice like a kid. What does he think of us? Where has he come from?

He took in Van's scrawny body. Every muscle was hard. Lines framed his eyes, and when his face was in repose – not fixed in his usual smirk – he looked old, and tired. How old is he? Wondered Martin. And why does he dance like a child in the road, without any reason at all?

2

Hardwick was in a reverie. They had been travelling for hours, cramped on the boat with little sound but the growl of the engine for company. Night had come without any preamble, a sudden closing in of the atmosphere that altered the tone of the journey for the worse, he thought.

Tiny midges gathered. Hardwick stared at the few feet of water he could still see in the cloudy moonlight. He listened to the putter of the engine and the low gurgle of the river. His mind drifted.

Yesterday. He pulled his thoughts away, and then berated himself for doing so. He was a coward. Worse, an automaton. He had experienced a similar numbness after Felicity's death, and wondered now if this state of detachment – of cowardice – was somehow integral to him. He closed his eyes. To test his responses, he forced images of yesterday to parade before him. He saw people running, their faces glazed with panic. He saw a young boy, his thin arms outstretched, his hair matted with blood. Hardwick did not know what had happened to the boy because he hadn't stopped to look. There it was: firm proof of his cowardice. He blinked.

He had hardly thought at all during the day, letting the stronger personalities take over: Martin to probe, April to argue and object. He had merely listened. It was a return to type, he knew. He was the old Hardwick again, not the resolute man who had comforted Martin yesterday. Not quite the old Hardwick, though. That person would not be here at all. He smiled, bending his long neck so that no one could see. He was sitting on a boat with three strangers and a child as they sailed up one of Asia's main arteries. Astonishing. He shook his head in wonder. The night embraced him. So warm. Whatever else was going to happen, he would savour this moment: the darkness, the water, the warm air. He felt –

not happy, it was too complicated, and after yesterday, too dreadful for that – but a tingling excitement that shivered through his body and made the hairs on his neck rise.

He had experienced the feeling before. With Lorraine. He closed his eyes and nudged her away.

Felicity. The thought came and she came too. He was lying in his bed in England and Felicity was beside him, frail as paper. That is how she had seemed in the last days: a woman made of paper with not an ounce of blood in her. He could blow on her, and she would float away. Strange images: Felicity on the end of a piece of string; Felicity kites sailing into the air. Felicity leaves falling. He reached out and touched the paper woman. The head flipped back, and a skull gaped whitely at him.

He gasped. He groped in front of him and there was no skull, no bones, only damp wood. He shook himself. How vulgar, to dream such a parody of death. How insulting to the real woman to make her a pantomime monster.

He shivered, and came back to the surface of his consciousness.

Van was sitting in front of him with his head bent on his chest. Hardwick thought that the old man was asleep, but a second later his head jerked up. Van's lips stretched over his teeth. After scanning the silhouettes of the near bank, he moved his arm on the tiller and steered the vessel closer to the shore. Ten minutes more, and Hardwick could dimly discern the grey outlines of wooden huts some distance from the water.

Van cut the motor. The night was quieter without it; more intense. Hardwick became aware of a host of insects in the air. His skin prickled. Were they mosquitoes? He wasn't sure – the bites seemed more like sharp pinpricks than leisurely feeding – but even if they weren't mosquitoes, he wondered what diseases the air might carry. An image of his blood crawling with infection entered his head. The flesh of his arm shivered. He wondered how he would sleep.

'Come. Come.'

Van took his arm. He shook himself into awareness. He stood up unsteadily, and with Van's help clambered out of the boat. There was a steep muddy bank to climb, rendered more slippery by the fact that it had started to rain, fine persistent drops that quickly soaked through his clothes. He climbed slowly and painfully. He soon lost his footing, and after a few attempts to regain it resorted to sliding up on his hands and knees, his neck spattered by rain.

Martin touched his shoulder.

'Are you all right?'

He started. It was an effect of the rain-blurred night perhaps, but Martin's eyes seemed huge and unnatural. He gasped.

'What is it?' Martin sounded alarmed.

'Nothing. It's nothing.' Hardwick lost his footing again, and slithered down the bank. Martin grasped him and hauled him up roughly. Above him, far away, he heard whispering.

'Is he okay?'

'I think he's exhausted. He's shivering too. Van –?' The last word was a shout, answered by a mumble in the dark. 'How far do we have to go? Hardwick has to get dry. We're all knackered. If he doesn't rest soon he'll get ill.'

Hardwick heard the sound of hurrying feet and saw Van's face peering down at him. 'You okay?'

'It's nothing.'

'How much further?' repeated Martin. He sounded angry.

'Not far,' was Van's reply. 'Over there, a village. Short walk, please follow.' He ushered Hardwick forward.

The party plodded through the mud. Hardwick leant heavily against Martin. He kept his eyes fixed on his feet, and afterwards, had this as a clear memory: the way the moonlight picked out his shoes as he trod through the rain soaked earth.

Out of nowhere he felt a hand tug at the fabric of his trousers. A small child – a girl, not much older than Sam –

had come out to greet them. A boy soon joined her, his face wet with rain and his eyes shining. The two children clung to him, fascinated, he guessed, by his height and his white hair. He tried to smile a hello, but their large brown eyes did not smile back. He moved and the children moved with him, clinging like little crabs to his trouser legs.

They reached the village, a scattering of wooden huts on stilts that raised the dwellings clear of what was now a sea of mud.

Van led them to the largest hut. A grey-haired man emerged on the porch, holding a kerosene lamp. It smelt powerfully, and the heat from it rose so that the man's broad features were blurred. He wore a pair of cut off jeans, and his bare shins were bowed like the limbs of a tree. He exchanged a few brief words with Van, then shepherded the group inside. The children watched from below and the man with the lamp beckoned. They climbed up, and crept quietly in.

Hardwick sat on the wooden floor. Though the place had no furniture it was clean and neat and warm, with a stack of shiny pots and pans in one corner and a pile of rugs in the other. The walls were bare apart from a framed, yellowing portrait of a man Hardwick recognised as President Vien Song. He saw that he had trailed mud and water into the hut, and felt bad to have brought the dirty night inside. He began to shiver. He removed his wet jacket and slumped against a wall.

The two children were sitting cross-legged on the floor opposite him. He wanted to say something to them, but exhaustion was hitting him in waves. His eyes lost their focus, fixing first on the children, then on the gaudy portrait in the corner. The face, in his mind, began to swell. It became a yellow balloon, with tiny blinking eyes. Someone brought in the kerosene lamp. Fumes filled the hut. A woman handed him a bowl of sticky rice, and a small cup of black tea. He ate and drank greedily. Soft voices flickered around him. The children began to sing.

Later he wondered if he had imagined it; another memory of happiness, separate from the arduous journey, or the violence of the day before. The children's voices were clear and sweet, their tune mournful. The music mingled with the sound of the rain hitting the porch, and melted into the edges of the glow of the kerosene lamp.

Hardwick's chest heaved. Beside him he saw that Sam was clinging to Martin, the boy's head buried in his father's arms. April was looking at the ground. Nobody spoke. The tune died away. The children left as quietly as they had come.

Gently, Martin laid the now sleeping Sam beside him and covered him with a rough blanket. He turned to Hardwick and pulled his fingers through his hair.

'Not exactly five star is it?'

Hardwick shook himself in an effort to dispel the peculiar feelings the children's voices had stirred in him. 'You know, I worry about mosquitoes,' he said, attempting levity in his tone as Martin had done. 'Do you think it is safe?'

'I've got some spray.' Martin started rummaging in his bag. He was whispering, Hardwick noticed. He noticed too that April had not stirred or spoken since the children had departed. He had a sudden need to reassure her. He took the mosquito spray from Martin, and as he did so, nodded in her direction. Martin rolled his eyes. A moment later, though, he coughed, and addressed her in a low voice.

'I always feel business travellers miss out on really experiencing a country, don't you?'

April smiled listlessly. 'Yeah. I mean, who needs a mini bar?'

Van rose and stalked out.

Martin blinked. He said, his tone detached, 'I agree. Or room service. Used to those things, are you?'

She straightened, making a visible effort, it seemed to Hardwick, to respond to Martin's approach. He strained forward to listen.

April said, 'Sure. I've stayed in hotels before.'

'So what do you do?'

'I'm a lawyer. Corporate.' She added, after a pause, 'There's a lot of money to be made in Asia.'

'Looks like it.' Martin's eyes travelled around the bare hut.

'Don't be naïve.'

'I'm not being naïve. I'm just –' He slumped. 'Never mind.'

'All right.' She drummed her fingers on the floor. 'So. What do *you* do?'

'I'm a teacher. Music.' He folded his arms across his body.

'Play anything?'

'Guitar and piano. I used to be in a band.'

'Figures.'

'What do you mean?'

'I mean you look exactly like someone who used to be in a band.'

Martin snorted. 'I'll take that as a compliment. Though I'm sure you didn't mean it as one.'

'I didn't.'

Hardwick stammered an interruption. 'So what brought you here, Martin? It is an unusual destination for a holiday.'

Martin stared at the floor. 'I don't know. I really don't know what to say, Hardwick.'

Hardwick shook his head, uneasy lest he had stumbled onto sensitive ground. 'I'm sorry. I didn't mean to pry.'

'I want to tell you, but –'

Hardwick raised his hands in alarm. 'There's no need. None at all.'

Martin interrupted him. 'I want to. We're alone. We might not even –' He shook himself. 'I need to tell someone. We might not even get out of this.'

Hardwick swallowed. 'That's – a pessimistic view.' He stopped. 'Of course,' he added, warily, 'If you want to talk –'

Martin regarded him for a while. He nodded. 'Yeah. I suppose I do.' He glanced at April.

'Sure.' She shrugged, without apparent interest. 'Go ahead.'

'Well.' Martin scratched at a splinter of wood on the floor. 'Well. The fact is I've not been getting on with my partner – Jen, Sam's mother – for a while. As you know. We've been living apart.'

'I'd say that pretty much defines not getting along,' remarked April.

'We've been separated for a while,' Marin said, tightly. 'As I said.'

April grunted

'It wasn't exactly my choice,' persisted Martin. 'She left. I don't know why. She hasn't bothered to explain yet.' He stopped, and clicked his tongue. 'She didn't get in touch for a long time. It was like she'd vanished. She and Sam. They could've been killed, for all I knew. Who does that? Didn't she realise how I'd –' He inhaled. 'I went to the police and reported them missing. When I told them Jen had packed a suitcase they laughed at me.' He stopped again, his voice catching. 'Anyway. She did get in touch. A month later. She was living with some bastard. Just *friends* she said, but I knew what she meant. She said she'd needed someone to talk to, and that he, this man, had listened to her. That I never listened. I didn't think that was true. I think I listened to her. I took her seriously. I wanted –' He shook his head. 'I wanted a lot. But anyway. This *friend*. This wanker. He told her she needed some *space*, and said she could stay with him for a while, until she sorted herself out. So how long was that going to be? She said, it's going to take forever. And in that time – that forever – she didn't want me to see Sam. She didn't even tell me where she was, because she knew I would try to find her. She wouldn't talk to me at all, and – well. I got angry. I shouldn't have got angry, I know, but there she was always saying I wouldn't listen, so why was *she* the one

147

slamming the phone down? I kept asking, what have I done? She said it wasn't what I'd done, it was what I hadn't done. What was I supposed to do with that? How can I be responsible for things I haven't done?'

Martin raised his hands as if to seek an answer to this question. Hardwick shook his head. He didn't have one.

'I tried to get her to explain,' continued Martin, 'But it was useless. I said, just tell me what it is and I'll try and do it. I'll do anything. I told her I was desperate. I *was* desperate. But I just I got angry and that was the end of that.'

Hardwick asked, gently, 'Did you find out where she had gone?'

Martin nodded. 'It wasn't hard, once I started thinking. It had been such a bloody shock. Everything was foggy. But Sam still had to go to his nursery, didn't he, so I just waited there one day and saw Jen pick him up. I followed her home. It was weird, watching her. I was like a spy. Yeah, really. Turns out, she was living in West London – nice place, much better than I could afford – and I saw her go into this house, a big Georgian place, white with black railings in front, really nice and – weird. When I saw it I knew I wasn't in the guy's league, and it occurred to me then that maybe *that* was it: I hadn't been rich or successful enough for Jen. Lots of things had gone through my head before but I hadn't considered *that*: that I might just be mediocre. I'm a schoolteacher who used to be in a band. Yeah. You're right, April. It's pathetic. Do you think I don't know?'

April stared at the floor.

'So anyway,' Martin resumed. 'Anyway. I looked at that big fuck off house and thought, yes, I'm nobody. That's it. And Sam's inside with somebody. And I'm nobody.

'My plan up to then had been to go inside and talk to her, maybe hit the fucker, I don't know. Make some stupid point. But once I'd got there I didn't have the heart. It drained out of me: seeing the house, thinking those things. You know what I did instead? I stood on the pavement and cried like an idiot.'

'But,' interrupted April, 'You could have gotten access, right?'

Martin nodded. 'Yes. I could have done that. I thought about it. Lawyers, all that. But that wasn't what I wanted. I didn't want all that, and for what? So I could see Sam once every couple of weeks like he was some sort of *acquaintance.* I wanted him back. I wanted them both back, actually. But Jen wasn't even talking to me and I started to think there was no hope. So. I took him.'

He paused, as if for dramatic effect. Hardwick watched him shyly, beginning to understand.

April cut in. 'What do you mean, you took him?'

'I took him. I found out where they went every day, cashed my salary, and took him. I brought him here.'

'You kidnapped him. In fact.'

'I suppose so. Yes.' Martin sat hunched, his arms folded in front of him, enveloped in shadows. 'You make it sound like – you have to understand, April, I had no plan. I wasn't thinking of anything, except that I had to be with Sam. That's all I wanted. So here I am. With Sam.' He smiled, a brief twitching of his lips.

She hissed a breath of air between her teeth. 'So. Now we know what you did. Why bring him here?'

'I dunno.' He did not look at her. 'I thought it was about as far away as anywhere. I doubt if Jen's heard of it. And the police – Interpol, whoever – I didn't think they would come here. And –' He hesitated. 'My dad came here once. He was a sailor. Merchant navy. Sailed up this river. Used to tell amazing stories.'

'So that was it? Your reason?'

Martin said, quietly, 'Yes. Pretty much the reason.'

'Jesus.' She compressed her lips. 'Well. Beautiful. A fine plan. And what do you intend to do now? Hide out in the jungle? Shack up with Van? What's your next dumb idea?'

'Yes. It was dumb, April. Yes. I know that. It's just I was desperate. I didn't care where I went, or what I did, as long as I had Sam. I didn't care about anything. Maybe I did think I could hide out here forever. Maybe I really did. It seemed far away enough. The kind of place people disappear.'

'So you wanted to disappear? Looks like you got your wish.' She tapped the floor with her fingernails.

'I know. I know. You don't have to tell me that. Don't you think I regret it?'

'You don't have a hope of getting custody now. Not a hope. '

Martin hung his head. 'Don't. Please.'

She stared at him, and seemed about to say more. Instead she turned to Hardwick, and asked, abruptly, 'So what about you, Professor? What dumb idea brought you here?'

Hardwick flushed, taken aback by April's question. He disliked the tone of it, and he had not expected her attention to be focused so suddenly on him. He could see Martin's distress, however, and wanted, somehow, to offer the man something. If not consolation, then a distraction at least.

He thought for a moment.

'Oh. Equally dumb, I'm afraid,' he said.

April smiled. 'Okay. Dumb too. Fabulous. Great. So are you going to tell us?'

Hardwick raised an eyebrow. 'My wife died. I took a sabbatical. I suppose I was running away – from a lot of things, I suspect.'

'Oh.' April drew back. 'I'm sorry.'

'You weren't to know,' he said, lightly. 'It's taken a while to sink in. Sometimes I hardly believe it happened. I don't suppose I shall ever really believe it.'

He folded his arms around himself and was quiet. The door of the hut was open behind him. Noises drifted in from the jungle: low whistles, distant screeches. His attention drew inwards. He had not once talked about Felicity's death, though well-meaning friends had probed. As for Lorraine –

150

The kerosene lamp flickered.

'Do you think it is possible to love someone,' he asked suddenly, 'without receiving anything in return?'

The other two were silent for a minute or so. Then, 'No,' said April. If she was surprised by Hardwick's question she did not show it. 'Of course not. All it means is you get hurt, spat on and used. Anyone who says otherwise is talking garbage.'

'Is that what happened to you?' Martin asked him, after a longer pause.

Hardwick blushed. 'Not the being spat on part. Not technically speaking.'

'But you loved somebody, didn't you?' Martin shifted closer.

'I believed I did. Yes. In fact it is disingenuous of me to use the past tense, because even though I know there is no hope, and there never was in fact any hope, if I had the slightest suspicion that this person might one day be pleased to see me if I happened to walk into a room where she sat – my ambitions are not great, as you can see – if I thought that to be true, I should feel happy. Stupidly happy. And there would be nothing rational in that happiness, because even if I should, for a little moment, matter to her, I would have no right to expect that moment to last. No right at all. It would be ludicrous. She was – is – much younger than I am, you see, young enough to be my daughter, if I'd ever had children. Which I do not.' He looked at Martin. 'I wonder sometimes if that was a mistake, a selfish insularity on my part. Felicity never wanted them.'

'Felicity was your wife?'

'Oh yes. Yes she was. Felicity was too busy for children. The whole idea made her shudder. And I – Felicity once said to me that the forces of inertia are strong within me.' He fell silent.

April asked, 'This woman. Who was she? A student?'

'Yes. I'm ashamed to say it.' He raised his eyes to meet hers.

'It's kind of an old story.'

'That's why I'm ashamed.'

'Well. My guess is you probably don't have much to be ashamed of. Did anything happen? Did your wife find out?'

Hardwick chose not to reply.

She shifted her position. 'How old was she? I mean, the student?'

'I'm not sure. About twenty, I suppose. They usually are.'

'Pretty?'

'Yes. Long hair. Unusual looking.'

'You taught her?'

'Yes, of course.'

'Was she bright?'

'I don't really know.' Hardwick considered this. 'Sometimes I think she was very bright indeed. She didn't try very hard. It occurred to me that she saw things in a different way, and had a kind of free-wheeling intelligence that can't be classified too easily. Now and then she would come up with ideas which struck me as surprising. It could be that she didn't understand the subject at all. Or else she understood it more profoundly than the rest of us.'

Martin interjected, 'I had a kid like that at school once. I kept wondering, do I have a genius on my hands? Or does he just not get it? I talked to Jen about it.'

'And what did she say?' Asked Hardwick, interested.

He smiled. 'She said I was too romantic.'

Hardwick nodded. 'That's the sort of thing Felicity might say. A very practical woman, Felicity.'

'And do you think she was right?' April asked him.

'That I was too romantic? I used to consider myself very far from romantic. Not practical – no, that was Felicity – but logical, at least. I preferred puzzles to enigmas, if you like.'

Martin said, 'I never could stand enigmas myself.'

'We're getting off the subject,' said April. 'This girl, professor. What was it about her?'

Hardwick regarded her coolly. 'I can hardly say,' he said. 'She was an enigma.'

'Okay, okay.' April smiled. 'I get it.'

'No.' He patted her arm. 'It's a relief to talk. Please continue.'

She snorted a laugh. 'All right. If that's what you want. Did your enigma have a name?'

'Lorraine.' He flinched.

'Lorraine.' She rolled the word round her tongue. 'Pretty, maybe bright, maybe not. You haven't exactly explained why you fell for her.'

'No. I haven't.' Hardwick sighed. 'Can these things be explained? Thinking about it now it seems completely irrational to me. I can't explain it, no. Except that – perhaps this is it – I felt as though she could see inside me. In quite a medical, rather than romantic, sense. As if I were transparent. It was not a comfortable feeling, not at all, because she could see all my faults, my great weakness. Perhaps we are condemned to love those who know us. Perhaps. Because there is this hope – the marvelous hope – that maybe they might see everything, and know everything, and forgive us still. Yes.'

Martin filled the silence that followed this with a cough. 'I don't think that's right.'

'You don't think so?' Hardwick raised an eyebrow.

'No. I don't.' Martin was rocking on his haunches. 'I think it's possible just to get along with someone, and have some laughs, and just – I don't know – just be happy. That's what I think. And maybe it didn't turn out that way with me and Jen, but –' He ruffled his hair. 'I think – I want – to be happy. And I'm not going to believe it's not possible. I *will* be happy. I'll find my way home, and I'll find Jen, I'll sort out this mess and I'll be happy. That's all.' He folded his arms.

April snorted. 'How's that going to happen? You've just kidnapped her child.'

'I don't know. I don't know. It just has to, April. Otherwise I've lost everything. And I can't do that.'

'But if you have lost everything,' said a soft voice behind them, 'then maybe you have nothing left to fear.'

The words came from Van. Hardwick had been so involved in the conversation that he hadn't noticed him creep through the door towards them, stealthy as a cat. He wondered how long he had been listening. For some time, he guessed.

Martin said, levelly, 'Look. Maybe you know more about this than I do. I can't say I know much at all. What I do know is it's time to sleep.'

Van nodded, and waved at their hut. 'Not comfortable. Not like a hotel.'

'We'll be writing to your tourist board for sure,' April grumbled, settling down. 'I'm getting old. I ache. I never did like camping out, even when I wasn't old. It's too bad.'

Van gave her a baffled stare.

She said, 'Lighten up, Van the man. We love your road trip. It's fun, fun, fun.' She stretched out on her stomach, making a straight line on the floor. Hardwick lay down stiffly, in between her and Martin.

'You shouldn't tease him,' he whispered. 'Van. We are relying on him.'

'I know that,' she whispered back.

Hardwick said, 'I didn't ask what brings you here. It was rude of me.'

She stared at him. Her eyes were large and soft. Martin, behind him, was quiet: listening too, Hardwick guessed. He waited, readying himself for what April had to say.

She smiled, slowly. 'Hey,' she whispered, 'I'm a woman of mystery.'

154

3

Corporal Paysonge was tired, hot, and dispirited. His men, he guessed, felt much the same way. It was important not to betray his feelings to them. He stirred his tin of rice, pausing for a moment before eating. His men were already tucking in hungrily. Like most of them, he came from a poor farming family, but he believed he should show them a more refined sensibility. Also they were well inside *Khia* territory, and though he was reasonably sure that the area where they had set up camp was secure, it would not do to let his guard drop. It had been a punishing day. He scanned the clearing once more, and then settled down to eat.

He thought about nothing for a while, until the warm sticky rice formed a comforting lump in his belly. He sighed, stretched, and took in the heavy indigo dusk and the clump of slender bamboo growing nearby. His eyes were vague. Someone had told him once that he had nice eyes, and he was proud of them: they were mellow and soft, and girls liked them. Not that there was much point thinking about girls right now. Apart from the fact that they were stuck in the middle of nowhere, he was aware of a whiff of sweat rising from his body, mixing with the smell of rain. He had been marching for twelve hours, and the slow absorption of his bodily odours into the rough army cloth offended his natural sense of cleanliness. Then again, he shouldn't be finicky about it. Fastidiousness was a quality he disliked in himself, thinking it womanish. It was one of the things he had hoped the army would erase in him when he had joined as an idealistic seventeen-year old. Eager and naturally intelligent, he had risen through the ranks quickly. Now, at twenty-two, he was proud to have been entrusted with this mission, his first solo command.

His sergeant had made much of it, praising him for his vigilance at the airport. The foreigners he had first seen there had joined a group of Khia fighters, his sergeant told him: ruthless insurgents intent on violence. Paysonge was to follow them upriver to their base, and from there to move against them. These were dangerous times, his sergeant had said, and the nation was under threat from several quarters. Malcontents – incited by foreigners – were stirring up trouble in the city, while unrest had flared again in the northwest. Paysonge was clear in his mind that both had to be dealt with swiftly. He bore no grudge against the upland people, and believed they should be treated fairly. But they should not be allowed to tear Mingoria apart. Mingoria, the Joyful Land, the land he loved. Mingoria was precious to him. He knew it was not a powerful country, but its fragility made it more precious. It could so easily be swallowed up by stronger nations – China or America – rapacious in the pursuit of their own power. That's what he had always been told. He would do everything he could to stop it.

Still, doubts troubled him. The army grapevine was alive with rumours about the trouble in the capital, and not all the stories he had heard matched what his superiors told him. Doubtless the usual troublemakers – students and the like – were involved. He'd heard whispers, though, that other people had been caught in the crossfire: ordinary people. A friend of his said that the unit responsible had panicked, shedding unnecessary blood. Some even whispered darkly that the protestors were only angry about the price of rice, an anger Paysonge shared. As a soldier he was shielded from the worst vicissitudes of poverty, but he was not stupid. He could see that times were hard. It made him uneasy.

Then there were the peculiar orders his sergeant had given him about the foreigners. Paysonge knit his brow. Surely it was no coincidence that they had arrived in the country on the eve of the worst trouble? Such things have meaning. There were depths here, patterns he could not fathom. The foreigners were, without doubt, part of the insurrection – and as such deserved to be shot on sight. At first his sergeant told him to do just that. Then new orders followed. Try to capture them, if possible. But if they died in crossfire, that would be no bad thing. Accidents happen. People get hurt. Paysonge was left, it seemed, to make up his own mind. He couldn't help feeling that this was so that if blame should fall, it should fall on him. There were things he hadn't been told. He didn't like it. He straightened his back. He placed his empty dish on the ground by his knees. The moon was full, and light from it silvered the edges of his tin. He was a soldier, and he had a task to perform.

Heat. Heavy, relentless heat.

Sam raised his arms to push it away, but the heat was too heavy and would not move. Why was it so hot? He tossed his head. He was on something hard. Why? His back hurt. What was happening? What was this darkness? He opened his eyes. He couldn't see. He looked harder. After a minute of staring he saw that the blackness contained deeper blackness. Crouching shapes, pieces of darkness, had crawled into his bedroom. They surrounded him. They sat drooling, licking their lips with purple tongues. Their breath wet his cheek.

Monsters.

He whimpered. There were monsters.

There was a leaden atmosphere in the hut, and the weight of it pressed April into sleep. She began a snatch of a dream, something about Mo perhaps – his face was fresh and vivid – then she heard a scream. The noise pitched her awake.

Why was a child crying? The sound horrified her. Her hands made marks on the sticky floor. She forced her body to relax, counting down from twenty. A trick she used often.

She opened her eyes and saw Martin bending over Sam. The boy was struggling, his body coiled with so much energy that Martin, for all his strength, could barely contain him.

'Sam. Please.' Martin was trying to keep his voice level but the boy's hysteria cut through it.

'No! I want to go home. When are we going *home*?'

'Hush, Sam. We can't go home yet. Hush.'

'When? When? *When*?'

'One day. I promise. Please.'

'No!'

'Please, Sam.'

'Where's Mummy? *Where*?'

Martin picked him up. He tried to soothe him. He shushed him and jiggled him in his arms. When this failed, he carried him onto the porch.

Slowly, as April listened, Sam's screams subsided. After a time they became quiet sobs, then hiccoughs. Finally they stopped altogether.

Martin returned. The child was limp, his cheek wet against Martin's shirt. April watched as Martin covered him with a blanket. She saw that Martin's eyes were rimmed red.

Sleep was impossible for her after this. The floor of the hut was hard and scratchy, and sharp splinters dug through her clothes. The restlessness of the jungle crawled over her skin. She heard cawing birds, screeches and laments like human cries. Her body itched.

She watched Martin hold Sam close. As the child calmed, she found her own breathing slowed too. She closed her eyes and drifted. She thought of other things: the small girl who'd met them by the river; the huddled children singing as the rain drummed outside. More than once, she thought of Sam. She saw him trailing his hand in the water, the golden evening light on his hair. Finally, as sleep stalked her, she saw Mo.

It was their third meeting. Mo had the urge to pray, he told her, and the urge could not be denied. He took her to a temple near his little room in Bangkok. The temple was small and garish. April removed her shoes and sat to one side. She watched while Mo performed his obeisance, lowering his head three times in front of an overweight Buddha.

He said, 'Why do you look concerned? Are you afraid?'

'Why should I be afraid?'

'You look at me as if I am mad.'

She laughed. 'That's about it.'

'Good. You are laughing. You are happy now.'

'Maybe.'

Mo sat up. He said, quietly, 'I think maybe you are not happy sometimes, April. This concerns me.'

'I'm fine.'

'I think,' he said, 'You must believe in something.'

'What, this?' She gestured at the shrine. It was overflowing with offerings: expensive bottles of drink, pieces of moulding fruit.

'No, of course not.' Mo shook his head impatiently. 'Too strange for you. You need something you can understand. Have you heard of Victor Hugo?'

'What, the guy who wrote *Les Misérables*? I saw the musical once in London, if that's good enough for you.'

'Yes. Precisely. Victor Hugo. A very fine writer. Did you know my country used to be colonised by the French? They left a great legacy. Many of our old folk speak French. My father does, although we youngsters prefer English.'

'You youngsters?' She asked with a half smile.

'Yes,' he said, ignoring her. 'And Victor Hugo is very much admired. So much so that in one temple he is worshipped as a saint.'

'You're kidding me.'

'No, not at all. And I feel perhaps, April, this would very much suit you.' He made a little cough. 'Because of the blend of East and West, you see.'

'You are seriously suggesting I ought to worship Victor Hugo?'

'Yes.'

She stared. Mo stared back, straight-faced. The corners of his mouth twitched.

'Oh come on. You bastard.' She made a lunge at him.

He shuffled out of the temple with his head bowed. April pulled on her shoes and hopped after him, taking playful swipes at his back.

It was dusk, and the sky was yellow. She wondered if a monsoon was on its way. Ahead of them, a scrawny cat stretched and ducked into an alley. The air was electric. Rain was coming.

'It is true, you know.'

'What?' She had forgotten Mo.

'Victor Hugo. It is true there is a religion that worships him. But not in my country. Vietnam. It is called Cao Dai.' She looked at him suspiciously. He laughed. 'Oh dear. I see I am in great jeopardy, April. You will no longer believe what I say.'

'No, I believe you. Why would you be crazy enough to make up something like that?' She shivered, feeling the first drops of rain on her hair and shoulders.

'Quickly,' said Mo, and pushed her into a doorway. A second later the sky opened. It seemed, to April, as if someone had pulled a trapdoor for all the world's water to fall through. She cowered against the wall, trying to keep some small patch of herself dry as the rain lashed her.

'This is awful.'

'Please, I will protect you.' He stood in front of her.

'Mo. Don't be crazy.' She began to laugh at his hopeless efforts.

Mo, seeing this, laughed too. Soon the two of them were shouting at the thunder, and cheering each flash of lightning. They ran out into the street and back to Mo's place, splashing through the rain and dodging marooned cars.

They drank tea in his tiny room. Once he had finished, Mo put down his cup on the floor with a precise movement. He said, 'April, you will make someone a good wife one day.'

She spluttered. 'Why, do you want to marry me? Oh please.'

'Not at all. I do not.'

'Well thanks. What's wrong with me?'

'Nothing. You are perfectly fine. But I am already married.'

'You didn't tell me.' She frowned. 'So your wife is back home?'

He nodded.

'You're a dark horse, Mo.'

'You mean a stalking horse?' he asked, eagerly.

'No, that's totally different. It means you're full of surprises.'

He looked puzzled. 'Why is a dark horse surprising?'

She made a helpless gesture. 'Trust me. But you know what? I used to be married too. So I guess I'm a dark horse as well.'

'Your husband is dead?' His face fell. 'Was it the horse?'

'God, no. There was no horse Mo. Forget the horse. And he is very much alive – my husband. Alive and fat. I can't believe I ever went ahead with it now. I was young, and incredibly naive.'

'You were in love?'

'I guess so.' She thought about it. 'I guess I thought I was. That was pretty stupid. All I really wanted was to get away from my dad and out of the dump I grew up in: that was the smart part. So I married George. He was a geologist – I actually called him *George the Geologist*. And Mo, if ever two people were unsuited, it was me and George. It took me about up until our honeymoon to figure that out. He insisted on taking me to some godforsaken national park because he wanted to look at rocks. I mean, *rocks*. Can you believe it Mo?'

'I cannot.' Mo rolled his eyes.

'So there I was, in this trailer, and it rained for two weeks by the way – seemed like two years – while he looked at his damned rocks. Jesus. And I thought, oh boy, April, have you made a mistake. Though it worked out in one way – it got me out of town. For a while.' Her voice trailed away. She shifted on Mo's bed. 'Poor old George. Actually he was a nice man. You would have liked him. He was like you in a way. He thought a lot. Always thinking about something. Except he was fat. I guess he's even fatter now. Good old George.'

Mo said, softly, 'You are sad to think of it.'

'No.' She chewed her lip. 'I'm not sad.'

He regarded her sceptically. 'One day you must have children.'

'Says who?'

'One day I hope to have children.'

'Well. Maybe. That's for you to say. But I don't.'

'Why?'

'Because I don't. And I can't.' She rubbed her arm. It was itching.

Mo pulled off his glasses, and stroked the wire frames with his thin hands. 'I am very sorry, April.'

'Don't be. No.' Her voice was low. 'Once, Mo, I thought it was something I wanted. Like I thought I wanted George and his rocks. I'm a different person now.'

He nodded. 'Like myself. Once I thought I did not like beer, and that I would never like beer. But now I have tried it and I find I like it. So I am a different person now.'

'Well.' She snorted. 'I guess you could call that an analogy.'

He put his glasses back on, and smiled at her. The lenses flashed. 'You are a very lucky person, April.'

'Yeah,' she said. 'Yeah. You're right, Mo. Lucky old April.' She pulled his sheet around her shoulders and stretched herself out on his bed. Her clothes were still damp. Though the room was hot, the heat did not reach past her skin. She murmured, her limbs softening as sleep took her, 'Good old April.'

She began to dream.

*

She woke, and met Martin's eyes.

Green eyes, she noticed. Next, she saw how pale he was. Sam must have slept after his outburst – in any case, she hadn't heard him again – but she guessed Martin had stayed awake through most of the night.

His eyes held her eyes. She looked away.

It was too intimate, waking so close to someone. Too close.

She pulled on a jacket and stood up with her back to him. Saying nothing, she slipped out of the hut. Cool mud oozed between her bare toes. She walked around the hut and climbed a gentle slope that took her clear of the mud. It was early. Her eyesight was fuzzy. The air was full of grey mist, and she couldn't see far. She made her way towards a line of trees. When she was enough under cover, she squatted down and peed.

She walked further. The leaves underfoot were white with dew. She bent and wiped her hands in it, then rubbed the moisture over her face, muttering. Her hair was a mess. She took a comb out of her jeans pocket and did the best she could. Her stick of lipstick was half melted, but she applied it anyway, smacking her lips together. She stretched. The sun was hot already, and the dewy grass was steaming. She retrieved her last cigarette, straightened it and lit it. She smoked it slowly, her eyes shut.

She began to sweat. Something crawled over her bare foot.

She dropped her cigarette, kicked out, and rubbed her toes. Seeing nothing, and with the cigarette dead at her feet, she walked back to the hut.

She heard loud voices arguing.

Sam said, 'I don't *want* it.'

'You've got to eat,' Martin shouted back. 'You might not get any more food.'

April sat down quietly.

'I don't want it. I want to go HOME. I want MUMMY.'

'We can't go home yet, Sam. You've got to eat your breakfast.'

'Where's Mummy?'

'She's back at home. Eat your breakfast now, Sam.'

'I don't WANT –'

'Eat it!' Martin thumped the floor, shocking Sam into silence. The boy's lip trembled. He began to whimper.

Martin put his head in his hands. 'Hush. It's okay. It's all right. Please, Sam.'

Hardwick handed April some rice, and black tea. She ate and drank listlessly, spooning her rice around the bowl. Sweat soaked into her t-shirt.

Van's face appeared. 'Good sleep?'

No one replied.

He scuttled into the hut, grinning at them. 'We move now. okay?'

Hardwick stood up uncertainly.

'You okay?' Van asked.

'I'll do.' Hardwick straightened.

April rose too. As she passed Hardwick, she patted him on the shoulder. She climbed out of the hut slowly, wondering at the impulse that had made her touch him.

She saw that someone had placed all their shoes on the porch in a neat row. She knelt down and banged her new trainers against the wooden slats, trying to shift the mud that had caked on them overnight. Van watched her, his arms folded, his eyes crinkling in a smile.

'Nothing stays beautiful forever,' he said.

She looked up, her mouth half-open. Before she could think of a retort – something sharp or funny – Van turned away from her. She stared after him dumbly, her mouth open, a muddy shoe in each hand.

*

Corporal Paysong shifted camp before the sun rose. It was better to start early, he knew, before the full heat of day could seep through his skin and sap his strength. He had slept abominably, and his back ached. A few hours of walking would loosen his muscles. Hopefully, too, it would free his mind from the anxiety that had plagued him all night.

He squatted on the ground, brushing his teeth carefully. Earlier he had shaved, scraping the razor over his soft skin. Important, such things. The line between an animal and a man is a thin one, and his small rituals of cleanliness kept him a man.

He sighed, straightened his back, and began to trudge forwards through the dense trees.

4

Back on the river, Sam was restless. He stood up, dangerously close to the edge of the boat. Martin tensed. Just as Sam tottered and overbalanced, Martin leapt at him, knocking him back down onto the seat. Sam screamed, his face puce, the veins bulging in his neck. He reached a small hand out for the far shore, struggling so desperately that Martin found it hard to contain him.

Van laughed until Sam was still. Then he squatted down beside the boy.

'You are naughty. You make noise and I am angry, okay?'

Sam's lip trembled.

Martin snarled, 'Don't tell him what to do.'

'You must keep him quiet.' Van turned his head sharply. 'Maybe people will hear.'

'What people?'

Van gestured to the bank. 'Some people. Any people.'

'The boy is frightened. It's not surprising, is it?'

'So why you bring him here?' said Van, his sibilant tones a note higher than usual. 'Very dangerous for a child.'

'I didn't know your bloody country would collapse as soon as I got here, did I?'

'Then you should listen. You should think,' snapped Van. 'Not just come here and look at lovely temples, yes, and lovely monks, and so pretty everything, everyone smiling, so nice. Think about what is happening before you come. And not be so stupid.' He tapped the side of his head.

Martin tightened his fists. Sam, he saw, had been cowed into silence. He squatted and gave the boy a brief, hard hug. Glowering at Van, he moved away from the others.

A moment later, April joined him.

'Hey,' she said. 'Forget it.'

He shook his head. 'No.'

'We've all messed up. Don't beat yourself up.'

166

He looked at her in surprise. Odd woman. Why choose now to be friendly? She had barely smiled since they'd met. It was obvious she didn't like him, and the feeling, as far as he was concerned, was mutual. Still, he reminded himself, she had been kind to Hardwick. He supposed that counted for something.

He pulled his hand through his hair.

'I didn't see it coming, April. Any of it. If I'd known, then—'

'Then what?'

He struggled for words. 'Maybe I could have done something. I don't know. Maybe a lot of things would have happened. Maybe she wouldn't have left me. I don't know.'

'Who?' April frowned, not following.

'Jen. Jen wouldn't.'

'Oh. Right.' She shrugged. 'I can't say.'

A pause.

She said, 'You want talk about it?'

'No.'

'Might help. Who knows?' April fiddled with her empty cigarette packet.

'I doubt it.' Martin looked away from her. Hardwick, he noticed, was listening. Martin slumped against the side of the boat, conscious, suddenly, of how tired he was.

He said — his question directed at Hardwick, not April — 'Do you really want to know?'

Hardwick replied, mildly, 'If you want to tell, Martin.'

'Christ, I don't know.' What did he want? He considered, looking at the water, feeling the rhythm of the boat in his body. He looked back at Hardwick.

He wanted to talk.

'All right,' he said. 'Okay. I'll tell you what happened. It was simple, really. One night I came home from school and Sam and Jen weren't there. Just like that.'

He clamped his mouth shut.

'Just like that, huh?' repeated April. She chewed her fingernails.

He glared at her, his antipathy returning. 'Of course, not *just* like that. Looking back the signs were there. I should have read them better, I suppose. Just – I don't know. It was just easier not to see.' He sighed. 'No. Looking back, I just didn't see.'

He paused.

'Jen called it my *head in the sand* mentality – one of the very many things she found irritating about me. Because I preferred not to talk about what she called the *issues* in our relationship. *Issues*.' He rolled his eyes. 'I mean, why rake over things that are painful? I just wanted to be happy. Was it such a stupid thing to want?'

April shrugged.

'I tried to explain this to her, but it only made things worse. Jen would say that if I really cared – if I really wanted to make things better – then I would listen to her. I'd say, okay, I'm listening now. Just tell me what to do. Tell me what's wrong and I'll fix it. Okay?'

He appealed to his audience, seeking a response. None came.

She didn't leave a note. He thought, at first, that she would soon be back. She'd had to go out. She'd been called away by a friend. Something. He would find an explanation, some reason for her silence. He waited for her to call. When she didn't, he sent her a text asking if she was okay. She didn't reply. He got himself a take-away and flicked through TV channels, trying to shake away his disquiet. He kept his phone beside him and he tried not to look at it: if he looked it would mean he was waiting for her answer, and that would mean she'd won whatever game they were playing.

Finally, the message came.

Can't come back Martin. So sorry. Have taken Sam. I love you.

That was it.

He stared at it for a long time. *I love you.* That was positive: she loved him. So this couldn't be a long-term thing, could it? But what did she mean, she couldn't come back? Tonight? This week? Or what?

He wanted to send another message asking her to explain. If he did though, she would win the game, and he couldn't have that. Better to stay quiet until she contacted him again.

She didn't.

He went to bed after midnight. The next day there was no message, and no Jen either. He broke, and called her number. It rang a few times before the line went dead. He started to search the flat, trying to find a note he might have missed the night before. Instead he found evidence of packing. Most of Sam's clothes were gone, and a few of Jen's too. He wondered how she'd moved everything out of the house. The car was still there, so either she had taken a taxi or she'd had help.

Horrible thought. He panicked.

He called Jen's friend, Amanda. It was eight thirty on Saturday morning.

He asked her if Jen was there. There was a long, heavy silence. Then, Amanda's mocking voice: 'Why, have you lost her?'

He said, 'She's out. It's fine. Forget it.'

Amanda said, 'It doesn't sound fine.'

He stammered, 'She probably told me she was going out, and I probably just forgot.'

Amanda said, 'Sounds like you.' A heavy sigh. 'Has Jen been out all night?'

He didn't know what to say. He put the phone down.

Amanda had sounded worried about Jen. Should he be worried? Perhaps she hadn't meant to stay away, and had got into trouble somehow. He didn't know what to do; couldn't remember ever feeling so helpless. He called Jen's number again. Nothing. He went to a nearby café. He wanted to cry. An awful feeling: sick and afraid. At a loss, he ordered a big fried breakfast, the kind that Jen would never let him have; though when it came he couldn't eat it. He sat and stared at it: puddles of yellow egg, pools of bacon grease. Finally, the thought came. Perhaps this is it. Perhaps she's really gone. He went back to the flat and put the TV on. It wasn't loud enough to fill the silence.

Martin faltered. April's hair had fallen into her eyes. He saw her flick the stray strand away. Hardwick looked down, and traced a line on his hand with his fingertips. Neither spoke. The boat puttered through the thick current.

He peered at the water. It was grey and lethargic, in no hurry to take them anywhere. The air shimmered, opaque and ghostly. His eyes blurred. His companions were obscured by a veil of heat, too distant for him to reach. London, the walk into school, the acrid smell of classrooms: these, not the boat or the river, or his strange companions, were real.

Over the next few days the thought came often: he was alone; she had left. As time dragged on it got harder for him to push it back. He went to work as usual, and laughed at the usual staffroom jokes, and it was like being crazy because all the time, while his own tinny voice echoed in his head, there was a dark pain inside him that he couldn't shift. He taught, he went swimming, he played the piano. And all the time, the pain remained.

At the end of the first week he decided to numb himself by going to the pub. He got drunk. The pain stayed. Nothing moved it. Not alcohol: that just sat on top, while the pain crouched underneath. He staggered towards home. The pain was so strong he had to stop to try and loosen it. He punched his chest. He couldn't shift it. He dropped down on his knees and cried. He couldn't stay like that. He made himself stop crying. He was cold. He thought about heading to the main road and taking a bus home. Instead he walked. The cold cleared his head. And crying – it hadn't stopped the pain, but it had done something. Made it sharper.

He lay on his bed, half drunk. The room was spinning. Questions buzzed around him. Jen had left him: he couldn't hide from it. He hoped she would come back, but she hadn't been in contact at all apart from that single text, and that made him fear the worst. Jen was a talker. And now – her silence was like an empty space on the edge of a cliff. Any minute he might walk over it.

He tried to make sense of it. She was punishing him for something. She would let him stew in this silence for a while, and then come back with Sam. She'd had an accident – she'd meant to contact him but couldn't, and he would hear the news from the police or a hospital. Or – the worst scenario – she had left him for a lover, and Sam was in the hands of another man. He saw pictures in his head: Sam watching Jen and this other man kiss. Sam alone in a car, waiting for the *man* to drive him home. Sam and Jen and the man, a nice little family photo.

Martin made an attempt to control his voice.

'I couldn't lose him, you see. I couldn't. I love –'

He stopped and dipped his fingers into the river. Van lit a cigarette and smoked it, his back to the others. The engine chugged and spluttered.

Sam crept towards Martin and put his head down in his lap. Martin touched his hair, stroked it with gentle fingers.

'Let me tell you about Sam,' he said. 'It's important, so I'll tell you.' He glanced at the boy, measuring the effect of his words on him. He gathered himself to explain.

He wasn't prepared. All through Jen's pregnancy he couldn't take it in. There were a few moments when it hit him. Her first scan was one: the sound of the baby's heartbeat, echoing with breathtaking intensity around the stuffy hospital room. Amazing sound. Martin had noticed of late that much of the time his senses were numb, as if the layers of habit that had built up around him like limescale were gradually deadening his nerves. Even music didn't move him, these days, the way it used to. That sound, though – the heartbeat – cut through the deadness like a high note on a violin.

The feeling didn't last. Towards the end Jen began buying things – pushchairs, a cot, baby clothes – until the flat was full of them, and all he could think of was that his life was going to change forever, and for the worse, probably.

Whatever Jen was going through totally absorbed her. He didn't blame her – he knew how it was – it's just that he felt left out. Jen kept telling him he was going to be a father, and the words sounded strange to him. He was young – well, youngish – and fathers were old. He had a father of his own, and he hardly admired him: not for being a father, anyway. Other things, yes. But fatherhood? Not that.

Sam's birth terrified him. Jen got up on all fours, vomited over the bed, screamed at him. It was frightening. He was scared, and hated the whole thing. He wanted to run away somewhere and smoke a cigar the way men used to do, but Jen dug her nails into his hand until his flesh bled, and told him to *never* fucking leave her.

The baby, when it finally came, was born blue. Jen passed it to him to hold. He thought he would break it, so he passed it back.

Jen asked him, 'How do you feel?'

He said he was fine. It was a lie.

He took two weeks off work to help out. He did help. He did the shopping, and cleaned up the flat, and watched the baby while Jen had a bath or slept.

Sometimes she would pass the baby to him and he would try to hold it properly and feel something. All he felt was fearful. The head was so heavy, the neck was so thin. Surely it couldn't be right? Jen was interested in the baby and not much else. He didn't mind that. If she ignored him she couldn't be angry with him. There would be peace.

There was peace, for a while.

One evening, a week after Sam's birth, Jen took a bath. Sam was sleeping in his cot, and Jen shouted that she thought she'd heard him, so he went to take a look. The room was dark. He didn't turn on the lights because he didn't want the baby to wake. He tiptoed towards the cot and bent over it. He bent low. He noticed something. The baby's scent. Fresh shortbread, buttery and sweet. When his eyes adjusted to the light, he saw that Sam's eyes were wide open. He was staring right at him.

What a shock. He stared back.

That was it. Nothing, really. They stared at each other. And after a while – minutes, hours, he didn't know how long – it dawned on him that this little thing – this weird creature with blue black eyes – meant more to him than anything he'd ever known. He touched Sam's cheek. It was soft, very delicate. Downy and warm. So strange, to think that he had made this thing. Somehow, without even wanting to, without giving it any thought, he had made it.

Sam's eyes grew heavy. His breathing slowed. His eyelids closed, and the skin there was so transparent that Martin could see the blue of his eyes right through it. He watched, and Sam slipped into a deep sleep.

Martin bent over him and said, 'I love you.'

Martin swallowed. He was crying, tears rolling down his cheeks in great blobs. His chest heaved. He felt foolish. He leaned forward and touched Sam. The boy was lying in a ball at his feet, quiet, listening.

Van revved the motor up a notch. The boat chugged on.

5

Corporal Paysonge's day had been difficult, and he knew the night would be worse. The terrain had forced him to leave the course of the river. The going was hard. At times they'd had to un-sheath machetes and hack their way forwards. In the heat each step was tortuous, and by midday Paysonge's back was bathed in sweat. His body ached. He tried not to show this. His men were suffering, he could see, and so was he, but he had to lead by example. How else could he lead?

He insisted his men march long into the afternoon before he allowed them to rest. When he finally did stop he saw that his fortitude had paid off: weariness was written on their faces, but nobody complained.

He ate his meal silently, a little apart from the others. They would need to rest before nightfall.

They had been climbing for most of the day, and now, as dusk came, Paysonge could see the river again, a fat brown worm winding through the green of the trees. He believed that nature was something to be tamed, not admired. His family owned a small piece of land, and had etched their lives on to it. It smelt of human beings, responded to their touch. This landscape was different. It had few human traces. Paysonge knew it well enough to negotiate it, but he did not love it.

He squinted against the last rays of the sun, and wondered how a place can have meaning if people do not live there.

Of course, he reminded himself, there were people out there somewhere, and not only in the miserable villages clinging to the riverbank. Paysonge scanned the river again. That must be how the foreigners were travelling, and it frustrated him that his own progress had been so slow. Even with his knowledge of the terrain they could be hours ahead. Unless he had miscalculated, of course, and they had not taken the river. He shook his head, dismissing the thought quickly. Even with the best guide he did not believe the foreigners would be hardy enough for such a march: his men were young and fit, and even they were struggling. He himself was struggling.

He rubbed his shoulder, trying to knead some life and softness into his rigid muscles. It was almost dark now. He turned away from the river and observed the slope of the mountain instead. He could see no trace of his own path behind him, and nodded in satisfaction. The jungle had swallowed him, and it did not give up its secrets easily.

And secrets, he reflected, could work to his advantage too.

The moon rose yellow and full. For the hundredth time, April wished she had a cigarette. She squinted at the far bank and saw a party of monkeys clinging to creepers, their eyes two shiny dots reflecting moonlight out of little black faces. She was suddenly sorry that Sam was not awake to see them, and thought, briefly, about tapping Martin's arm to point them out. She glanced at him. He was sitting as he had been for the past few hours, his eyes fixed on a small patch of water by the side of the boat. She sat on her hands and said nothing.

Van eased up on the throttle and the boat puttered along quietly. They were approaching one of the banks again. April saw an overhanging rock that cast a shadow across the water. She wondered how they would climb it to reach dry land.

'Are we stopping?' She was tired. More than that: drained. Martin's story had disturbed her in a way she could not really fathom. She was beginning to feel truly frightened, and not for any obvious reasons. Her fear was insidious, unspecific. There was too much going on she didn't understand. April believed herself to be resourceful: she believed practical problems demanded practical solutions, and for now, staying on the boat was the safest option. Even so, if she didn't get out soon she would scream.

175

The vessel was cramped. Everywhere she looked, she caught someone's eye. She needed a cigarette.

'No. We are not stopping.' Van's face was barely visible. She could just see the orange glow of his cigarette and his white teeth. She inhaled, trying to catch his smoke.

Van turned away from her to Martin.

'The boy is sleeping,' he commented.

'He is,' Martin answered, without removing his gaze from the small patch of water it was fixed on.

April shifted. Impossible to get comfortable. She wanted to move, do something, say something. She leaned over and tapped Hardwick's shoulder.

'You all right, Professor?'

Hardwick smiled, his eyes crinkling. 'Thank you. Surviving. I hope you are.'

'I'm dying out here.'

'You are?' Hardwick looked alarmed.

'Nicotine. Cancer stick. I need one. It's killing me.'

Hardwick coughed.

'Oh God.' April covered her mouth. 'I'm sorry. Jesus, why do I do that? And with your wife and all. I'm truly sorry.'

Hardwick smiled. 'Really, it doesn't matter. I'd rather it, to be frank. Rather that than the appalling – oh, I don't know – false sympathy mixed with embarrassment that most people offer. Talking around the subject. Squeamishness.'

April laughed. The laugh came out too loud, its raucousness not muffled by the dense air. She caught her hands, and whispered another apology. A chill passed through her.

Van steered towards the bank. He cut the motor. The boat clunked against a wooden jetty. 'This is a famous place. Good to stop here. You wait if you want.'

'What's so special about this place?' Asked April. She was shivering. She dug a jacket out of her case and pulled it around her.

176

'It is a cave. Very old. Many statues inside. If you want to come, you come. If not, it doesn't matter.'

She shook her head. 'I won't come.'

'I'll come,' said Martin, looking up suddenly.

Hardwick said, 'I would like to see it too.'

The jetty was a narrow platform between the rock and the water. April could make out rough steps beyond it. Van slung out a rope and lassoed the edge of the platform, then pulled at it deftly to moor the boat. He turned the engine off, leapt out and secured the rope.

She listened to the water lapping against the edges of the platform. It seemed loud now that the motor was dead.

Van started up the steps. Martin struggled out of the boat, groping in the dark for something to hold on to. Hardwick followed. April hesitated, torn between desire and suspicion. Martin leaned over the boat and whispered, 'Will you be okay? Can you watch Sam?'

'You want to leave him with me?' April heard the panic in her voice.

'You want to come?'

'No. Why are you playing tourist all of a sudden? What do you think this is?'

Martin leaned closer to her, pressing his body against the boat. He whispered, 'I want to make sure Van doesn't run off. I don't feel like being stranded out here.'

'You have a point,' she conceded.

'Then help me with Sam.'

She nodded, and lifted the sleepy child in her arms. He was heavier than she had expected: it was as much as she could do to hand him to Martin, and the boat rocked alarmingly as she did so. Martin swept him up with ease.

She climbed out of the boat. On solid ground, her feet were unsteady.

Martin whispered to Sam, soothing him awake. The boy whimpered, groggy and confused. His eyes opened. Martin set him on his feet.

'Come on. We're going to see a cave. Hold on to my hand.'

'What cave?' Sleep had made Sam's hair stick up at angles.

'Do you remember, like the one in Derbyshire?'

'Where it was dark?'

'Yeah, really dark.'

'Do they have Blue John?'

'I don't think so,' said Martin. 'Maybe we can find out.'

'Okay. Because maybe its treasure.'

'Maybe it is.'

Sam nodded his assent, and they groped forwards. April followed behind.

The stone steps were wet and slippery. Walls of rock rose up on either side of her, and she found she could steady herself by placing her palms flat against them. Even so, she was close to losing her balance with each step. The rock was slimy, and a cold draught funneled down its sides and caught the back of her neck. She moved with difficulty. The rock closed in over her head. One by one, the stars went out.

Ahead, Martin plodded on steadily upwards through the narrow cavern. He was stoical, she would give him that.

The steps were made for tiny feet, so Sam progressed well. Just as she thought this, the boy skidded and lost his balance. He had been holding Martin's hand, and in a moment he was dangling from it with no other means of support.

Martin slammed his back against the rock. April saw naked fear flashed across his face. She reached forward and caught hold of Sam's shoulders. Between them she and Martin steadied him, and with an effort that made her groan they placed him back to the steps.

He clung to Martin's knees and shook.

Martin said, his voice strained, 'It's okay. Hush. Are you okay?'

Sam nodded.

'Do you want to go on?'

Sam nodded again. Martin glanced at April.

'Thanks.' He exhaled. 'Are you all right?'

'Sure. I'm fine.'

His fingertips brushed her hand. She curled her fingers away, recoiling from the contact. He shrugged, and turned back to the blackness.

She reached out and found her balance against the side of the rock. When she was steady, she stepped forwards again. After thirty or forty more steps – she lost count – the passage opened out into the mouth of a cave proper. She could tell this because the left hand wall fell away suddenly. The cold and darkness deepened at once, and she uttered an involuntary cry. She felt, but could not see, Martin turn back to her.

'All right?'

'Wonderful.' His hand reached for her. Misjudging the distance, he hit her face, catching her eye.

'Sorry.'

'It's okay.'

His hand paused on her cheek, then fumbled downwards to rest, briefly, on her shoulder. It was heavy there. She was breathing hard.

'I'm sorry.' Martin removed his hand.

She started forward. She could see nothing at all now, and relied on the sound of Martin's footsteps, and the wall on her right – against which she pressed her whole body – to guide her. She was disoriented. After a while of staring pointlessly into the blackness, she shut her eyes. It was as if she had been inside the cave for years already. She was tired.

She began to remember things. Running from the casino. The boat. Mo, lying in the road. She opened her eyes. Nothing. She closed them again, took a few more steps forward. Nothing there. Splashes of orange and red floated across her closed lids. She saw the sun. She took a step. The cave seemed to expand around her. It had become a vast, roofless place. She was tiny, a dot under the stars. She began to smell incense, sharp and unmistakable. She swallowed back the dryness in her throat. Her scar was itching maddeningly, and she resisted an urge to drag her fingernails across her damp skin.

She groped forward and saw, through the film of her eyelids, more than one sun swimming before her. She saw flowers of light, dancing, growing.

She opened her eyes and the soft lights were still there, flickering halos around a thousand candles.

The candlelight stuttered, making a weird play of shadows around the rocks. Here was a monster, here a witch with a long hooked nose. Everywhere she looked, she saw a statue of Buddha. There were hundreds of them, of all shapes and sizes: some were tiny and made of metal, others wooden; some painted gold, others half rotten. Skinny, standing Buddhas. Fat, squatting Buddhas. Many were carved into the rock. In the centre of the cave a thick stalagmite served as a pedestal for a makeshift alter. A happy swollen Buddha, the largest in the room, sat on top of it. Clumps of choking incense burnt around it.

Van was kneeling before it, holding lighted incense of his own in each hand.

She saw Martin and Sam standing awestruck a few steps ahead. She made her way towards them. The ground was soft, covered in some sort of slippery grey matter. Martin looked at her ruefully.

'I think it's bird shit. Or bat shit. See up there?' He pointed to a patch of shadow on the cave roof. 'It's the sky. If you look for a while you can see stars. Birds must fly in and nest, I suppose.'

'This place is freaky,' breathed April.

'Yeah.' They were both whispering. 'All this. Where do you think it comes from?'

'Who the hell knows?'

'He offered, 'Monks, maybe?'

'Yeah,' said April, her voice shrill. 'That or Jehovah's Witnesses. What do you think, Professor?'

'Hmm?' Hardwick was standing in the centre of the cave, next to the stalagmite pedestal. He was stooped, but even so his shock of white hair brushed the ceiling. The way the candlelight flickered on him made him look iconic, as if he too was something to be worshiped.

April whistled. 'Hey, look at you. The God of this place.'

'No,' said Hardwick quietly. 'Not me. I never did believe in God, you know. But if he were to be found anywhere, it would be somewhere like this, I imagine.'

'You've got to be kidding me.' Her voice echoed against the walls of the cave. She backed into the shadows, breathing hard.

'Why should I be?' queried Hardwick.

'It's only a cave. Only rocks.'

Van said, looking at Hardwick, 'It is a nice place. A good place. A very good place.'

'Yes,' said Hardwick. 'A very good place.'

April stared at him in disbelief.

'It's peaceful,' he added. 'Strange. Pervading strangeness. But peaceful. I feel at home here. Curious.'

'Why is that, Professor? Why at home?' She asked. She pointed at a rotting carving with haunted, hollow eyes. 'It's not even pretty.' Her fingers were itching. Everything was itching.

Hardwick stood in thought, his body another statue. 'I'm not sure. Perhaps… A memory. I once went to a museum – not so long ago – and I saw an icon there. I remember it vividly. There was nothing very remarkable about it, but even so I kept wondering, why that curious expression? Not a human expression, not even a happy one. So what did it mean? Was it self-satisfied? Distant? Warm? I thought I understood something, but it was too elusive, like a very distinct dream one might forget on waking. I wish, now, that I could catch it.'

Van said, abruptly, 'We can go.'

April turned quickly, eager to make her way out of the cave. Looking back she noticed Hardwick linger, as if trying to fix it all in his mind.

The journey back was easier. The cave mouth was lit by moonlight, and this made something to aim for. Still, heading downwards on the slippery steps was treacherous. Martin led the way, holding Sam with an iron grip. April followed, her eyes locked on to Martin's broad back. Hardwick was behind her. She looked back occasionally to check on him, and he nodded lightly when she did so, though his steps were slow and shaky.

They climbed into the boat in silence.

Her scar was itching. She wondered if it was fear that made it itch, and whether her fear could be smelt on her, like an animal pelt.

She reached under the tarpaulin and groped for her black handbag. It was there still. She swore to herself. The dollar bills crunched under her hand.

Corporal Paysonge shivered. The sallow moon made him wakeful. He sat up, dusted himself, and walked to the brow of the hill to take another look at the river below. The moon had turned it silver, a bright road twisting through the forest. He nodded to himself, pleased: a romantic thought. As he scanned it, squinting for any object that did not belong there, it occurred to him what it was this landscape made him feel. Not fear: he knew it well enough not to be afraid.

Sadness. That was it. It made him sad.

6

Van steered them just a little further upriver before he announced that they would be stopping for the night.

Hardwick was the last out of the boat. He noticed this: that he lagged behind the others. And not only, he thought, because his pace was slower. April and Martin seemed able to switch their attention so quickly from one thing to the next. His thoughts, as the boat travelled ever further up river, were still in the cave.

They landed by a group of huts clustered close to the water's edge like stooping men. They carried their packs ashore and climbed upwards.

Van hallooed. His voice echoed back without reply. There was a splash.

Hardwick jumped. 'What was that?'

'Frog. Nothing. Just frog.' Van shook his head. 'Nobody here.'

They walked past the deserted huts, treading quietly for fear of disturbing whatever might be crouching in the vegetation ahead. One structure was bigger than the rest. It was around two storeys high, as wide as a hay barn. A semi circle of trees spread out from either side of it, making it the focal point of a rough clearing in the jungle around fifty metres across.

They dumped their bags on the ground by the deserted barn, and followed Van to the centre of the clearing.

Hardwick panted, exhausted by the climb. He looked about him, trying to decipher messages in the silence. There were, he thought, signs that people had left the pace in a hurry. He saw a silver object glinting in the moonlight by his foot, and on closer inspection it turned out to be a cooking pot lying upside down. He saw the scattered ashes of a fire nearby. It reminded him of certain archeological sites he knew, preserved at a particular moment before calamity struck.

He returned to the others. Even before it had been deserted, it struck him this must have been a sad place. Dirt poor: he hadn't truly considered the meaning of the phrase before. He sat on the ground, and tried to smooth out a space in the earth where he could sleep.

Nearby, Van squatted down and began to assemble a fire. Soon flames silhouetted his thin body. Hardwick thought, looking at him, that he resembled a shadowy insect moving over the earth. He wondered how the comical figure they'd met in the bakery had turned into this creature, so spidery and purposeful.

The fire, though, was cheering. The others gathered round it, and soon Hardwick joined them.

Van prepared a quick meal, using rice that the villagers had given them the previous night. Hardwick ate mutely. It was their first meal since the morning, and it was meagre. Not, he reflected, an encouraging sign.

Crickets started to sing. The air closed in, warm and soupy.

Once they had eaten Sam moved to sit beside Hardwick. He smiled at the boy, pleased to have been sought out. He cleared his throat.

'Do you like fires?'

'Uh hum,' Sam assented.

'Yes,' said Hardwick. 'They're good, aren't they? Cheerful.'

'You got flames.'

'Yes. Yes, you do.'

'Like a rocket.'

'Oh?' Hardwick raised his eyebrows.

'You know.' Sam pointed to the moon. 'In space.'

'Would you like that? To be an astronaut?'

Sam shrugged, as if he didn't much care either way. Hardwick considered what to say next. He was unpracticed at talking to children, and was anxious lest the conversation dry up. He tried another gambit.

'Do you like trains?'

Sam shrugged. He said, 'I'm hungry.'

'I know,' said Hardwick, sadly. Van's supplies appeared to be dwindling. He did not seem, to Hardwick, to be the type to horde anything. He hoped that his judgment – often shaky when it came to character – was correct. How else were they to survive?

He drew some lines in the dirt. Naughts and crosses. 'Can you play?' He asked Sam. Sam nodded, and they began a game.

Van watched them. Before long he moved away, and sat with his back to them, facing the high barn. He lit a cigarette. The smell drifted over their heads, wove itself in with the smoke from the fire. April and Martin began to talk all at once. Their words floated over him, muffled, nonsensical. He stared at them both. He could see something in their faces so clearly, that he was surprised how little he had noticed it before.

Fear.

Hardwick gazed at them. It was visible, the fear bearing down on their shoulders. He squeezed his eyes shut. A line of sweat ran down from his temple to his chin. He wiped it dry with the back of his hand. The same trickle ran down again. April's voice interrupted his thoughts.

'Well. This is nice.'

Martin said, before Hardwick could reply, 'Why do you have to do that, April? Why do you have to say such stupid things?'

'Don't you think it's funny?' She arched her eyebrows. She wore her jacket pulled tightly round her. Odd, thought Hardwick. It was hardly cold.

'No. I don't think it's funny.' Martin sat hunched, his knees drawn up to him. He looked, to Hardwick, bulkier than usual. Troll-like.

'A joke. That's all.' She made a dismissive gesture.

Martin muttered, 'It's not a joke for the people who live here, is it?'

'I don't know.' April tossed her head. 'Maybe they're happy.'

'What would you know about happiness, April?'

'What would you know about it?'

He shook his head. 'There's no point talking to you.'

'I mean it. Just because I can buy leather shoes – does that mean I live in paradise? Does it mean my life is perfect?'

'No, but –'

'So why the judgement, Martin? What is it you think you know?'

'I don't think I know anything.'

'Then fuck you.' She turned away from him.

Hardwick raised his hands. 'It does – really, it does seem odd, here. This place. Something seems wrong.' He peered down at Sam. The boy had dug up the upturned cooking pot with his fingers, and was throwing stones into it. They clanged against the iron.

April sighed. 'I guess you never imagined you'd end up somewhere like this, Professor.'

'No. I don't suppose I did.'

'And you did it all for love.' Her voice trailed away.

He stared at her, wondering if he was being made fun of. 'Is that what you believe?'

'Sure. Isn't it true?'

'Perhaps.' He swallowed. 'I don't know.'

'Tell me more about her.'

'Who?'

She threw a piece of dry grass into the fire. It fizzled. 'You know who. The enigma. Your puzzle. Lorraine.'

He gave Martin a pleading look. The younger man was twisting his fingers through his hair. He seemed disengaged, only half listening to the conversation. Catching Hardwick's eyes he said, absently, 'If you want to.'

Hardwick was not sure what he wanted. His lifelong habit was of privacy, but he found, now, it was tempting to talk. He was barely aware of where this temptation came from, but something – Martin's frankness of earlier perhaps, or the oddness of their experience in the cave – had acted on his mood. In normal circumstances he would say nothing about himself.

These, however, were not normal circumstances.

A monkey whooped. The sound cut through the vegetation. Leaves trembled.

'Would you like to hear something more about me?' He asked, cautiously.

'Of course.' said Martin. 'Please.' He raised his green eyes to Hardwick.

'Yeah, Professor,' said April, casually. 'We all need a story.'

Their faces were anxious; eager, it seemed to Hardwick, for a distraction from other thoughts.

'All right.' He frowned, weighing his words. 'Maybe it will help.'

He cleared his throat. Where to begin?

His audience waited, tense.

He closed his eyes, dredging his memory until something surfaced. The text message he had once sent Lorraine: *You are so beautiful.*

He returned from hall late, his mind racing and his skin tingling, the phone clutched in his hand. Felicity was asleep already, and he crept into bed beside her, clumsily quiet. He did not expect to sleep but fell into a troubled doze nevertheless.

He was woken by the sound of whimpering. It was an animal sound, and he thought at first, in a fuzzy half conscious way, that a cat had wandered into the room. Once he realised that the sound came from Felicity, he sprang upright.

'My God. What is it?'

Felicity's lips were shiny. 'Get me those pills please. The yellow bottle.' Spit bubbled out of her mouth.

He fumbled with the pills on the dressing table, spilling some. Felicity swallowed two but gagged on the glass of water he offered her.

'Should I call the doctor?'

'No. Leave me alone.'

'You want me to –?'

'I want to be alone.' Her voice was barely a whisper. He shuffled out of the room and sat on the sofa in his pajamas.

He reached for his phone and checked it, for the hundredth time. The message he had sent Lorraine was a disciplinary offense – at worst, a sackable one. His hand shook. The phone's buttons were made for a child's fingers – his adult ones slipped. The screen glowed pale and blank. Lorraine had not replied. It was to be expected, of course. What else had he thought would happen? That she would declare some sort of love for him? That she would say anything at all? His stomach clenched with shame.

He crept back in to see Felicity. She had fallen into a sleep of sorts. She was breathing shallowly. Her lids were thin, hardly covering her eyes at all. The skin on her face was translucent. He had the peculiar feeling that he was looking at a body already preserved by anatomists, and that if he pulled the covers down he would see her organs through her skin.

He panicked and reached for the telephone.

'Hello? I want an ambulance. My wife is –'

'What, sir?'

'She's very ill. I'm afraid she may be dying.'

He sat with her on the way to hospital. The ambulance crew was sufficiently impressed with her condition to usher her straight onto a ward. A nurse tutted and administered morphine.

He squatted beside Felicity's bed, hardly noticed and not consulted, and wondered when it was that she had become not his wife but a mere body.

He gazed at her. Her features, so familiar, were transformed by pain. She looked old. He too felt old.

By mid morning her eyelids flickered open. She was awake, though not fully conscious. She was confused: the drugs, he supposed. She mumbled something he could not hear. Her eyes swam towards him.

'What's that my dear?'

Her lips moved. '– always looking at me.'

'I am?'

'No. The others. Always.'

'Which others?'

'The people. Why are they looking?'

'There aren't any others, dear Felicity.'

She turned away. After some time she whispered, 'I've looked into it. It must be clean. They don't let us wash here.'

'Would you like me to bring you clean clothes?'

'Yes.' She lowered her lids and lapsed into sleep.

He returned early the next morning fearing the worst. Felicity, however, was propped up in bed admonishing a young nurse over the state of hospital food. She turned to him as he entered.

'How do they expect people to get better if this is what they serve?'

'I'm not sure.' He tried to suppress a foolish smile

Felicity asked the nurse, 'Don't they have nutritionists? Haven't they heard about diet?'

'I don't really know,' the woman simpered.

'You'll kill more people than cure them with this stuff.'

'Would you like to make a complaint?' volunteered the woman.

'I am making a complaint. I'm complaining to you.'

The nurse promised to pass it on. She backed out of the room.

'Of course she won't say anything,' Felicity remarked. 'Totally indifferent.'

He sat down beside her. 'It's marvelous to see you.'

'I've only been away a day.'

He shook his head. Their eyes met. Felicity was the first to look away.

'I'm discharging myself.'

'What?'

'There's nothing they can do for me here.'

'But the morphine?'

'It gives me bad dreams. I don't want it. If I'm going to die at least let me die a sane woman. At least let me have that.'

They held hands in the taxi that drove them home.

He gave up all pretence of work to care for her. Despite her complaints – which he suspected she only made for form's sake – he nursed her with as much skill as he had. He saw lines of pain draw deeper on her face by the hour, but she did not mention her suffering, and he did not allude to it. He spared her his pity.

Death filled their bedroom. He saw it in every shadow. It skulked behind the wardrobe, hid under the bed. Struggling against it, he found he was not afraid, only exhausted.

He left her for only an hour each day. He told her this was to buy supplies, and there was some truth in this: on his way back home he passed the local supermarket and filled a trolley with randomly chosen goods. The rest of the time, though, he gave to Lorraine.

He saw her by the riverbank on the first day of Felicity's return from hospital. Instead of approaching her – his imprudent text message made that impossible – he kept his distance and followed her. He did the same thing the next day. Soon a pattern was established which he was powerless to help.

He loved to look at her. She often seemed deep in thought, stopping to stare at the most unlikely things: shop

190

windows, advertisement hoardings, office buildings. Lorraine, he decided, was a visual magpie: any flash of colour or incongruous object would attract her attention.

He began to feel as if he knew her.

One day she appeared wearing glasses. He soon guessed that this was because she was developing a cold: he saw her sneeze and wipe her eyes. He surmised that she normally wore contact lenses, and that today they were irritating her eyes. He was amused to see, when she met someone, that she whipped off the glasses and held them in her hand as she talked. This little vanity made his heart go out to her. She must think that the glasses made her ugly. He shook his head in wonder.

It pleased him that she should have these insecurities. He was protective of her, and he felt, when he followed her, as if he possessed her in some way. Ownership of her unguarded moments was a paltry kind of power, he realised. But it was power nonetheless.

Power to the powerless. He muttered it to himself as he walked home to Felicity. It was not an encouraging slogan.
He had seen it often: the unlovely sight of an aging teacher falling recklessly, ridiculously in love with a student. He had thought that he was immune. What troubled him most was not his frailty in falling, but that his awkward longing ran in perfect parallel with his grief for Felicity. As one feeling grew stronger, so did the other: delicate, nuanced grief, and intoxicating desire. He tried to banish both emotions, but as soon as he shut the door to one, the other entered. He ached for Felicity, quietly and without fuss. He ached for Lorraine, compulsively and upsettingly. To satisfy the ache he sought her out.

His best afternoon was one in which she had chosen to slump on the grass beside the Radcliffe Camera. He found he could settle himself a little to her left, across the square towards the entrance to All Souls, and observe her unseen. The circular building – picked out in gold by the afternoon sun – cast a soft shadow over her childish-adult face. She was wearing her glasses once again, and as she tipped her head forwards they slipped, slowly, down her nose, so that at intervals she had to prod them up again with her forefinger. This delighted him. He watched for an hour or more as the glasses slipped and ascended, slipped and ascended, and her long hair fell across her shoulders.

He found himself in tears as the sun set.

She left. He raised himself, knees creaking, and returned to Felicity's small room. He drew its heavy curtains against the falling light.

Felicity's end was not sudden. For days the line between life and death in her was blurred. A doctor came every day, and every day he asked if Felicity wanted to be hospitalised. Every day she refused, and when she could no longer refuse, Hardwick refused for her.

He had never studied her face so intently before. Knowing it better, seeing it revealed so unguardedly, he came to love it better. Was it not the same with Lorraine?

'I'm glad you are here,' Felicity whispered, and he knew that the end would be soon.

One afternoon he followed Lorraine to the Ashmolean museum, and talked to her over a smiling Buddha.

That night, Felicity slipped away, quietly and unremarkably.

He stayed beside her through the night. He talked to her, relating odd snatches of thought which came into his head. He remembered things he had to tell her – about the post, about appointments to be kept.

Later, friends would tell him he had been in shock, and that when at last he had descended from her bedroom he was white and trembling. This was not what he remembered. He remembered the first peace he'd had in many months.

7

Martin woke. Someone was shaking him.

Hardwick's story had crept into his dream, and for a moment it was he, Martin, who was the one battling death, and it was Felicity's cold hand on his arm. He shrieked, brushed it away. A pair of black eyes met his.

He gasped. 'Christ. Don't do that.'

Van's face hovered above him.

'What is it?' Martin sat up. His heart was racing. Something flared in the distance.

'We must go,' said Van, urgently. 'Now. Fighting.'

'Who's fighting?' Martin rubbed his head. His eyes were glued with sleep.

'Army. There is a village nearby. Army attack village. '

'What?'

'We leave now. Oh dear. Very dangerous.' Van began to shake the others, scuttling between them like an insect.

April stirred. 'What's going on?'

'We've got to get out of here,' said Martin. 'We're being attacked.'

'We are?' She stared at him, open-mouthed.

'Nearby. We've got to get back to the river.'

She sprang forwards and made to grab her black bag. Hardwick too had woken, and was making laborious work of putting on his shoes: they were caked in mud, and he was trying to clean them by scraping them against a charred log. Martin thumped the ground. 'Christ man, they're not going to stop shooting us if you have clean shoes. We've got to go.'

Another flare blazed overhead. His heart lurched. He scooped Sam up in his arms, turned his back on the others, and ran.

He ran wildly, crashing through leaves and branches. Twigs snapped his face like whips. It was a bright night, and the ground sloped downwards in front of him. He guessed the river must be that way. The flares in the sky confused him: they seemed to be coming from everywhere.

He heard Van shout, 'Not that way. Stop, you stupid.'

He turned and stumbled, twisting his ankle as he fell. Pain burst in his head. He crouched on the wet earth, panting like an animal, his body curled around Sam's. Another flare lit up the night. The trees around him turned white.

He saw a face loom over him.

The face belonged to a man. He was younger than Martin, handsome in a doleful way, with large eyes and fine high cheekbones. He wore a neat army uniform with shiny buttons done up to his neck. Like Martin, he was breathless and flushed. He had a rifle slung across his body.

The man shouted, raised his rifle, and aimed it directly at Martin's head.

Time slowed.

With great delicacy, the soldier pressed the mouth of his gun against Martin's temple.

The soldier's eyes met his. They stared at one another.

Slowly and deliberately, Martin stood up. He gathered Sam to him. The boy clung to him, his hands little claws. Martin trembled, his knees wet and smeared with earth. The gun throbbed against his skin.

Nothing happened.

He held Sam tighter. Fixing the man with his eyes, he spoke to him in his mind. *My child. Can you see? My son. He's only little. I'm rubbish: a complete bloody failure. Honestly, you can do what you like to me. Thing is, I've only done one good thing in my entire life, and he's here. Please don't hurt him.*

He began to back away, locked in the man's gaze. The soldier did not stir. His doleful eyes, and his gun, stayed level. Martin heaved in a breath, turned, and ran to the sheltering trees. He ran hard, tripping, ankles twisting.

*

Corporal Paysonge felt sick. He had killed before – twice, in fact – and each time he'd had the same terrible elation, which, each time, he had suppressed with alcohol. This time was different. The attack had been messy and confused, even though it had been well-planned and he accepted that killing was always messy.

Well-planned? No. He stopped and leant against a tree, panting. He had been told that they were to attack a dangerous bandit encampment. What he'd found was a miserable village full of sleepy old men and naked children. True, after the initial shock of the attack had passed, a couple of men had emerged with crude rifles and taken a few frightened shots at them. But the noise of the guns hadn't muffled the sound of children screaming.

Had he killed a child? He didn't know. People had been hurt, certainly, but it was too dangerous to go back and check exactly who; and anyway, the sick elation of killing was still on him, and he did not trust himself not to shoot again. His own soldiers were his priority: one of his men had been injured in the confusion, and he'd needed to move him away as quickly as he could. He'd dragged his comrade through the trees, then swooped back to tell his men to withdraw. It was then that he'd seen the foreigner.

Paysonge's stomach heaved. He'd been so stupid. He thumped his arm to punish himself. There was no question where his duty lay: he should have killed the man. So why had he let him go? It was the child, of course. The shock of it. He would have had no compunction otherwise. The sight of the boy clinging to his father, his bottom in the air and his knees bent like a frog, was so unexpected that he had not known what to do.

It was the first time he'd seen the younger foreigner at close quarters. In the airport he'd only seen him at a distance. The man had looked frightened, yet his fear did not hide what Paysonge imagined was a film-star attractiveness about him. He was a rugged cowboy type, he thought, just like John

Wayne. Paysonge loved cowboy stories: three years ago, as a fresh recruit, he had seen a John Wayne film in the cinema.

Paysonge smiled. He would not, he resolved, tell his men what had happened. Not because he was afraid of their ridicule – he was not, he believed – but because he did not want them to take his own vacillation for a model.

He straightened, and made an attempt to neaten himself. He flicked his fingers across his chest, dispelling imaginary dust. It was important that his men did not feel that their raid had been futile, so he would try to explain the circumstances as best he could. The place had been abandoned by the fiercest fighters, he would say: it is well known that the *Khia* could up camp quickly. This time, though, they must be pursued.

His resolve stiffened. Like John Wayne, he would never give up. He picked up his rifle, and strode towards the thin trail of smoke that signalled the abandoned village.

Martin slid through the red mud that oozed towards the riverbank, not looking where he was going, clutching Sam in his arms. He smashed into April.

'What is it? What?'

He gripped the sides of her head and mouthed wordless sounds at her. He was so relieved to see her he could, at that moment, have embraced her. She snatched at his arms, pulled them away from her, and dragged him forwards. He stumbled behind. The professor followed; Van was ahead: his sure feet found the way through the mud and trees to the water's edge.

They scrambled onto the boat together. Van flung their luggage down and started the engine, just as Hardwick clambered aboard after them. The jerk threw the professor backwards, and as the boat chugged towards the centre of the river he lay motionless on top of Martin's rucksack, inert as a dead fish.

Martin dug his nails into his palms, too shocked to check if Hardwick was all right. He could still hear gunfire coming from the river bank. He was pressed against April's side, and the bare flesh of her arm was damp and cold. He waited, frozen. The firing became more distant. He unpeeled his skin from April's.

Sam asked, 'Are they shooting?'

'Not at us Sam. It's safe.'

'Why are they shooting?'

'I don't know. I don't know, Sam.'

'Are there baddies?'

'I'm not sure. I don't know. Maybe.'

'Oh.' Sam sat up and scanned the riverbank for any baddies that might be hiding there. His expression was pensive. His eyes shone.

Martin followed his gaze. The hills beyond the river were low dark humps, crouching giants poised to spring. He strained into their depths for signs of movement. The sky was scrawled with a thousand messy stars.

Van revved up the engine. Water lapped around the boat.

Martin leaned close to Sam. 'Listen,' he said, his lips brushing the child's soft cheek. 'Listen to me. Whatever happens, I'll keep you safe. Do you understand?'

Sam stared at the passing bank.

He heard April, sitting close to him, exhale. He turned to her. She had been listening. Catching his look, she swiveled backwards. She hit the rucksack where Hardwick was still lying inert. She gripped her arms as if to compose herself. She turned, and tapped Hardwick on the shoulder.

'You okay, Professor?'

Hardwick looked up. 'I suppose we're not dead, then?'

'No. No, we're not,' said April.

Martin tested this thought. They were alive. He felt a rush of euphoria. In the light of this new perspective – their continued life – the sight of Hardwick spread-eagled on the

197

pile of luggage, his wild hair on end, seemed suddenly hilarious. He spluttered out a laugh. April sank into the floor. Hardwick craned at her. 'Are you all right, my dear?'

'Yeah. Yeah, I'm fine.'

Hardwick sat up. He was wobbly and pale but, as far as Martin could see, sound. Hardwick held up his hands and stared at them, apparently surprised to find them attached to his body. 'It's strange,' he said in a conversational tone, as if picking up the thread of an interrupted chat. 'I didn't think I feared death. I faced it before, you see, and I didn't feel afraid. But just then, I was petrified. I'm sorry. I am ashamed.'

Martin reached past April and touched Hardwick's arm, his mood crashing. 'Listen. Don't be ashamed.'

Van cut the engine. They floated.

Sam was scanning the river bank still, oblivious to the others. He lifted a small fist and pointed. 'Bang.'

Martin asked, 'What are you doing?'

'Fighting. Bang. Killing the baddies.'

'Okay, Sam. That's okay. Only do it quietly, so they can't hear us. We have to –' He leaned closer. 'We have to take them by surprise.'

Sam nodded. He set his face to the shore and raised his fist again. He whispered, 'Bang.'

Martin squeezed Sam's shoulders. He was light headed, drunk on the mixture of emotions – tension, adrenalin, relief – that he'd experienced in the last hour. Above all, relief. He scanned the boat, checking everyone was there. Sam, staring out across the water. Hardwick, sitting on his rucksack, his hair crazily tangled. April, her thin arms hugging her slight body, staring fiercely at the far bank. He smiled, finding her fierceness – just at this moment – funny. He closed his eyes and sank against the sides of the boat.

'Boy oh boy. That was fun.'

No one responded.

He continued, half to himself, 'You know, things are going to be so different after this. Things will change when I get home.'

April asked, without looking at him, 'So how will things change, Martin? How is that going to happen?'

'I don't know,' he said. They just will. Things will be better.'

She snorted. 'You're not exactly complicated, are you?'

He frowned. Strange how she could make this – his not being complicated – sound like so a grave fault. 'No?'

'No. Believe me.'

'So you're complicated, I suppose?'

She shrugged. 'What I don't get is what you want out of life? Do you ever make plans beyond the next five minutes? Don't you have any ambition?'

He said, 'My ambition is to be happy.'

'Yeah? That sounds easy.'

'I thought it would be easy. What does it matter?'

'So.' April sat back. She peered at him. 'What makes you happy?'

'Oh. Nothing complicated.' He smiled. 'Maybe you're right about me, April. Maybe there's nothing to me at all. I just want – I don't know. Some good friends. A few beers every now and then. I want to feel – just that I'm okay, I suppose. I want to have someone I can love, someone who might be happy with me. And I want to be able to see Sam. That's it.' He paused, reflecting. 'Not exactly profound, is it?'
She was quiet for a while. Then, to his surprise, reached out and touched his arm. He held his breath, not knowing how to respond. Was she offering him pity? Her fingers were light and cool. He didn't want pity.

Van was guiding the boat, ignoring the others. He was placid, his eyes concentrating on the water. April tossed her head at him.

'Hey,' she said, suddenly. 'You.'

Her voice echoed across the water. The hairs on Martin's neck began to rise.

Van's head flicked up. April strode towards him. Martin watched them both, and bunched his fists.

'Listen,' she said. 'You. Listen to me.'

Van took his hand off the rudder.

'You may not have noticed,' she said, 'but we were almost killed just then. And my guess is you knew all about this. Right? Right?'

Van did not reply.

'Look–' April pointed at Sam. Martin saw her hand tremble. 'We've got a little kid here. He's terrified. The professor's terrified. We're all terrified. If you're going to take us into danger you have to let us know, so we can make some kind of a choice about it. Okay? *Comprende?*'

Van narrowed his eyes. 'I understand,' he said, quietly. 'And do *you* think, April, you would have survived one day without me?'

April started.

Martin moved between them. He said, placating, 'We're grateful to you. All of us.'

'No. That's not good enough.' April pushed Martin aside. 'We don't know where we're going. We don't know what's going on. We don't know who you are. Tell us. Now.'

'April– 'Martin began.

Van stared at her levelly. 'What is your question?'

'Okay.' She was breathing hard. 'So, how did you learn to speak English like that?'

Van shrugged. 'I had a good teacher. Missionaries.' The old man closed his eyes. "*And God so Loved the World that he gave up his only son…*"

'Oh, spare us. Don't give us that crap.'

Van turned his back on her.

'Have you been listening to us the whole time?' She persisted. 'Have you been listening to everything we said?'

'Yes. I listen.'

200

'It was damned rude. Why were you listening to us? '

'Because you are interesting.'

'Yeah. Sure we are. Sure we're interesting.' She hissed at his back. 'And who the hell are you?'

'I am Van.'

'Fine. You're Van. I get that. What I don't get is what you're doing here. Nobody does anything for nothing. So what was it? Money?'

Martin said, through clenched teeth, 'April, leave it.'

She ignored him. 'Okay,' she said. 'Not money. What? Because you're such good buddies with this Karasin? I don't believe it. Is Karasin paying you? Is that it?'

'You think money is everything.'

'For most people it is. It is for me. Why not? How long can you survive without it? Don't give me that shit.' She gestured at his back. 'Okay. So what does matter to you? Us?'

'I don't want to let you die,' he said, turning to look at her again. 'So I helped you. Is it strange?'

Martin watched her redden. He leaned forwards, all his muscles tense, certain of impending danger. April had the look of a bated animal: her eyes were glazed; her cheeks pinched. She had, it seemed, moved from fear to anger without any intervening gears. He wiped away the sweat from his forehead.

'Money is not the only thing that matters to you, April,' Van remarked, suddenly. 'I know you went to the casino that night. My friends told me.'

'They told you, huh?' She muttered. 'Seems like you know a lot.'

Van ignored this. 'What were you doing there?'

She said, 'It doesn't matter.'

'Why did you try to help us?'

Martin looked at her in surprise.

April blinked. 'I didn't try to help anyone. Not you, anyway.'

'You are good.'

'Yeah. Sure. Good old April.'

Van's face broke into a smile. It lit up his face.

April persisted, 'You haven't answered my question. Are you doing this for Karasin?'

'No.' Van shook his head. 'Though Karasin had the same thought. You three –' He pointed at them with splayed fingers – 'You are the only foreigners who saw everything. All of the shooting. Because of this, the army is frightened of you. They want to find you. We – everyone wants you.'

'Oh right. We're fucking popular.'

'April,' warned Martin. 'April. Stop this.' He was beginning to feel desperate. To antagonise Van was idiotic: they were dependent on him. Martin was responsible for Sam's life, not only his own. April did not seem to realise this, and if her recklessness put Sam in danger, he would not forgive her. He glared at her. Her neck was bent, and her hair fell forward, covering her face. It made her seem timid. The appearance, Martin knew, was misleading. She was full of uncontrolled anger, and the intensity of it disgusted him.

She turned on him. 'What do you want me to do, Martin?' She asked. 'Sit quiet? Do as I'm told?'

'Yes,' he said. 'Yes, if it saves your life. And Sam's, too. Stop – I man stop – being so selfish.'

'You're calling me selfish?' She retorted. 'You? I didn't bring Sam here. Who's selfish?'

Martin said, furious now, 'What do you care about that? You care about yourself, and that's it. Don't pretend otherwise.' He sucked in his cheeks. 'You're disgusting.'

He watched the colour drain from April's face. His heart beat in triumph.

Van cut in. 'Listen,' he intoned. 'Be quiet and listen.' He pointed at them again. 'You want to know what I want. I will tell you. I want this. When you return, speak about this. Say what happened. Say, and tell people they must help. Please. I will make you safe. You will go home and be safe.' His jaw twitched. 'What I want is, please, tell. This is what I want.'

April folded her arms deliberately, turning her face from Martin. 'So that's it, right? You want us to tell your story. That's why you're helping us. That's your angle.'

Van ignored her. He directed his question at Martin. 'Is it right, what you have seen? Women, children killed? Is it right?' His eyes flickered nervously over each of them.

Before Martin could answer Hardwick interposed, his voice weary. 'No, it's not right. Of course it isn't. But would anyone believe us? We're not that important, you see. We'd like to help you – of course we would – but you have to understand that what we say won't necessarily make any difference. You think that we're more powerful than we actually are. I'm afraid the fact we've seen something doesn't mean anything. It doesn't mean anyone will listen to us. Not at all.'

'They will listen to you,' said Van, urgently. 'I am nothing. You are something.'

Hardwick said, 'I'm sorry. You have an inflated idea of our importance.'

Van muttered, 'You are important. You are good.'

'Sure. We're all good,' spat April. 'Everyone's good. Wonderful. Fine. You have absolutely no idea, do you? The professor's right. No one will give a damn what we say, and nobody will care about you. You need – God knows – an earthquake or something. Something big, something to make the papers. Maybe then people might notice you for a while. That's how it happens, see? The three of us – like the professor says, nobody gives a damn.'

Van shook his head. 'You will tell.'

Martin said, hastily, 'We'll tell. Don't worry. We'll tell. Just get us to safety.'

'I will help you,' said Van. 'Please help me too.'

'And if we don't help you?' April asked. 'What then?'

Van began to speak, but his words were drowned by a piercing cry. A child. Martin's head jerked up. How could he have forgotten? He watched, stiff and helpless, as Sam fell.

8

The young man might be dying. Corporal Paysonge couldn't be sure. The wound in his leg had not looked too bad at first, and Paysonge had done his best to clean and disinfect it. During the night, though, the man had slipped into a fever.

He suffered. Paysonge hated suffering, and he hated his comrade for making him witness it. He held the man's hand. It was cold, and weak as a child's. He met the man's eyes. They wandered, searching Paysonge's face like fingers. Paysonge wondered what the man might see in his face that made him search it with such longing. His brother? His father? Impossible to say. Paysonge did not think his face was memorable. It was young, and too unformed for stories to be written on it.

He gripped his soldier's hand tighter, and whispered in his ear. 'Sleep now. It is a beautiful night.'

He had a sudden vision of himself from above: he was slender but upright, his face was passive. He looked like a soldier. The thought reassured him. If the man died, he thought, he would wear white gloves to bury him. He glanced behind him, an involuntary check to see if any of his men had spotted signs of weakness in the movement of his shoulders, the twitch of his neck.

The man sighed, turned, and sank in Paysonge's arms.

Sam thought about the young soldier who had appeared out of the trees. Was he the baddy? He looked at the far bank through sleepy eyes. He could see the shape of hills, dark against the darkness. He couldn't see anything else, only stars and the reflection of stars.

Sam frowned, vexed. If the soldier was the baddy, why hadn't he chased them? The man wasn't following the usual rules. It didn't fit. He needed to think.

He lived on a boat now. That meant that no-one on the boat could be the baddy. He stuck his fingers in his ears, trying to block out the sound of the adults' voices. It was hard to concentrate when they quarreled, batting words backwards and forwards like ping pong balls, while he had work to do.

He needed to find out who the baddy was.

He screwed up his face. The boat rocked. His eyes were heavy. He sank down onto his knees and leaned his face against the damp wood. The water called him. He looked into it and saw his face, floating whitely above it. It drew him. He squirmed over the edge. Like a magnet drawn to iron, he fell.

There was nothing for it. The young man needed help, and Paysonge did not want to leave him alone. They must cross the river and head west. He had heard about the teak plantations, though he had never actually visited them. The two largest – one Chinese owned, one French – were several hours walk in the wrong direction. It couldn't be helped. Carrying their comrade on a makeshift stretcher, progress was tortuously slow. At least the man was quiet now. Earlier, his groans had wrenched Paysonge to his gut.

They arrived at daybreak. Paysonge looked up, and knew they had reached the right place because half the hill to his left, and the entire hill to his right, was denuded. Tree stumps littered the ground like broken teeth; the earth was naked and raw between them. Logs were piled high as houses.

A cluster of buildings ahead were surrounded by a low wall, roughly painted with white Chinese characters. A man with a gun was asleep in front of it.

Paysonge nudged his shoulder. The man sprang up, shouted, and pointed his weapon at them. Paysonge put his hand gently on the muzzle and lowered it. He explained the situation, briefly, and asked if he could leave his comrade here for a day or two.

The man looked at him uncertainly. He whistled. Two more men emerged from the nearest whitewashed building: one thin and immaculately dressed, the other with a pot belly, wearing a vest and underpants. They asked what he wanted. Paysonge repeated his story, and the pot bellied man scratched and spat on the ground. No, he said. No, he didn't want trouble. It wasn't his fault. He wanted to help – they were his countrymen – he loved the army, he loved Mingoria – but his bosses, you see, wouldn't allow it. No, there was no question. There was nothing he could do.

As the fat man talked, more armed men emerged from behind the wall.

Paysonge saw, quickly, that his company were outnumbered, and while the fat man's tone was friendly and placating, there was really no point in arguing. He asked if they could have water.

Yes, yes that would be fine.

Medicine?

The fat man looked sad. He would help if he could – he wanted to – supplies were limited – maybe try the French? Paysonge nodded, ordered his men to pick up the stretcher, and together they shambled on.

The French plantation was some eight miles further. Four miles on, they were greeted by shouts, and a volley of shots fired into the air. Quietly, Paysonge gestured to his men to lower the injured soldier to the ground. He shouted to the distant figures squatting on the naked hillside ahead.

We need help. We need medicine.

His voice echoed over the hard ground. He walked on a pace, and another shot ricocheted against a pebble near his feet. He nodded.

He knelt by the wounded man and touched his face. The man's skin was cold. His eyes rolled open. Paysonge smiled at him. He sat in the dust and waited.

*

April lay on some damp tarpaulin, her neck twisted underneath one of the wooden planks that served as seats. Her mind flitted in and out of consciousness. She dreamt she was on a boat drifting rudderless under a star-washed sky. A breeze wafted over her.

Sam was falling. Or, she was falling. Which? She had to break his fall, but she was wedged between two wooden planks and though she tried to move she couldn't reach him. Her lips were cold. She was falling into the cool depths of the water, into the night sky, into the cave with a roof of stars; and though part of her wanted someone to catch her, another part wished to fall forever, and never hit the ground. She gasped, and woke.

She knew where she was without opening her eyes. It was barely light. The boat was rocking gently, caught between some low branches hanging over the bank. She lay still, and listened. No other voices, no movement. She opened her eyes. She was stiff. She massaged her neck, digging her fingers in sharply. A dull ache remained, like a bad day at work. She took a few scoops of water from the tank. She looked about her.

Sam was curled up beside Hardwick, lying more or less where he'd fallen. Hardwick's long arm was curled about him. She remembered: they had settled down like that immediately after Hardwick had broken Sam's fall. No one else had moved: she, Martin and Van had sat frozen as dummies as Sam had pitched head first towards the water. It was like watching a film on half speed. Of everything that had happened so far, this was the worst moment. Only, just before Sam had hit the water, Hardwick had seemed to appear from nowhere, all long limbs and wild hair, and grabbed the boy in the crook of his arm. Sam had hung there limply, a puppet boy with his strings cut. Martin had sprung forward with a cry of such anguish that it turned April's stomach to think about it. Hardwick, however, had cocked his head and said something dry and ordinary. *Quite a fall.* He had laid Sam down gently, and cooed into his ear until the boy slept. And, miraculously, April had slept too. Everyone had slept.

She sat up, awkwardly. She was bruised, a line of purple blotches along her arm. She rubbed her face. It was early. The sun was only just beginning to break through the mist. She shuffled towards Hardwick and Sam, and knelt over them. They seemed peaceful. Sam's face was pale, and misted with dew. She retrieved a jacket and tried to dab Sam's wet cheeks. Gently, she placed it over the boy's body.

She moved to the prow of the boat. Martin was there, awake already. She hesitated, unsure, after last night, whether to go any nearer.

Martin saw her and said, flatly, 'I've got a coat you can wear if you want.'

'I'm not cold.'

'Suit yourself.'

She stared across the water to the range of mountains that loomed ahead. These had become imposing overnight, she realised; they now dwarfed the boat and its occupants. She shivered. She recognised a tang in the air, a freshness at the edges of the all-enveloping humidity. The mountains' upper flanks were dense with foliage; further down they were obscured by powdery white mist.

Martin said, following her eyes, 'They're beautiful.'

'That cave was beautiful,' murmured April, 'But it still fucking terrified me.'

She looked across the water. The river was wide and slow.

Martin cleared his throat. 'You know, last night – when I panicked – I ran straight into this man. A soldier. Just a young man. He had a gun. I swear he was about to shoot me. I mean, I really thought we were for it, me and Sam. But, he didn't shoot. He just looked at me. Just a boy, really. We looked at each other for ages. It was like – I don't know, like

208

we knew each other. It was weird. I was so scared. I was just terrified. But he didn't shoot.'

'You should've been scared,' April muttered. 'These people are crazy.'

'What about Van? He's trying to help us.'

She shrugged, and shut her mouth.

'He needs us,' Martin pressed. 'You heard what he said last night.'

'I heard. He wants us to take sides, that's all.'

Martin rocked on his heels. 'What's so wrong with taking sides?'

'I'm on my side.'

'I see.'

She chewed her nails.

He asked her, 'What did he mean last night? About that casino?'

'Nothing.'

'April –'

'Come on.' She shot a look at him. 'Just because the rest of you have told your sins doesn't mean I have to. This isn't the fucking Catholic Church.'

'You don't have to do anything. But, as you once so wittily pointed out, we're all in the same boat.'

'I make the rules so I can break them.'

She saw Martin smile, then lower his head to hide it.

'God. Listen to me.'

'Forget it.'

'I need a cigarette. Soon, before I kill someone.'

'Me, probably.'

'Probably.' She did not smile.

'So, what were you doing there?' He persisted. 'At the casino?'

'I was helping a friend.' She looked at him askance. 'Yes, I have them. Except that he wasn't what I thought he was. He let me down.' She fell silent.

'I see.'

209

'Yeah. Well.' She shrugged. 'And now we're stuck here.' She chewed the tips of her fingers.

'At least we're alive,' said Martin. 'I'd rather be here than back in the city.'

'You think we're safe here?' She tossed her head, finding him exasperating. 'Because some guy liked the look of you?'

He frowned. 'I don't know.'

'No. You don't.'

The mist on the mountains had begun to clear. She was sticky. She couldn't remember when she had last washed or changed her clothes. The skin on her scalp prickled.

He asked, 'Is that it then? Just give up? Is that what you think?'

'You mean you haven't already? Lucky you.'

He turned away from her.

She wiped her forehead, hot again, frustrated. She didn't want Martin to hate her.

She dipped her hands into the water and splashed her face. The water ran down her neck and onto her shirt. She smoothed her hair behind her ears. She remembered she had some sun lotion in her black bag. She reached for it and smeared it on her face and the back of her neck. She offered it to Martin. He took it silently and dabbed it on his cheeks. He had tanned, she noticed. His eyes looked paler and greener in his dark face. Three days of stubble had become a beard, brown flecked with grey. It suited him, actually. She took back the cream.

'I wish I could shower.'

Martin grunted.

'I want to shower. And put on clean clothes. And sleep. I'm so tired. I wish I could sleep.'

Martin said, 'Sleep now. Why don't you?'

She shook her head. 'It's too hot to sleep.'

'I'll shade you.'

'I'm fine.'

'I'll sit over you and shade you.'

'I don't want you to.'

'Suit yourself.'

She shuddered. 'I didn't mean that. I meant thanks.'

'Of course you did.' He raised an eyebrow.

'Look. Martin, just – leave it. Okay?'

'Fine. I don't honestly care.'

She sighed, and packed the sun cream back in her bag.

Van woke and started the engine. The boat made fast progress through the brown water, leaving a trail of white foam behind them.

Hardwick and Sam were still asleep. April thought, observing them, how at home with one another they looked. Hardwick's hair was flapping about in the wind, and occasionally a wisp of it brushed against Sam's cheek.

Hardwick groaned and sat up. Sam whimpered and began to wake too, confused and little in the bottom of the boat. Martin moved from April. She held herself tightly, and watched as he squatted beside Sam and stroked his face, till the boy's alarm at waking abated.

'I'm hungry,' he said.

Van looked at the child sorrowfully. 'Nothing more now.'

Sam began to wail. April thought of something. She slapped her forehead.

'*Stupid*. Stupid of me.'

'What is it?' Martin turned to her, a look of alarm on his face.

'I'd forgotten. Wait. '

She started rummaging furiously amongst her luggage, pulling out clothes and flinging them across the boat. She sat up, triumphant. 'Here. I don't know why I'd forgotten. It's kind of melted, but –' she handed Sam a sticky, half eaten bar of chocolate. 'I bought it in Bangkok. Didn't think of it till now.'

Sam took it, cautiously.

Martin hugged him. 'What do you say?'

211

'Thank you,' Sam mumbled. He buried his head in Martin's chest.

'Sure.' April grinned. 'No problem.'

Sam began to eat the chocolate.

Hardwick stretched. 'Kind of you, April.'

Van asked, 'And you have nothing else hidden?'

April froze. 'What's that supposed to mean?'

Van smiled at her.

'And what about you Mr Van?' She asked, coldly. 'Any more secrets you'd like to share?'

'Nothing,' Van said.

'Sure. Fine. Just checking.'

Martin mouthed at her, 'Keep it to yourself, April. Keep it.'

'We can all trust one another now,' said Van.

She muttered, 'That's for me to judge.'

Martin slammed his hand against the side of the boat.

'No.' he shouted. 'No April. No. It's not for you to judge.' His blow echoed across the water. She stared at him.

'I've had enough,' he said, his face red. 'Enough. Of you, your big mouth, your stupid secrets. Sam's the child here, not you. Don't you get it? Christ. You talk about trust, but why should we trust you? Why, when you won't tell us anything?'

She said, through tight lips, 'So that's how it is, huh?'

'Yes. Yes, April. That's how it is.'

'So I have to talk. Or what, Martin?' She began to throw her clothes back into her case. 'Jesus. As if there's anything to say.' She stopped. 'Do you know what the stupidest part is? You want to know?' She grabbed bunches of t-shirts and underwear and flung them aside. 'The stupidest part is, it only happened because I didn't go to the office one morning. Funny, huh? Don't ever do that.'

She snorted, and sat back on her heels.

'So. It's my turn, right? You want to know about me. All my creepy little secrets.'

No one replied.

She zipped up her case. It snagged on her skin, making it bleed. 'Only here's the thing. I don't want to talk about me, see? I hate that. Why should I do that, Martin? Just because that's what you do? Because it's what you want? No. I'm not going to talk about me. No. I'll tell you about Mo.'

She sucked the blood from her hand. She saw Van watch her.

'Yeah, she said, quietly, looking at him. 'Yeah, I'll tell you about Mo.'

She wiped her hand across her sleeve.

'Mo. Okay. He was this funny little guy who wore clothes that didn't fit.' She shook her head. 'Big round glasses. Bad shoes. I met him in a bar one night and we got talking. Mostly I would've left it at that, but with Mo – I liked him. I don't know why. I actually liked him.

'The last time I saw him he was bleeding his life away on a crowded sidewalk. It was the day – didn't it just have to be that day? – we had our only argument.'

9

It was a weekend. She and Mo had agreed to spend the whole day together. Usually this was impossible: she often worked weekends, and Mo had to report to the air conditioning company that employed him at five each morning. They had planned the trip a long time in advance, Mo promising, mysteriously, to show her something she had not seen before.

He met her outside his apartment wearing a fresh shirt under his usual tight green jacket. He stood there shielding his eyes from the sun. She guessed he'd made an effort with his appearance.

She strode up to him, carrying a bottle of water and her briefcase.

'So. What's the big story? Where are we going?'

'Do you want to meet my friend?'

'Sure.' She looked at him in surprise. 'I didn't know you had anyone here. Except me.'

'Oh yes,' he said, gravely. 'I have many friends. There are many people like me here.'

'What, illegal air conditioning engineers?'

'No, April. Many different kinds of illegal workers. Not only air conditioning.'

She smiled. 'Then lead on.'

They took a bus out of town. The bus station reminded her of cattle markets back home, with buses not running to schedule but, it seemed to her, going to the highest bidder. It was a case of market forces at their purest, and she imagined that her colleagues – self-avowed capitalists all – would have been impressed. Although it was hard at first to see a method in the madness of pushing and shouting, she guessed that routes were determined on the spot, depending on how numerous and vocal the potential customers were. Once a driver had signalled the direction he was going to take, a scramble ensued, with interested parties surging on to the battered bus and waving their money wildly.

Mo, it turned out, was an adept player of the system. April was awed. He came to an agreement with a driver, reached out to her and yanked her aboard. Other passengers pushed and scrambled behind.

The bus had no air conditioning, and the tiny seats were hot plastic. April tried to make her body area smaller by squeezing her arms against her sides.

'Ugh. Do you do this often?'

'It is very difficult and painful for you?'

'I wouldn't go that far. But I could use a shower. I smell disgusting.'

'Yes. You suffer very much,' said Mo, sadly.

'You'll suffer once you smell me. And I think you're making fun of me.' But she didn't complain for the remainder of the journey.

The driver dropped them off at a dusty town far enough away from the city to seem alien to April. Gone were the international chain stores and high-rise hotels; instead she saw a garage with a single shop selling local branded goods, and Coca Cola. She guessed she was the first foreigner to have appeared there in a long while.

The town was strung out along the main road, with non-sequitur side streets meandering away dustily. Traffic hurtled past, scooters mainly, and a few long-distance trucks. A couple of bare-chested youths rode by on a shared motorbike, their rolled-up jeans spattered with oil.

'Now what?' She squinted. The light was hard and unforgiving.

Mo signalled she should wait by the shop. He disappeared into one of the side streets. April stood by the highway, feeling uneasy. After a few minutes she went into the shop and bought herself a can of coke.

She re-emerged and sat on the ground by the roadside. She opened her can and drank. The drink was warm and flat.

215

A fly crawled across her leg. Her skin twitched. She began to think about work. She was due in Singapore in a week, and she needed to prepare for the trip. Better to be in her cool office, the grey carpet under her feet muffling every noise, than here. She sighed, and wondered why she had come.

Mo appeared sitting astride a motorbike, behind a glum man with iron-grey hair. A younger rider pulled up beside him. The space on his back seat was empty.

'We take motorcycle taxi,' said Mo, and smiled, obviously pleased with himself.

April spluttered. 'You've got to be kidding.'

Mo's face fell. 'My friends live too far away to walk. Even for you.' He winked at her. 'I got taxi.'

'That's no taxi. It's a death trap.'

'No, it's very safe.'

'I've seen how those guys ride.'

'Are you afraid?'

'No, but –' Heat beat down on her.

Mo took her hand. 'I'm sorry,' he said softly. 'I will not hurt you, April. We will not go.'

'No.' She shook her hand free. 'Of course we'll go.' She climbed up behind the younger man.

The bike roared under her. She clung to the man's thin back, her eyes shut tight. She heard Mo shout,

'Are you all right?'

'I'm fine.'

'I have never seen you afraid before.'

'I'm not afraid,' she said. 'You think I'm afraid?.'

'If you are not afraid, then open your eyes.'

She opened them to tiny dots, screamed, and shut them again. She heard her driver laugh. Mo said something to him, his voice sharp. She opened her eyes wider.

Mo caught her looking at him and gave a sudden yelp. His black hair whipped behind him. She saw the look on his face, and grinned.

'It's good, April,' he said. 'It's good!'

She threw her head back and laughed too, and for a few moments nothing mattered: they could go anywhere, she and Mo, and do any damned thing they pleased.

They rode for fifteen minutes through narrow deserted streets, until they reached the far edge of the town. Their drivers dropped them by a row of small concrete houses with plain walls that caught the glare of the sun. April stepped to the ground unsteadily. She brushed her fingers against the white wall of a house. Mo knocked at the door. It opened a crack. April heard an exclamation, and the door opened wider.

An old man appeared, a round little man with a puffy face and a big belly. He was panting. 'Please will you be so kind?' He ushered April in. He carried a heavy battered case, which he handed to Mo without a word. Mo leaned towards April, and said in a stage whisper as they followed the man,

'His name is Mr Shay. Everyone knows him. He has a degree from a university. He is a qualified dentist.'

'Right.' April raised an eyebrow, wondering if she should be impressed by this. Mo lowered his voice even further.

'He is part of our government-in-exile. He is brave. There are many spies.'

'I see.' She suspected Mo of melodrama. She walked inside.

They were in a small room, its walls covered with pages of newspapers by way of decoration. There was no furniture. Mr Shay asked them to sit down, and pointed at the floor. April sat. The floor was sticky, covered with blue plastic tiles. Mr Shay bustled out, returning a few seconds later with a tray of tea. He set it on the bare floor and beamed at them. He looked, to April, like a small round Buddha.

'Please,' he said, panting. 'You are too kind to visit me here.' He had old-fashioned sounding British English, more accented than Mo's. He handed April a cup. 'You are the lady known to my friend.'

'I guess that's me,' she said, brightly.

'We are so happy to have a visitor from foreign parts.'

'It's my pleasure.'

Mr Shay heaved himself onto the floor. He stuck out his small stumpy legs from underneath his large belly. Not a Buddha, thought April: Humpty Dumpty. She bit back a smile.

'It's a very hot day,' she said.

'Oh yes, very hot weather we are having.'

Silence.

Mo asked, anxious and polite, 'Are you accustomed to the heat, Mr Shay?'

'Oh, I am accustomed to it.'

A further, longer silence.

Mo broke it. 'Mr Shay would like to ask you questions April, but he is too shy.'

'Go ahead and ask,' she smiled. 'Sure.'

This set off a peel of giggles from Mr Shay, followed by a stream of coy questions:

'Where are you from?'

'I live here. But I was born in America.'

'How old are you?'

'Twenty seven.'

'Are you married?'

'No. I was once. Big mistake. It won't happen again.'

A pause.

'Do you like it here?'

'I do. It's a beautiful place.'

'Why do you come here?'

'I like to travel. And I found work here.'

'What do you do?' He asked, eagerly.

'I'm a lawyer. I work for big companies. It's kind of a stupid job, but the money is good.'

'No no.' Mr Shay tutted. 'The law is very important.' He leaned forward. 'How much money do you make?'

'More than I deserve, but less than I want.' April was used to this question, and had a pat reply. She asked him, 'So what do *you* do?'

'I am an illegal worker,' he answered, unabashed. 'I work in a factory and make shoes. Very beautiful shoes. I can get you a pair.'

'It's nice of you, but I have plenty.' April shifted her position. The floor was hard. She took a sip of the bitter tea.

'What a pity.'

Mo said, 'Mr Shay is no longer being paid for his services.'

The round-bellied man regarded her mildly. 'However, my boss is very kind and lets me live here, in this nice room, for free.'

A further silence followed.

Mr Shay asked, 'Will you visit us one day in our country?'

'I would love to. Thank you.'

April glanced at Mo. She guessed he had brought her here for a purpose, but she couldn't fathom what it was. If it was for her education, then she resented it.

Mo tapped Mr Shay on the shoulder.

'Are you busy just now?'

Mr Shay nodded. 'We are immensely busy. We have the new materials, and have been putting together our next edition. It is very good. I would be very happy if you would peruse it.'

'I would certainly like to. There is no problem with the printer?'

'No, we have been given great help. But the – how do you say it? We –' he lapsed out of English, and the two continued talking for some time. Suddenly – or it seemed sudden to April – Mr Shay broke off. He shook his head, making funny little noises in his throat. He ruminated for a while, then stood up and heaved a heavy sigh.

'You will think I am very rude, speaking in my own language.'

'No. It's your language.'

'And now I have to leave. Disgraceful behaviour.' He smiled.

'Not at all.'

'It was charming to meet you.' He took her hand and shook it warmly. She returned his smile. He ushered them to the door. As he shuffled out she noticed the way his shoulders sagged. She caught a flash of something underneath his smile: a wince, as if of pain.

Mo and April walked down the lane to meet their motorcycle taxis. He asked eagerly,

'What do you think of Mr Shay?'

She shrugged. 'I guess he's a nice man. Kind of funny.' She sensed Mo was unsatisfied with her answer. 'I mean, he's sweet,' she continued. 'What else can I say? He seemed like a sweet old man.'

Mo frowned. 'I see you do not think much of him. I am sorry.'

'I didn't say that. I said he was sweet.'

'It doesn't seem much to you that he is a qualified dentist. You think he is only funny.'

'I said he was sweet,' She insisted.

'I know you. When you say sweet, you mean you do not think much of a person.'

'Come on Mo. That's unfair.'

'It is true April.'

She sighed. 'I don't know why we're arguing about this. There's nothing to argue about.'

He marched along beside her in silence. She could tell he was hurt. To pacify him she asked, 'So who exactly is this Mr Shay. Now he's not pulling teeth?'

'Actually sometimes he still does that. If someone has a problem with their teeth they will go to him.'

She guffawed.

Mo ignored her. 'He is trying to write a newspaper to show what is happening in my country.'

'What, like propaganda?'

'No. Not propaganda. The truth.'

'Whatever you say.'

'It is not easy, April. We have lost much, all of us.'

She could see the two motorbikes ahead. 'Look, Mo. Your country is a mess and I'm sorry for it. I'm sorry for Mr Shay back there –' she gestured – 'killing himself working for free. It stinks. But the fact is I am *not* personally to blame. Okay?'

At Mo's insistence, she returned to his apartment before going home. 'You need to refresh yourself,' he said, though he didn't explain how that might be accomplished in his tiny room.

It was dark by the time they got there. They sat quietly. This wasn't unusual; they often sat in silence, and normally April was comfortable with it. Tonight, however, the silence contained something. She heard Mo sigh, then shuffle and click his tongue. She was restless, and wanted to leave.

Mo hadn't turned on the light. His face was shadowed on one side while the other was lit by the pink and blue neon sign outside his window. She lit a cigarette.

'I've got to go now.' She stood up. Mo nodded distractedly. He picked up the battered case that Mr Shay had given him earlier, and followed her softly down the stairs. When they reached the entrance he stood watching her, a forlorn expression on his face.

'Okay, Mo. I'll see you some time,' she said.

'April –'

'It was nice. Thanks.'

'April, may I speak to you?'

She closed her eyes. 'I have to get home. I'm tired. I still have work to do.'

'Please. For a moment.'

221

'What is it?'

He took a deep breath. 'I need your help, April.'

Her heart sank. So this was what had been coming. She asked, resignedly, 'Do you need money?'

'What? No. I have money.'

'Sure. Kleenair Systems pays well. Everyone knows.'

'I have money April. I am not begging.' He put a hand into the battered case and pulled out a large brick of dollar bills. 'I have this.'

She gaped at him. 'Jesus. Mo, where did you get this?'

'From Mr Shay.'

'Mr Shay is a millionaire?'

'You will listen to me April? You will help me?'

'I haven't said that.' She hesitated, her heart fluttering. 'What is it you want?'

Mo began to walk rapidly. He indicated that she should walk along beside him. He seemed nervous. He spoke in a hurried whisper. 'I cannot go back to my country. Mr Shay cannot. But my friends are still there. I want to help them. I want you to bring something to them.'

'Bring them what?'

'Bring them money.' He held out the case. 'I have money'

'What do they want the money for?'

'To buy guns.'

She stopped. 'Well. That's new.'

'So we can fight the army.'

'Fine. Sure. Good luck to you.' She began to walk again.

'If I try to bring them money I will die.'

'And if *I* try?'

'You are a foreigner. Nothing will happen to you.'

'I don't believe you.'

'Please.'

'Are you crazy?' She laughed out loud. 'All of a sudden you want me to run guns so you can fight an army?' She scanned his scrawny body disparagingly. 'You don't have a chance in hell. You couldn't fight anything, Mo. You couldn't even *hurt* anything.'

Mo flushed.

'Listen,' said April. 'All I can say is don't get involved. And especially, don't get *me* involved. I'm disappointed in you, Mo. I thought we were friends.'

Mo said, quietly, 'We are friends.'

'Then why spring this on me now? You don't do that to friends. You don't ask them to do stuff they can never do.'

'You must understand.' Mo's voice was low, and passionate. 'We have to try to do this. We have suffered. You saw Mr Shay. He has nothing. You laughed at him. It is worse, far worse for those left behind. April, I have no choice.'

'Oh, there's always a choice,' she said, bitterly. 'You have a choice to die or live, and if you're going to take on an army you may as well shoot yourself now.'

'You say that because you can,' replied Mo. 'You can go where you want. Yes, and do what you want.' He was upright now, blazing with anger. 'And what do you do? You drink whiskey and complain. You think your life is *so* bad. Things are *so* terrible. No, April. You have everything and you value nothing. You say I have a choice? No. My friends have been killed. Others are in danger. I have no choice.' He stopped, his face red.

She shut her eyes. Her head ached. 'Look. I'm sorry. If what you say is true, about your friends and all that, then I'm really sorry, Mo. Truly. It's just that this isn't me. I tried to explain a long time ago. I tried to tell you who I am, but you kept seeing someone different. You say I'm good. I'm not good, Mo. Maybe you are: I'm not. And there's no way you are going persuade me to carry this –' she pointed at the case – 'to a bunch of students, or dentists, or fucking air conditioning salesmen, so that they can buy weapons. Are you out of your mind? Find some other foreigner. Pretend to be their friend. This one is going home.'

223

Mo stared at her. He said, so softly she could barely hear it, 'I did not pretend to be your friend, April.'

'Look.' She shook herself. 'I sympathise. Really. If there's anything else I can do for you – get you a better job, get you into school, whatever – I will seriously try and do it. But not this: it's insane. You haven't a hope. Just look at you.' She threw her hands up, words failing her.

Mo looked down at himself, at his too-tight green jacket and crazy tie. He said, 'If you are my friend you will help me.' 'No. If you were my friend you wouldn't ask. End of conversation.'

She began to walk away. She tried not to look back, although she sensed him following. She wanted to shake him off. She was truly angry now.

He caught up with her and thrust a piece of paper into her hand.

'Here,' he whispered. 'This address. Big casino. It is all written down. They will know you, they will take the money.' He tried to put the case into her hand.

She brushed him away. 'What do I have to say to convince you? Leave me alone, Mo.'

She started to run. She could think of no other way to lose him.

She emerged onto the main road and dived into a crowd, glancing backwards to see if he was still following. His jacket was easily spotted. She rolled her eyes. She looked about her for a taxi. She saw one in the distance, its light glowing red. She stuck out her arm and the taxi pulled away from the main stream of traffic towards her.

She was good at drawing lines under things. This, she decided, would just have to be another of those things.

She tugged at the taxi door and was about to step inside when a commotion behind her distracted her. She heard an odd hiss, a gasp. She turned.

A group of people were gathered in a tight knot a few feet from her, beside a cart selling street food. The seller, an old man with a face like a pudding, was holding a ladle in mid air. She told the taxi to wait. The knot of people unwound. One or two remained, their arms folded. The street seller gave a whimper.

Mo was lying on the ground at her feet in a foetal position. His neat, ill-fitting jacket was soaked with blood.

She knelt down beside him.

'What happened?'

The onlookers shrugged and stepped back. One of them shouted into a cellphone, calling an ambulance she guessed. A fumbled check of Mo's pulse confirmed what she already feared. He was dead.

She turned away. She knew what she was seeing. Something cruel inside her wanted to laugh. Her eyes fixed on the battered case, the handle still encircled by Mo's left hand. Ignoring the astonished glances of the spectators, she prised open his fingers as swiftly as she could, and pulled the case away. She ran back to the taxi without looking behind her.

She drove through rivers of neon, blazing shop fronts, crowds of people laughing, eating, buying, selling. Two boys dashed out of the skeleton of a house, their fists full of spoils from the building site. A man with a moustache flung his head back and laughed. A woman thumped her boyfriend on his arm with rough affection. Nothing seemed real, except a case full of money and a piece of paper in her hand. The address of a casino in a country she barely knew.

She reached her apartment block and saw two men in dark shirts and jeans get into a car and drive rapidly away. She ran to the lobby, her heels skidding on the marble.

'Did anyone come up to see me just now?'

The receptionist shrugged.

April banged her hand on to the desk. 'Tell me. It's important. Who came?'

'Two men came. I don't know.'

'They asked for me?'

'Sure they ask.'

'What did you tell them?'

The receptionists eyes glinted malevolently. 'I tell them you run away.'

'Jesus.' April rolled her eyes. 'You let me know next time, Okay? Telephone.' She pointed. 'You telephone to me. Okay?'

The woman blinked. April hurried to her room

She locked herself in. She didn't cry. She was dried up inside. She fumbled with the case, her hands slipping on the catch.

It was stuffed with hundred dollar bills, neatly tied in bunches of a thousand each. She didn't count them. She didn't need to: a glance told her that she had an incredible amount of money in her possession. There was no way that Mo – or his Mr Shay – could have come by it legally.

She upended the battered attaché case and emptied its contents into a large black handbag of her own. Then she began to throw clothes into a suitcase. She retrieved her passport, and the crumpled address that Mo had pressed into her hand. Finally, without asking herself why, she added her father's letter.

She hesitated. She had been acting impulsively so far. It was not prudent. Her first instinct was for self protection. It was obvious. She must go to the police.

She sat down, and kicked off her shoes. The police would not help Mo.

No one would help Mo. Only her.

April stopped talking. Martin, beside her, was looking at the water. She looked at it too. The light on its surface danced and glittered.

Martin swallowed, and said, 'I'm sorry.'

'Sorry? Why?'

'I thought you were somebody else. I thought you were the kind of person I hate. I should have thought more. That's my problem: I don't think.'

'Yeah. Well.'

'What you did was really brave. I couldn't have done it.'

She said nothing.

He touched her shoulder. 'April?'

'What?' She shivered, brushed his hand away.

'Tell me something.' He was looking at her with intensity. She shifted, uneasy.

'What?'

'When your friend – Mo – when he died, you didn't have to do anything, did you? I mean – no one would have known any different. You could have just walked away. You had a choice.'

She shook her head. 'No,' she said, after a long pause. 'No, Martin. Sometimes there is no choice.'

Hardwick, sitting some distance from the other two, said nothing, though his thoughts were loud in his head.

'April is brave,' they said. *'When have you ever been brave?'*

IV

1

They reached their destination on the afternoon of the third day. They were deep in the mountains, and the air was fresher. As the mountains rose higher and the trees thinned, Martin could see jagged escarpments of rock poking through a thick white mist. At river level the heat was still intense, though dryer and sharper than before.

Van moored his vessel. They clambered out.

'We have to walk now. It takes maybe one hour, maybe less. Sam can walk that far?' Van directed his question at the boy.

Martin answered, 'Five minutes at the most. I'll carry him.'

Sam pouted. 'I want to walk.'

'What about our luggage?' asked April.

Van frowned. 'Difficult. I will take some,' he nodded at Hardwick. 'You –' he pointed at April, 'You leave some behind. Maybe we can come back later.'

April sighed, and to Martin's surprise did not argue. He offered, 'There's space in my pack. If you want.' She nodded, and she and Hardwick took out a few things from their suitcases and re-packed them between Van and Martin's backpacks. April kept her large black handbag.

At first their progress was tortuously slow, paced to match Sam's tiny feet and curious meanders. To Martin's surprise, Van was patient. The old man laughed as he walked alongside the boy, stopping at intervals to crouch to Sam's height.

'Look. A butterfly.' Van pointed to a butterfly the size of a bird, resting on a palm leaf. Its wings were velvet black. Sam stared at it, then reached out a hand in speculative awe. The butterfly rose, hovered, and landed amongst a crowd of purple bougainvillea. Sam's hand hung in mid air. He turned to Van, his eyes wide.

'Yes,' Van said. 'It is beautiful here.'

He was right, Martin thought. A shiny emerald beetle, which Sam now squatted down to stare at, sat in the middle of their path and dared Martin to make comparisons with the tiny scurrying creatures back home. The insects, the plants, were preternaturally swollen with life. Orchids leaked moisture from their lips; thickets of delicate bamboo knocked and groaned together. Gross palm fronds, the size of umbrellas, shivered with drops of water. Martin put his hands in his pockets. Fine in a garden, he thought, or in a glass house, but out here, uncultivated? There was something – he teased out the word – boastful about it all. He walked gingerly, as if at any moment one of the plants might reach out a creeping tendril and grab his wrists. Triffids, he thought. Bloody Triffids.

Sam, though, was entranced. Van took his hand.

'Yes,' he cackled. 'Yes!' He capered around Sam like a boy himself. 'Come on. The view is better up here.' He scooped Sam high on to his shoulders. Sam screeched with pleasure and rocked his small body back and forth.

They walked on, making slow but perceptible progress uphill. A rough path, at times barely discernible, had been hacked through the trees, making their passage relatively easy. Martin and April fell into step. Hardwick walked a little way behind.

Martin stole glances at April. Her upper lip was beaded with sweat; her mouth was half open. She tramped patiently, not seeming to mind the thin air. Martin wheezed beside her. He was impressed by her. He wanted, somehow, to tell her this. He peeked at her again. Her faced was flushed, and she breathed more heavily as the incline increased. Her purposeful expression reminded him of some of the children he'd once taught, their faces showing the strain of inner resolve as they tried to hold down a piano chord. He brushed her arm. It was damp. She turned to him, her face sharp and enquiring. He looked away.

They walked steadily uphill for about an hour. Gradually, the trees thinned. Lush green grass sprang up underfoot. The rustle of the jungle took on a secret, concentrated quality. A bird gave a thin high whistle; a mile away, another answered. They walked down a steep depression, their feet kicking up dust. From somewhere, Martin heard the sound of running water. He licked his lips – they were parched. Hunger clawed at his stomach. He found he didn't mind any of this. What he felt was quite simple: hunger, thirst. These things were easy to understand. Life, stripped of its usual complications, had become navigable.

They came to a clearing and stopped. Ahead was a circle of nissan huts, their tin roofs shining in the last rays of the sun. Van marched directly into the middle of the circle. A group of bare-chested men, about twenty in all, stood waiting. Each had a rifle slung casually over his shoulder. They were perfectly still. Their faces were scarred and pitted, and seemed to Martin oddly flat and expressionless in the half light. Their bodies, like Van's, were knotted, their sinews standing out like wires. They stared at the travellers and did not blink.

Martin gasped. The men stirred at the sound. Martin clenched his fists, remembering his encounter with the soldier the night before. The rush of water was louder now, some distance to his left. He watched the men. They stared back, motionless.

Van took Sam from his shoulders and shouted a greeting. The men sprang forward. They began to talk all at once. Van answered them, pointing and making gestures. At one point he made a sound like gunfire. The men listened, their brows furrowed. Martin guessed they were talking about the attack on the village downriver. Sam hopped around, apparently unperturbed by the strangers. The men smiled, though they did not shift their eyes from Van. Eventually, as if on a signal, the group broke up.

Three of the men remained, and under Van's direction helped the foreigners with their packs. The men led them to a row of empty huts at the far edge of the clearing. Van pointed out a drum of lukewarm water standing nearby; Martin threw down his pack and dipped his arms into it. He splashed his face and neck; rivulets of muddy dust ran down his chest. He carried Sam to the nearest hut. He talked to him and stroked his head, and as he did so, found his own eyes lowering. His exhaustion was physical, his mind light and untroubled. Here they were. Something will happen. Things will work out. He lay beside his son and slept.

He woke at dawn, parched and hungry. He sat up, crawled out of the hut, and tried to take in his surroundings. Though it was early, the light was fierce. It crashed down on the camp unmediated by the thin air, reflecting back off the dusty ground and the wretched tin huts, flattening everything. It was this flat light, Martin decided, that contributed most to the dejected appearance of the camp.

He began to shamble over the already baking earth, like a fly crawling across a desert. A figure at the far end of the camp beckoned to him. He shaded his eyes and saw it was Van.

'You slept well?' Van asked.

'Okay. I was knackered.' Martin stretched, trying to smooth out the knots and creases in his back.

'You want breakfast?'

Martin nodded. His stomach rumbled. 'I'll go and get Sam.'

Van waved dismissively. 'Sam is sleeping. Eat. Let the boy rest.' He handed Martin a bowl of thin noodle soup and squatted on the ground to eat his own. A group of men began to gather round, smiling shyly, showing rows of white teeth. Martin snatched glimpses of them, trying not to seem self-conscious. Their faces were burnt by the sun, set in a rictus of strain. They squinted at Martin with eyes that were vague and unclear. When Martin stared back they lowered their heads. They were dressed, in the main, in vests and

234

shorts, though one man wore a pair of jeans. A thin brown toe wriggled through his trainers as if it was an independent beast, curious and bent on escape.

Martin began to eat. The men clustered closer, following each movement of the spoon to his lips. Martin made an awkward move and spilt some of his soup. He laughed pointedly. The men laughed too, fluttering backwards.

He muttered, 'You're hardly an army, are you?'

The men hissed at the sound.

Van said, 'Yes, they are an army.'

Martin frowned. 'So what are they fighting for?'

Van watched Martin with hooded eyes. 'Many reasons.' He pointed to a thin youth, barely older than a child. 'Him. Perhaps his village was burnt down one night. Or him.' He pointed to a cheerful looking man with a streak of grey in his hair. 'Perhaps his father was killed. Perhaps his son was taken. Perhaps he had a desire for sacrifice. Many reasons, but only one life. No home, no family. Just this.'

'A hard life,' said Martin, and slurped on his soup thoughtfully. The air was hot already – too hot to think much. 'Hard all the time, it must be. Boring too – they must get bored as hell, out here.'

Van nodded. 'Malaria is the worst thing. Everyone has it many times.'

Martin looked at his bowl. 'What do you do for food? For water?'

Van sighed, and kicked at the earth. 'Water is not a problem. You see over there? It is an underground spring: it comes to earth and flows round the camp, ten minutes walking from here. Food and other things can be found, or bought from across the river. That way, the other side of the river –' Van pointed – 'is China. There are soldiers, but there are sometimes ways to cross. And for other food –' Van frowned. 'Sometimes people from nearby villages help. Sometimes, if the men are starving, they take what is not theirs.'

'They steal?' asked Martin.

Van nodded. 'They steal.'

One of the men, who had been listening closely with cocked head, imitated the sound: 'DEY-STEEL'

Van winked. The men laughed uproariously. Martin, feeling it would be wise to be friendly, laughed too.

Sam woke and clambered outside. It was hot, and he was thirsty. Where was his daddy? He tottered towards a knot of men squatting in the dust.

'Hello,' he said. 'I am from Camberwell.'

The men laughed.

'So,' continued Sam conversationally. 'I'm fine. How are you?'

The men grinned blankly.

Sam frowned. 'I know my phone number. It's 020 8577 7939. What's yours?'

Silence.

'What's your phone number, then?'

Silence.

'Is there a TV?'

Silence again.

Sam scratched his head. He was angry and confused. Why didn't they speak? Maybe they couldn't, he thought. He sniffed at them.

'I'm thirsty, actually.'

One of the men held out a piece of stick with two twigs sprouting from it like wings. He made it fly through the air, whistling as he made it swoop. Sam watched, unimpressed.

'Do you have juice?'

The men laughed.

'Oh, shut up,' said Sam.

Seeing the failure of the wooden bird, one of the men found a discarded coke can and kicked it towards Sam. Sam responded competitively, kicking it back with force. The first man kicked the can to his companions, and others, drawn by the noise, began to watch and laugh. One of them tapped the can to Sam. He returned it with an uncoordinated thump. He would show them, the stupid men.

Soon, a full-scale football game was underway.

Martin looked up from his noodles. He saw a cloud of dust ahead, with the small figure of Sam, surrounded by wiry men, in the middle of it. Van squinted.

'Football. You come?'

'No. Not me.'

'Yes. Come.' He tugged Martin's shirt, grinning.

'Oh God. I'm not fit. I can't run.'

Van pulled him up.

'Please, man. Have mercy.'

'Come. No choice.'

'No choice?' Martin groaned, but allowed Van to drag him towards the game. The can landed near him; he loped towards it and gave it a half-hearted kick. Several of the men began to clap. Encouraged, Martin ran at the can with greater attack. A youth darted past him, kicked the can nimbly, and rushed ahead. Martin, his pride at stake, gave chase. He began to rasp for breath.

Van jogged to his side and slapped Martin's belly. 'Eat too much,' he said. 'You get fat.'

'Too many beers,' Martin gasped. 'At least I'll lose it out here. Should be grateful, really. Fat farm.'

'Yes. You can tell other foreigners to come here. Lose weight.'

'I'll be sure to pass it on,' Martin wheezed. He caught up with his opponent and looped the tin can over Van's head. It landed on the tin roof of a hut with a clang. A cheer went up. The thin boy in jeans who'd been Martin's main opponent strolled up to him and shook his hand, giggling like a schoolgirl. Soon others clustered around him, slapping his back, giving thumbs-up signs.

'Cheers,' said Martin. 'Thanks. Cool.' He gave a thumbs-up sign back, feeling touched. They pulled at his sleeve and beckoned. One of them said,

'Hey, coca cola!'

Martin wiped his forehead with his sleeve. 'Okay. Sure. In a minute. Great.' He muttered to Van, 'I've got to get my breath. This is murder.'

Van nodded. He shooed the men. 'Go away. He is tired. Go away.' They sauntered off reluctantly, looking over their shoulders and nudging one another.

Martin collapsed to the ground. The sky, a great cloudless disk, swirled above him. He closed his eyes. Heat stroked his body.

Fun. That had been fun.

He smiled.

Two soft hands closed over his eyes. A voice tickled his ear.

'You beat them,' whispered Sam. 'We won.'

'That's right.' Martin opened his eyes. He touched Sam's hands, enclosed them in his own. 'We won.'

2

April saw him, lying in the dust. A jolt passed through her body. What was he doing there? Why was nobody helping him? She started forwards. She saw him sit up and rub his hands through his hair. She stopped, angry with him for making her afraid. She moved on, dragging her feet. There was something about the way the camp caught the light, trapped it as if in a bowl, that oppressed her. Her mouth was dry and tasted bitter.

She reached Van. 'Before you ask,' she said, tightly, 'I slept beautifully.'

Van grunted. 'Now everyone is awake.' He squatted on the ground and began to draw delicate circles in the earth with the tip of his index finger. He said, 'There is a village near here. Sometimes they give us food. If you want, you can come.'

April was surprised. She regarded herself and the others as little better than prisoners. If Van was prepared to trust them on a visit out of the camp, it suggested that their imprisonment might be finite. She nodded.

'Sure. We'll all come.'

She took her soup. Shortly, Hardwick joined them. He sat in the dust beside her, shaking as he lowered himself. She asked, 'Want to eat? It's pretty dull, but it's food.'

He touched his chest. 'Not yet. Later, maybe.'

She chewed her lip, worried. Hardwick had not eaten the previous night. He looked frail, and his eyes, she noticed, had taken on a yellow cast. The sun had darkened the liver spots on his hands. She drank her soup. There were some specks of meat floating in it – chicken, possibly – which a few days earlier she would have picked out. She ate the meat now, chewing carefully, not minding the gristle.

Sam said he wanted bread. Van indulged him by shuffling back to the cooking pots and unwrapping a small hard loaf.

239

He broke off a piece; Sam snatched it and ate it with his back turned.

Breakfast complete, she and the others followed Van out of camp. Martin carried Sam on his shoulders; she and Hardwick followed behind. She trudged with her head bowed.

After twenty minutes Van veered to the right and struck out for the mountains, further upstream than yesterday. April climbed woodenly, fighting the fierce temperature with each step. She screwed up her eyes. Her blood pumped through her head.

She looked up and saw Martin carrying Sam ahead of her. She caught herself, not for the first time, admiring his fortitude. It struck her that he rarely complained; certainly not of any physical discomfort. She had thought stoicism a quality she possessed. Now she wasn't so sure. It occurred to her that she endured not because she was strong, but because she was afraid of being weak.

She stopped abruptly, on the edge of tears. Her eyes filmed over. She was not in the habit of self-pity. What could be gained by it? She rebuked herself and bit her lip. The tears came anyway. She'd hardly noticed, until now, how lonely she was. Now it struck her as something physical: a blow to the chest.

Ahead, Martin had gained distance. She fixed her eyes on his back and forced herself on.

Hardwick caught up with her. She heard him panting hard, and saw a strange brightness in his eyes. She thought of cigarettes for the first time that day.

She asked, 'You okay?'

He smiled at her awkwardly. 'I should be asking that of you.'

'I'm fine,' she said quickly. Hardwick stared at her, a lingering look with peculiar warmth in it. She pursed her lips.

They walked for some minutes through the green and purple landscape. Once they'd climbed a further fifty metres or so, Hardwick turned to her and announced, abruptly, 'You know, I learnt to play the guitar once.'

'What?' April raised her eyebrows. 'Why'd you tell me that?'

Hardwick stopped and caught his breath, leaning forwards at a disconcerting angle. He said, 'I don't know. A train of thought. It was a few winters ago. I was recovering from a bout of pneumonia, confined to bed.' He peered at her. 'Can you imagine being cold?'

April thought about it. 'I can't,' she said.

'Neither can I. It seems like something that happened to someone else. But apparently, it was me. I was the one –' He frowned, as if he had forgotten what he'd been saying.

April prompted, 'Everything, before now, seems like a long time ago.'

'Yes.'

She reminded him, gently. 'You had pneumonia.'

He recollected himself. 'Yes. Yes I did. And April, I am a bad patient. I complain. I dislike inactivity. But at that time – the illness, you know – reading gave me headaches and I was too weak to walk, as I would normally do, to clear my head. I do like to walk, April.'

'Yes,' she said. 'I see.'

Hardwick said, 'So I taught myself to play the guitar.'

'What did you play?' Asked April. It was a strange image: Hardwick in his pajamas, propped up in bed with a guitar in his hand. Winter outside.

'Nothing well. Some simple songs. The Bee Gees.'

'Yeah? You played the Bee Gees?' She laughed.

He looked coy. 'I found the songs soothing, and quite easy to learn once I'd mastered a few chords.'

'It's quite a picture. You, singing the Bee Gees.'

'It passed the time. Because it was a physical skill, it was satisfying. I was like a child again. Having to learn something basic. And when I got it right – after much practice – well, the delight of it.' His voice trailed away.

'Yeah.' April nodded. 'I get that. That's good. Hey, you should tell Martin –' She tossed her head in Martin's direction. 'He's the musician.'

Hardwick smiled. 'No. He would expect some miracle of me, and I wouldn't want to disappoint him.'

'Martin? How could you disappoint him?'

'How?' Hardwick walked for a while. 'Because Martin takes music very seriously.'

'He told you that?'

'He did.'

April frowned, displeased that they might have had such a conversation without her. 'So what does *he* like? The Bee Gees?'

Hardwick raised his eyebrows. 'He mentioned some early music I hadn't heard of, all of it rather religious.'

April whistled. 'Serious, huh?'

Hardwick nodded.

'I doubt that.'

Hardwick said nothing.

'So when did you talk about all that, huh? Music and all that?'

'Oh.' Hardwick looked vague. 'I don't remember.'

'I wasn't there?'

'I'm sure you must have been there. It was a very small boat.' He smiled shyly.

'Did you wait till I'd gone to pee?'

Hardwick blushed. 'I don't recall.'

'Perfect. Just perfect.'

April sped up. So that was the picture: Hardwick and Martin, cutting her out, talking about things they didn't think she would understand. She dug her nails into her hands. She reached Martin and strode past him without giving him a glance.

She arrived at the top of a steep incline. Van called out to her to stop. She bent over and gasped, clutching the tops of her thighs.

'Man. I hope the view is worth it.'

Trees sloped down below her like tight woolly hair. Hills rose up behind, rippling into blue. The muted colours and the mild roll of the hills should have been gentle, yet the relentless sweep of the landscape was far from soothing.

Van reached her shoulder. Without saying anything, he pointed. April followed his hand and she saw the river lying directly below them. Spanning it, in one long graceless arc, was a concrete bridge. April looked at Van in surprise. It was the first bridge they had seen on their journey, and she had not expected such a sight in this remote place. It was very plain, a thing of function rather than beauty.

'What the hell is that doing there?'

Van nodded. 'China. Over there. Look, and you see.'

She squinted through the haze. On the far side of the bridge she could make out the beginnings of a small town, and hear the hum of – yes, she was sure of it – busy traffic. A horn tooted. She jumped at the extraordinary sound.

Martin reached the top, swung Sam from his shoulders, and sat down.

'Christ. I'm knackered.'

April pointed to the bridge. 'See?'

'Bloody hell. What's that doing here?'

April muttered, 'It's the border with China. There's a town over there.'

Martin whistled. 'That's brilliant. That's brilliant though, isn't it?' He looked at her brightly.

She narrowed her eyes. 'Maybe.' The bridge did not seem to April to be guarded on the near side. She craned forward.

Van, watching her, pointed to a tower in the distance. 'A checkpoint,' he said. 'Soldiers. See?'

Two uniformed guards stood in the middle of the bridge, on the far side of a white line that was all that demarcated the border. April examined them. The soldiers looked young and nervous, their heavy green overcoats surely hot and uncomfortable. Their fingers toyed with glinting rifles.

'What happens if you try to cross?' April whispered.

'If you try?' Van dropped his voice. 'Bang, bang.'

'You're sure about that?'

Van nodded. 'Let's go now.' He turned. April followed wearily as he trekked back into the foothills.

The village they were seeking was, it transpired, perched on the top of a low hill shaped like the crown of a monk's head, a semi circle of trees surrounding it like a tonsure. As they approached, a pack of half naked children gathered around them. They looked sickly, with bellies barrelled with hunger. They whispered, and tugged at April's clothes. One sloe-eyed girl touched April's skin and breathed, 'sweetie?'

April took a step back. A scar disfigured the girl's face, a river of churned up skin which travelled from her cheek to her neck and down along her arm. That wasn't the worst. The girl's arm ended in a stump just above the elbow. The skin on the end of it was pink and smooth; whatever blow had severed it had been a clean one. April felt her own scar itching.

The girl nudged her. 'Sweetie? Sweetie ma'am?'

'No. No sweetie. Leave me alone.' She pushed the girl away. It was too much – the arm, nudging her. She had no sweetie.

Sam, she saw, was clinging to Martin, demanding to be picked up. April understood why: there was something feral about the way the children hissed and swarmed. She wondered what they might do in order to pluck a few morsels from the strangers' pockets. She grimaced, scooped Sam up, and handed him to Martin. The children, as if they'd received a sign, stopped still.

Van said, 'Come on,' and beckoned. April folded her arms across herself and followed.

A single track, churned and pitted, served as the village's only thoroughfare. Four or five shabby huts crouched on either side of it, low to the ground and roughly thatched. A mangy dog growled at them as they passed, one eye wounded and full of maggots.

Van shouted, 'Yar.' The dog shuffled away.

An ancient woman emerged from one of the huts and squatted on the ground. Her eyes were caught like two flies in a web of wrinkles; her body was so thin that it seemed almost transparent. She gestured to the children. They scattered. She sank forwards.

Van sat in front of her. He muttered a few words. The woman lisped back, her voice barely audible. Her head sank onto her chest. Van shut his eyes.

Abruptly, he stood up and began to pick his way back through the village. April remained where she was, bewildered by this short exchange. The pack of children watched silently, their faces sharp and hostile. April realised, suddenly, what it was that was so weird about the place. The village contained children and old people. Nobody else.

She walked alone to the edge of the hill. The children had gathered there, close to Van but not too close.

She turned to the girl with the stunted arm.

'So what happened to you, honey?' she asked, her voice conversationally bright.

The girl scowled, spat on the ground, and walked away.

3

Hardwick walked across the cracked earth, his body stooped against the brutal light. He raised his hand to his forehead and, squinting, saw April amongst the children. He halted. A short tree offered a meagre patch of shade; he fell to the ground and held his head in his hands. He remained there for some minutes, noticing his chest rise and fall. He wondered if he was ill. Despite the heat he was shivering, and the hairs on the back of his neck were standing up. He tried to compose himself. His belly was empty: perhaps it was hunger that accounted for his feeling of hollowness? He was tired too: it had taken him many hours to fall asleep the night before, and though he'd had a rough blanket to lie on it hadn't softened the cracked wooden floor. Thoughts had buzzed round in his head like restless insects.

An old man with bare feet walked by. Hardwick watched. The man noticed him and recoiled: he gave a yelp, and ran back to the village. Hardwick groaned. Was the man afraid of him? Why? He wanted to sink into himself. He gripped his head. It ached.

He'd had the oddest sensation when he'd woken that morning, face down in the darkened hut. It had seemed to him then that he didn't have a body at all, just eyes in an aching head, and the world was a vast bowl in which his eyes were floating. He touched his face to make sure it was there. It was soft and plastic, like the face of a shop dummy. His skin was slick with cold sweat.

He watched April say something to a girl with a scarred face. April was kind. She was also brave; that's what Martin had said, and Hardwick believed it to be true. She had done something extraordinary: risked her life for her friend. Martin too, the day he'd taken Sam from the park, had at least acted – even if it was an impetuous, ill-considered act. And Hardwick? No. He did not act. He observed and did nothing.

He had followed Lorraine from a coward's distance, and watched, helpless, as Felicity died. He was a bystander to his own life.

He rubbed his eyes. Somewhere along the way he had lost his sunglasses. When? He couldn't remember. He bent lower. The heat beat down on the back of his head. He put a hand on his neck and swayed as he stood up. He resolved to walk back to the others, but noted, with dispassion, that his legs wouldn't move. He wondered why. A strange dreaminess had come over him. It was not that he couldn't walk, but that the choice between moving and not moving seemed so finely balanced that it was easier to drift and do nothing. He muttered to himself: Zeno's Paradox. Achilles will never catch up with the tortoise; an arrow in motion is – at any single point in time – at rest.

He sat back down with a sigh. Helplessness settled on him, a heavy and cumbersome blanket. He wanted to be rid of it. He had hoped, two nights ago, that telling the others his story might lift it; but his words had cloyed and stuck on his tongue, repeating on him like a bad meal. And too soon afterwards he had heard shots, and they had scrambled back to the boat, and the oppressive journey onwards had continued; and rather than being distracted by the present, the past pressed down ever harder on him.

Except – that was – the moment Sam had fallen.

Hardwick gave an involuntary shudder. Van had been speaking – he and April had been arguing – and Sam had been standing erect in the boat, his red t-shirt a smudge against the indigo sky. Crickets had been whining somewhere, water slurping against the side of the boat. And Sam had swayed, and a second later had plunged head first towards the yawning water. And in that single moment Hardwick had acted. He had swooped forwards with great speed, and yet somehow so slowly. He remembered catching the boy, clutching him in his thin arms just before his head hit the water. Martin – who had uttered a cry a second before

– fell silent. Everyone fell silent. Hardwick's legs had buckled, and he had collapsed – with Sam on top of him – onto the floor of the boat.

But he had acted. Time had frozen, and he – Hardwick alone – had moved.

What else? His heart beat fast. There must be something – some other act – he could recall? His memories were fragmentary, and though some things stood out clearly – April's story, Sam's delight at the inky butterfly in his path – others were blurred. He held his hand out, caught memories in the air.

Just now. What had happened? He panicked, as his mind struggled to recall the immediate past. He remembered, and relaxed. Yes. He had tramped, tramped up the hill beside April, and they had talked about music. He had enjoyed the walk, and their conversation, though he couldn't work out why that story – his illness, the Bee Gees – had popped into his head. He savoured the pleasure of the walk, and the easy conversation. It triggered a further recollection. He used to go on walking holidays with Felicity. It was one of the things they once did. He sat upright. Yes. Early in their marriage they would go to Derbyshire and walk in the Peak District, wearing thick woolly socks and trousers that came to just below their knees. They used to talk as they rambled, and their conversations, he remembered, were as easy and aimless as their walks.

Long ago, on one of these walks, he'd established with Felicity that he had no memory whatsoever of his early childhood. She had laughed at him and called him a dunderhead, and he had lifted up his hands and told her there was nothing of interest to say.

He found, now, that this was not quite true. He could recall a sensation – the tramp, tramping walk – most clearly. Yes.

He wiped beads of sweat from his forehead, taken aback by the rush of memories. It was true – he'd taken many walks with his mother, long rambling walks, mostly in silence – he recalled the silence – gripping his mother's hand and walking fast, his steps matching her steps. He must have been lanky, even as a child. He recalled the languor of those walks, the fact that they seemed neither to begin nor to end but to be conducted in an in-between space where his mind could wander in tune with his mother's footsteps. He remembered thick grass snagging against his shins. He remembered thistles prickling his legs and his fingers – how tall they must have grown – and dandelion sap smearing his skin, and pollen irritating his eyes, and he realised that even those sensations carried with them a kind of pleasure because they came with the warmth of the sun and his mother's cool hand in his own. And, thinking of Sam on Martin's shoulders, he wondered why, given how intently the boy studied everything he saw, why he, Hardwick, could remember so little. He shook himself. The present came into focus.

Van was squatting near the wizened old woman. Martin and April were kicking their heels, ignoring one another. The children cowered a few paces back. No one saw Hardwick. He turned his back on them.

He began to walk downhill, his knees buckling. He wanted to walk: it was good. He fell into a rhythm. The rhythm carried him downwards, and soon he couldn't hear Van's voice. He reached the tree line. The vegetation thickened. He marched on. It began to rain, a few slow hot drops at first, then harder, more rapid ones. He sped up. There were large palm leaves growing by the side of the path. He stopped and pulled at one. It snapped easily. He held it above his head and it made a reasonable shelter, keeping his hair dry at least though his clothes were soon soaked through. He didn't mind. The rain was warm, and the downpour had released a gathering tension in the air. He loosened his stride, sheltering from the worst of the rain under his palm parasol. The earth became slippery. He trod nimbly, without any particular aim or direction. He wasn't sure if this was the way they'd come; in fact he felt sure it was not. He skidded and flung out his arm. The rain poured down his neck. He discarded his makeshift shelter. It was appropriate, he considered, that the rain here should be extravagant, a far cry from the thin unrelenting drops that fell on him in England. *Don't go out in the rain*, his mother had always told him, and he never had; only watched as it slid down grey window panes. So it was pleasant, exceedingly so, to feel this hot large rain smack against his skin like a kiss.

The ground levelled. He swung his arms. A bulky rock barred his way and he climbed over it, slipping a little on the thin covering of sandy earth. The rock was sheer on the far side, and he was forced to jump off it. He twisted his ankle as he landed. He knelt on the ground in the mud and saw, a few inches from his nose, a fat python with green and yellow skin coiled beneath the rock. It was, Hardwick guessed, a good ten feet from tip to tail. Its tongue flicked in and out. Hardwick squatted. Apart from its tongue and its lidless eye, the snake was motionless. Hardwick gazed at it for a long time. The rain stopped.

Someone tapped him on the shoulder. He shuddered, and turned. April.

'Professor. Step backwards. Slowly.'

'There's no harm.'

'You don't know that.'

He stepped back, reluctantly. April was flushed. Her hair was dripping, clinging to her face in dark streaks. She said, 'We're leaving.'

He shook himself. 'Yes, of course.'

'Are you okay?'

'I was miles away.'

She narrowed her eyes. He did not elaborate.

She said, 'The sooner we get out of here, the better. This place stinks.'

She sped up, leaving him, as usual, travelling behind.

He mulled over her words. He wouldn't have used her phrase, was shocked by it. An abrupt judgment – not one he would have made. He groped for something more nuanced, but was disappointed by each effort he made. His mouth filled with saliva. He swallowed. He wanted it all gone, suddenly: the children, the village, the whole ugly place. He wanted it destroyed.

He stopped, bent over, and retched.

The ground lurched towards him. He fell on to it. April ran back.

'Professor.' She gripped his hand, tried to tug him up.

'Oh, God. Oh, God.'

'What is it?'

'I've committed a crime, April. God help me, I've sinned.'

'What are you talking about? Put your head down.' She urged him to sit; pushed his head onto his knees. 'You're hot. It's the sun.'

'It's not the sun.' He gagged. His mouth filled again. April's hold on his hand tightened until it was painful: this was useful; kindness would not have helped. He shut his eyes to stop the ground spinning.

He heard her voice from far away. 'Professor. Talk to me, Professor.'

'Talk to you?' His voice was equally distant. It sounded weak and tinny.

'Talk to me. Tell me something.'

'Tell you what?'

'I don't know what. Anything. Tell me your name. Tell me your favourite food.'

She was worried. It was touching.

He mumbled, 'Cheese.'

'Cheese?'

'My favourite kind of food. Cheese.'

'What kind of cheese?' She was a great distance away; could have been in the heavens.

'Stilton. Strong blue stilton. Gorgonzola. Roquefort.' He retched again.

April said – her thin, faraway voice edged with fright – 'Okay. Shit. Not cheese. Not food. Tell me something. God, I don't know. Shit. Tell me something you know that I don't know. I know about sin and hell and all of that crap. Don't tell me about that. Tell me something else.'

Hardwick searched his mind. It was hard. The ground was steaming; the sun was sucking the rain back up in to the air. April held his hand. Her grip was firm. He thought of walking, another hard grip on his hand, dandelion sap on his legs, his mother following in a patterned dress. He thought of Sam falling into his long arms, falling so slowly and so very fast. Zeno's paradox. He gritted his teeth and tried to think of something to tell April. Not those things. Not all that. The effort was tremendous. Images rushed at him. Felicity; Sam; walking by the river; Lorraine.

Finally, he whispered: 'Thermopylae.'

'What?'

'The battle of Thermopylae, April. A defeat. But an extraordinary one, against great odds. Have you heard of it?'

'No,' she said, gently. No. Tell me.'

He sat down in the mud and told her about the Greek defeat by the Persians in the gorge of Thermopylae. The rain started again. It fell on his bare head in hot thick sheets.

That evening, as they ate, Hardwick asked, 'What was that horrible place?'

'That?' Van grinned mischievously. 'That is my horrible village.'

Hardwick blushed deeply. 'I'm sorry.' He had rested on their return. He felt – not better, but calmer, less muddled.

Van batted away the apology. He bent over his bowl, grunting as he shoveled in his food. April stared at her bowl.

Martin said nothing. Neither of them, it appeared, wanted to know more. Hardwick, however, did.

'It's quite extraordinary,' he said, his voice hoarse, 'that given the – er – circumstances – that your English is so fluent and you are so – ah – well versed in the ways of the world.'

Van looked up from his food. 'I was taught by missionaries. American. Though my accent is one hundred per cent BBC.'

'Indeed?'

'Of course. You know, the first time I saw a missionary – a foreigner – I thought he was a monster. And then, when I knew him better I thought –' Van laughed, wheezily – 'I thought that all foreigners must be free as birds, and all of them are unhappy. I didn't know why.'

Hardwick leaned forward. 'Do you think you know now?'

Van didn't answer this directly.

Hardwick pressed, 'Won't you tell us more? Please.'

April picked at her rice.

Van demurred, though it seemed to Hardwick only for show. 'I think I am not interesting,' he said. 'I have never travelled. I have only lived here.' He pointed to the ground. 'Not like you.'

'On the contrary,' said Hardwick, 'I've hardly travelled myself, despite appearances.' He paused, and looked at his hands: they hung limply in his lap. 'In any case I am not sure travel is the best guarantor of wisdom. So please. We truly would like to know.'

'About me? You are kind.' Van shut his eyes. He said nothing for a long time, just inhaled softly through his nose.

His eyes snapped open.

4

Van asked, 'Where can I begin?'

Hardwick thought. 'Tell us about meeting foreigners for the first time. What was it like?'

Van put down his bowl. Hardwick could hear the drone of a mosquito somewhere near his ear. He batted at it. His skin trembled.

'You want to know?' Van asked.

Hardwick nodded. Martin and April drew closer.

Van breathed out softly. 'I try to remember,' he said. 'It is so far away that sometimes I think it is a dream. I do not know if the time I imagine is just what I imagine. Not real.' He turned to Hardwick and smiled. 'But you want to know my history, so I must do my best.'

Hardwick bowed his head.

'This is what I imagine. A small boy. No shoes, like the children you see today. But happy. More food, more peace. A better place. It is hard to use words to describe his world, because his world is made of tastes and colours, not words. Like all children. Like you. Can you imagine? The patter of rains when they come, and the deep sound of the river. The brown of the water. The smell of rice. Can you imagine this boy, this child who was once me?'

Hardwick thought of Oxford. He thought of walking barefoot through a daisy-covered meadow, of holding his mother's hand. Sunlight making the air shimmer with gold; his mother's grip, strong and comforting.

He said, 'Yes, I can.' He observed a small change in Van's expression, a flicker of a muscle in his cheek. He asked, 'Who else was in your family?'

'My grandmother – the old woman you saw today – and my father. It was a very small family. My mother died when I was born.'

'What was your father like?'

'So many questions.' Van's voice was sharp, but his eyes glittered. 'My father was quiet. Very quiet. A soft man with a hard life.'

'Why was his life hard?' Hardwick judged that his questions were not rude. A wave of nausea passed over him. He swallowed. 'Why?'

'Because our land was not good,' said Van, apparently willing to humour him. 'Other families had better, but even the best land was not good. A long time ago my ancestors went into these mountains to get away from big taxes. My grandmother told me that the life they left behind was better. My grandmother – my mother's mother – talked about it. She talked about my ancestor who made profits from opium farming. He hired lowlanders to work for him in his fields. Can you imagine? But his money swelled his brain, and he began to think he was the *Pha Nom,* this means The Big Man, a God Man some people believe will come one day. He attacked a tax office; he told people he was the *Pha Nom*, and other villages joined him. He spread the rumour that any bullet fired at him would turn into a jasmine flower, but when he was fired on – Bang. He was dead.'

Van gave a rasping laugh.

Hardwick asked, 'Why did you leave your village? To find more land?'

'No. I saw a man in the jungle – a monster, like I told you. I thought he was a Japanese ghost come to make revenge, because before, in the war, we killed many Japanese.'

'And was he? A ghost or a spirit, that is?'

'Of course not.' Van looked at Hardwick awry. 'A missionary, come to save us.' He sat back and intoned, 'And God so Loved the World, that he gave up his only Son, Jesus Christ… The man gave us presents: little Bibles, gold crosses – and a photograph of a puppy. I loved that photograph especially. He came with others. They said they would teach us, so I began to learn. I began to learn how to give the world

255

a new shape, with strange words. I liked having such a power. I stopped being a child.

'I grew into a man. I was restless. I hated the things I once loved. I wanted to see a motorcycle, and a refrigerator. I wanted to leave my village. I talked about this with my friend from the mission school. He was called Bob – an American. He said he had come to Mingoria to escape those things, motorcycles and things. And I said, you can only say that because you have had them already. You can only escape what you already have.

'Bob liked to argue things, and prove things by logic. He did not want to agree, but logic told him my point was true. So. Every two months a pair from the mission school had the duty of walking to the road – three days or more – and then a friend would meet them in a jeep, and they would walk back with supplies and letters. In special times – if they needed medicine, or to make arrangements with the French – one of the missionaries would return to the city to stay for a while. It was Bob's turn to do this. He said I could go with him.

'I told my family. It was not easy. As I said before, I had just two in my family, and after my mother died my father was very quiet. I thought he was weak, soft in his head, the way he looked at something I could not see. But he was only quiet, after all. When I told my grandmother my plan, she was angry and said I could not go. My father had never disagreed with her before. I thought my plan was over, but I was surprised. He said I could go. He said, you must be strong, and knowledge will make you strong. And though my grandmother was very angry, he did not change his mind.

'The missionaries gave me new clothes. They cut my hair too. I was given writing paper and a new Bible. This, as well as a little golden cross and my photograph of a puppy, was what I had. I left my village, and went into the world.

'My father watched me go. I remember it very well. He stood still. He did not wave. There was a bright hope in his eyes. I did not watch him for long.'

Van sighed and looked down. Hardwick waited, breathless. Insects chirruped; something rustled nearby.

Van scratched his leg. He said, 'It took us three days to walk to the road. Our skin was cut by twigs that whipped us as we passed. I thought the jungle was punishing me because I left. A jeep was waiting, as Bob had promised. It frightened me, because I had never seen a car or even a road before. Our driver was American. His name was Frank. When he saw me afraid he laughed and called me a peasant. Bob said, do not say that – he is educated. Frank said, it is a free country, and told me that this was his joke. I laughed, even though I did not understand. Was I not free? Why was this a joke? Frank's skin was sweating, and I smelt for the first time the sour smell of a fat white man.

'It took us another day to reach the city. When we arrived I was asleep, and I saw nothing. Bob woke me and led me through a stinking alley to a small room with no air. I spent my first night in a bed. I woke sick and aching. My tummy was very bad. I tried to stand up but I fell down instead. I was sick over the side of my bed and onto Bob's shoes.'

Van laughed. 'I was very friendly!'

Hardwick asked, 'What was it like, being there for the first time, in the city? It must have been extraordinary.'

'Yes. Yes, very. So big. For me – you cannot imagine.'

'Please tell.'

'Tell. Yes.' Van paused, and chewed the tip of his finger. 'So many people. I had never seen so many people, and although the city was vast I wondered how they can all fit. And, no one looked me in my eyes. I thought they were angry with me but Bob said it was because my existence was not important to them. I thought about this. When I was a child I imagined I was invisible. Here I was visible but I could pass through a crowd and nobody could see. This seemed to me a useful thing.

'Bob took me to a church built by the French, and I liked the peace inside. The green light from the glass reminded me of the green jungle, and it was the only time that I felt homesick. Bob said we should have a short siesta, but I couldn't stand to sleep indoors, so I said I would walk around the city alone. First of all Bob did not want to let me go, but afterwards he changed his mind and agreed. When I found him later, he was snoring and there were empty beer bottles by his bed. I understood why he had let me leave.

'The city was wonderful to me. Bob soon stopped asking me where I was going. He did not want to return to the mission, he said. He wanted motorcycles and beer again. After a week, he left me. I was alone in the vast city, with little money and no friends. I needed work. In my many walks I had discovered something that interested me greatly: a nightclub. On my third night I walked inside.'

Van shut his eyes.

'Oh, it was very beautiful. Such light; such beautiful sounds. Smoke, like magic. Most of the people were foreigners, French and American and one young Russian guy called Karasin. The foreign men wore white jackets and black ties. There were also women there. Foreign women with bare shoulders, and a female from my country. She stood in the centre of the stage and she sang a lovely French song. She wore foreign clothes, and she too had bare shoulders. Her hair was cut short and it curled around her ears. She wore pink lipstick. I wondered what Frank the driver would think of her.

'Someone tapped my shoulder. It was Frank himself. He was more friendly now than before. He asked me what I was doing and I said I was looking for work. He thought this was funny. He bought me a drink and gave me a cigarette. He went away for a while. I thought he had forgotten me, but then he came back. He said, you are very lucky, I have found you a job. I said, really sir? He said yes, and don't call me sir.

'It was for a man called Sisavong, a friend of his. He needed a secretary, someone who could speak English and someone he could trust. This someone was me.'

Hardwick sprang forward. 'You mean Sisavong the politician? That Sisavong?'

'Yes.' Van raised his eyebrows. 'You are surprised?'

'It's extraordinary.'

'Maybe.' Van hummed. 'Maybe not. My good fortune is not so strange if you consider that, at that time – 1950s – not many young men in my country could speak English.'

Hardwick nodded, and settled down again. The wretched camp, the crawling, restless night, seemed illusory; Van's story, the nightclub, the vast city – these seemed real. He noticed that the others, like him, had edged further forward. April's eyes were closed. Martin sat close to her, watching.

Van resumed. 'I will describe Sisavong. He was an aristocrat. His father was a prince. He had lazy eyes. I liked him, though others did not. He asked me questions in English, and he quickly saw through Frank's lie that I was a student from the south. He asked me questions about our southern capital, and when I could not reply, he smiled at me. I confessed the truth. He looked surprised, but he clapped me on the back and said it was very good. He said he was ignorant of the northern peoples, and my English was first class. He hired me.

'When I was hired he was finance minister in the government. Later he was Prime Minister It was a time of hope. You know this. The year was 1958, and I was seventeen years old. Sisavong talked to me about the modern world. He liked to be modern, and he liked to teach me. *Van*, he said, *if you can be modern then everyone can be modern*. He bought me white shirts from Paris. He laughed very loud when the American Ambassador told jokes, even though I thought the jokes were not funny at all.

'Sisavong lived in a big house with shutters and a garden full of butterflies. Sometimes I stood out in this garden and I took off my shoes, so I could feel the cool grass on my feet. Very nice. But the best thing about the house was the library.

I sat and studied and I read. I wanted to be like Sisavong. A modern.'

Van giggled. 'We survived because of American money. Sisavong knew this. Mingoria had only three cash crops: teak, coffee and opium. We were small. We needed friends, whoever they might be. But not everyone laughed so loud when the American Ambassador told his jokes.' He sighed. 'You have heard of Vien Song? He likes to be called General Vien Song now.'

'You met him then? Vien Song?' Asked Hardwick.

'Yes. I met him once. He came to the big house, and in the company of Sisavong and his friends he seemed stupid. He was covered in amulets to protect himself from harm, and this, and the things he said, told me he was superstitious. He had big gums, and a big mouth in a flat fish face. He told his own jokes. But, like the Ambassador's, they were not funny at all. It is wrong, though, to say he was stupid. He was cunning. He understood power. He said that Sisavong was not patriotic enough. He criticised that he was friends with America, and said we should find friends nearer to home. He himself had many friends. 'So. Not long afterwards came the coup. And after the coup, the war.'

'If it is painful,' said Hardwick, after a pause, 'You don't have to tell.'

'No. I will tell.' Van stretched his hands in front of him. His fingers – Hardwick noticed this – were long and fine, like Martin's. Hardwick wondered, for an absurd moment, if Van was a pianist, as Martin was.

Van said, 'Let me tell what it is like to be in a city during a civil war.'

'Thank you,' responded Hardwick, humbly. 'If you can.'

Van nodded. 'It is impossible to go out at night. The nightclub, with the little singer inside, is closed for good. I spend the evenings at Sisavong's house, hiding in the dark. Around me, the sound of mortar shelling. Boom. Boom. The electricity is not working. There are blackouts; food is scarce, though we suffer less than people in the countryside. I think of my father, and how he waved to me when I walk away. And I am sad, terribly sad, with no words to say it. Fear is everywhere. Fear and madness. After five years of fighting, Vien Song marches into the capital. People throw flowers. They are happy, I think, that it is over. They are sick of war. Many in the government have run away abroad. Sisavong made plans to run away, but he was too late. He was arrested that night. I was arrested too.'

Van heaved in a breath. 'So. I will not say much. I was blindfolded and my hands are tied. I was forced rough into the back of a truck. We drove around the city, and I heard cries around me. Night became day. I did not know where we were going. I try to think of nothing. I endured the baking sun on my body, and the flies that crawled over my face. I was given no food and no water. Next morning I was allowed to drink, and my blindfold was removed. I was with twenty people. I did not know them. We did not speak to each other, or look in one another's eyes. Each man is alone.

'After another day's driving the guards force us out and we walk. We walk for a long time. I knew the jungle, and the mountains, but not this flat place. Nothing there but gloomy teak trees. No colour, no flowers or cheerful plants. Everything without life. Sometimes we saw curious people who stopped and stared at us, and it seemed from their faces that we were criminals because our hands were tied and our eyes were full of fear. We walked through this place until we were ordered to stop. There were more soldiers. They greet each other with cheers, and do not look at us. We fell on the ground until a soldier hand us bowls of rice. We ate like starving children.

'We were given tools and ordered to dig. This was our first task: to build our own prison. We chopped trees, until they were dead stumps and rotten teeth. Our own teeth rotted. Every day we said words to praise General Vien Song, and every day we made confessions of our crimes. This was so we could be reformed. We thought about our mistakes, of our love of foreigners and our greed. Hard work will clean us, the guards said. One day we will be new men.

'Rumours began to reach even that place, so far away from the world. It is surprising, how thirsty we were for knowledge, more thirsty even than for water. I began to hear about fighting near my village, and I think about my father. Why did I not wave to him goodbye? Why did I not look at him longer before I walked away? I became a shadow. I did not want to live. But I lived.

'Eleven years after I was captured, I was freed. The camp commander shook my hand and congratulated me kindly. After all, he had kept us alive. He gave me my watch, and some coins. They were wrapped in a piece of brown cloth, and I signed a piece of paper to say I had them, and also that I was reformed. I thanked the commander very much for keeping them so nice.

'I returned to my village. I had nowhere else to go. During Vien Song's war, some *Khia* thought they had a chance to get land. When Vien Song got power he made them pay. Many villages were destroyed.'

Hardwick asked, 'Was your village destroyed?'

Van shook his head. 'My village was not destroyed. It was there. You saw it. The little village you saw today, with children and wild dogs. Is it always true that when you leave a home it is smaller when you return? I stood in my village and had this thought, and I laughed, and my laugh came back to me. Something was not right. I started to feel sick. Where were all the people? I stood still. No noise. I walked on. I wanted to cry. I reached my little house. I climbed up and look inside and there is a tiny shape. I ask the shape, is it father? The shape says, no it is not father. I ask, who is it. The voice said, Me. I say, is it grandmother? The shape nods. I crawl towards it. The shape looks up. I see two hard little eyes. She does not speak. She is tiny as a bird but the eyes are hard and bright. I said, I have come back grandmother. She said, I can see that. I ask, where is father. Gone a long time ago, she said. Is he dead, I ask? She nods. Because of the fighting I ask? She says no, they made him work. I ask, what work? She said, making the bridge, as if it is very obvious. I try to ask again, but she tells me to go away.

'I do not go far. I sit down outside my home, not knowing what to do. I sit there for a long time. I start to fall asleep, but then I hear footsteps. I see a man come. He is limping. I sit silent and still. When he sees me he jumps.

'He is a farmer from our village. He told me there had been fighting. Most of the men had fought, my father too. He had fought with an old Japanese gun that had no bullets. Others fought with sticks and knives and stones. Eleven people from my village died. My father survived.

'Then the army said, in the name of peace and development my father must help them build a bridge. A big, modern bridge across the river to China, which is a modern place. It would, the army told him, bring us civilisation and money. It will make us modern. My father must build it.

'My father was an old man. Too old for work as hard as that. He died slowly, and afterwards, they threw his body in the river. My friend told me this. Then he left me alone.

'I thought, then, for a long time. I thought about being a child. When I was a child I believed in many things that were not true. I believed what the missionaries told me. I believed I must laugh at jokes I did not understand. I believed my father was weak, but he was not weak. He was quiet. That is not weak.'

Van stopped. Hardwick studied him. His face – so changeable during their journey, at times candid, at times watchful and closed – was old, and streaked with tears.

5

Martin thought, as Van spoke. *'What am I doing here? What the fuck is all this about?'*

A memory came to him. An odd memory. One day – Sam must have been about two – he had walked into work early, and experienced a sudden, wrenching panic as he approached the concrete school playground. He was supposed to teach that day. He had taught every day for twelve years. But he knew he could not. He thought about running. The idea was insane. He shut his eyes and tried to control his fear. He took a few halting steps. His stomach churned.

He managed to get into the classroom. He sat down at his desk and leant his head on it. Cool plastic. A large cupboard stood to the left of him. A bell jangled and he jumped, his panic worse than ever. Without thinking, he stepped into the cupboard and closed the door. He stood confined in the dark space. His lungs ached. His whole body trembled. He listened as the children entered and sat down. He waited. He shivered. It was ridiculous. A child giggled. Another banged at a desk. The class descended into chaos.

He heard a colleague's voice asking after him, her tone one of anxiety and surprise. He shut his eyes. He leant into the darkness, wishing it would snuff him out. The bell rang, the children left, and he stepped, shaking, into the light.

He had wiped the memory until now. It was such a bizarre, childish thing to do. Yet even now the thought of it – so vivid and shameful – made him tremble and sweat.

He'd had nothing to be afraid of that day, and yet – he couldn't deny it – he'd been sickeningly scared. And there were so many days like it: of panic, of baseless fear. Shivers on the underground; chills in the road. Why? What was it, this fear without a purpose? Depression, was that the word? Martin pondered. Meaningless fear. He'd been afraid of nothing – and with nothing to fight, he had no chance of winning.

Things were different now. It had been creeping up on him, this change, manifesting as a slow tingling in his blood, a quickening of his heart. He'd known real fear lately, and instead of it leaving him hollow and destroyed, he felt more alive than he'd done in years. He wanted to survive, as Van had survived the prison camp and left it – not a shadow, but a man. That day in the classroom he'd wanted the darkness to annihilate him: a scared teacher in a cupboard. Now he wanted to live.

Hardwick moved apart from others.

Martin asked him what was wrong. Hardwick shook his head, and the younger man did not inquire further. Hardwick appreciated this delicacy. A kind soul, Martin.

Thoughts chased across his brain. He thought, first, about the nature of history, and how far a single individual might change or be changed by historical events. There was a certain comfort in this speculation: he found that through it he lost the grainier details of Van's story, could remove himself from its harsher elements. Even so, certain images came to him: the green canopy of jungle, the quiet church in the city. He pictured the prison camp and recoiled. He tried to imagine the seventeen year old Van forcing himself through the undergrowth into the unknown.

His thoughts turned inwards. He recollected, with anguish, how little he had done in his life – for himself or anyone. He thought about Felicity. He thought about Lorraine. He thought about the little nightclub singer with her neat hair tucked under her ears, and wondered, with a pang, what had happened to her.

Van's story threw April back into a memory of her own. She was there now, in it and of it. It had happened many years before and she had built a wall around it, guarding it with layers of cynicism and disdain. Until one night, after a day of fruitless walking, she caught herself telling a funny little man with puppy eyes wearing a green jacket that plainly did not fit.

She had been living with her husband George for a year and the misguided marriage was failing. She went home to tell her mom and dad. Looking back, she could think of no reason why: she did not need her parents' approval for a divorce. She knew that her mother would weep, and her father would yell. What had she hoped to gain?

She told them in the afternoon. Her mother was cooking fries and her father, a big man, was turning over the corner of his newspaper.

She said, pitching her voice loud and strong: 'There are two things you need to know. First is, I'm pregnant. Second is, I'm leaving George.'

Her mother left the room, clutching her head. Her father – and silence – remained.

He sat heavy in his chair, his fists pink balls on the table. When the silence became too much for her, April spoke.

'Dad, I'm not the first person that this has happened to.'

The silence thickened. April stood up, scraping her chair back.

'Sit still, young lady.' His voice was soft. His eyes, pale blue and remarkable for their mildness, shone in his face.

April stopped, frozen in mid-movement. She said, pleadingly, 'You're over reacting. It's not what I wanted, but it is what has happened. I feel sad, Daddy.'

He rose. Something creaked. He'd been complaining, recently, of arthritis. He turned his back on his daughter. She thought at first that he was walking out of the door, and her muscles relaxed a bit.

He did not walk to the door. He stepped, very carefully, towards the deep fat fryer bubbling on the hob. He picked up an oven cloth and wrapped it, like a bandage, around his big hands. He lifted the fryer from the hob and carried it towards April.

He stood before her. Very slowly and carefully, he tipped the contents of the fryer over her lap.

She registered three things. The first was disbelief. Her eyes saw, but her mind did not accept, what was happening. The second was pain. Scalding oil burnt through her clothes and began eating into her raw flesh. The pain, thankfully, was brief: it travelled like lightening up her spinal chord and burst into her brain, shutting everything down.

She remembered one last thing – the third – before blackness descended on her. It was her father's face, not twisted in triumph or fury, but mild and sad.

Martin took Sam to bed. He sang to him softly in the twilight.

> *What shall we do with the drunken sailor?*
> *What shall we do with the drunken sailor?*
> *What shall we do with the drunken sailor, early in the morning?*

> *Hooray and up she rises; Hooray…*

The boy's eyelids drooped.

Martin returned to find Hardwick and April sitting some distance apart from one another, their faces barely visible in the moonlight. He sat down and fidgeted, wanting to do something to lighten the atmosphere. He asked Hardwick, 'So, what's the first thing you'll do when you get home? Me, it's a cold beer.'

Hardwick lowered his eyes. 'I'm not sure. I don't know what I want to do.'

'There must be something,' Martin insisted.

Hardwick shook his head. 'No. I can't honestly say there is. I'm not even sure if I want to go home.'

'Come on.' Martin was irritated. 'Of course you do. I mean, we're not going to be here forever, are we.'

'I don't know, Martin. I don't know.' Hardwick sighed. 'I've lived according to a pattern. All my life I have. And I'm simply not sure what the pattern is any more. I may as well be here, as anywhere.'

'Oh, come on. That's rubbish,' said Martin, exasperated. He didn't want Hardwick to feel defeated: not when he felt the opposite. He slapped his hands on the ground. 'Cheer up, everyone. No-one's died.'

Hardwick looked at him inquiringly.

April stood up. 'I'm going for a walk.'

Martin opened his mouth to say something. She turned away from them. He watched her back retreating into the night.

Voices were ringing in her ears. She needed to walk in order to silence them. She walked towards the pool that bordered the camp, along a path marked by many feet.

She was dirty. She examined her hands; her fingernails were black and cracked. She imagined dirt soaking through layers of her skin. Her scar was itching. She wanted to tear at it. That was dirt too, a layer of filth permanently stuck to her. Boiled skin.

She reached the pool and squatted down beside it. She had come here earlier in the evening, and seen a black dragonfly hovering over the water. She'd sat and watched it for a long time, half forgetting where she was.

She kicked off her shoes and dipped her feet in the water. It was unexpectedly cold. The pool, she guessed, must have its source in an underground spring, and be cooled by the earth as it emerged.

The night was full of stars. Their light made it easy to see. She stared at her feet. They looked like two white potato lumps cut off at the ankles. She wiggled her toes. It was good, feeling the water flow over them. She reached down and rubbed her skin. A cloud of mud rose and then dispersed as the river ran clean. Stars swam on the surface of the pool. The air was earthy and fresh.

She needed to wash. She stood up and began to take off her clothes, removing them quickly and folding them with care on a dry patch of bank beside her. She stripped to her underwear, then looked down at the scar snaking from her belly to her thighs. She shuddered, and stepped in to the pool.

She murmured with pleasure at the shock of the cold. She squatted and splashed her shoulders. Her skin shivered as drops of water rolled down her back. She splashed her belly and let water run down her thighs, over her scar, down her legs.

She began to scrub.

She scrubbed so hard that flaky layers on her shoulders, burnt by the sun, began to peel away. Not satisfied, she scooped up a handful of pebbles from the water bed and began to grind them into the skin on her legs. She worked methodically, as if she could rub the scar tissue entirely away. She scraped until she bled.

She began to sob.

'April?'

Martin's voice was querulous, barely a whisper. He was standing a few feet away from her, staring at her with a mixture of shock and pity on his face.

She spun round. 'What the fuck are you doing?'

He stepped backwards. 'God, I'm sorry. I didn't – '

'Leave me alone.'

'April. Are you all right?'

'No.' She shook her head. 'Do I look all right?'

'You're bleeding.'

She stared at him.

'Is there anything I can do?'

'No.'

'April. Poor April.'

As coolly as she could manage, she said: 'Leave me alone, please.'

'Your clothes. Can I get them?'

She nodded, but made no attempt either to approach or turn away.

Martin picked up her bundle of clothes, stepped into the water and waded towards her. He passed her a t-shirt. His hands, she saw, were trembling. She looked at the shirt.

'Thanks.'

'You're cold, April. You're shivering.'

'Yes.'

'Are you going to come out of the water?'

'Yes.'

'Sometime this week?'

She smiled. He was holding out his hands. She looked at them. She took them. She allowed him to pull her back to the bank. She saw his eyes flick down to the scar, still visible on her thighs. She muttered,

'You've been spying on me, Martin.'

Martin blushed. 'I'm sorry. I didn't know you were – I was worried about you, and I thought – well, anyway, I didn't know you had gone to wash, and –'

She cut across him. 'You saw me crying.'

'April, I'm sorry. I shouldn't have seen that.'

She began to cry again. It was his gentleness: she could bear anything else. She sobbed into her hands. Her shoulders shook. Martin wrapped his arms around her. She leant against him. He did not flinch.

He pulled her t-shirt on over her head. Because he hadn't flinched before, she didn't flinch as he did this. She watched him stare at her face. His eyes flicked down to the point where her scar began.

Tentatively, he touched the scar with the tip of his finger.

His touch was light and tender. He traced the scar down, over her hips and then to the insides of her thighs. She shivered. His hand stopped just above her knee. He knelt down onto the wet riverbank, leaned towards her, and kissed her lightly on that spot. April knelt down too. She placed both hands on either side of his face. They stared at one another. She drew Martin's face towards her. She kissed his eyelids, his hair, his salty skin. His mouth. She thought: this man is kind. I love this kind man.

She held his arm all the way back, unable to speak.
As they reached the camp, he turned to her and kissed her once again, lightly, on her forehead.

'Night then.'

She said, 'That was nice.' Her voice air-stewardess bright.

She saw a brief, puzzled expression flash across his face. 'Well. It was definitely my pleasure.'

'It really was nice.'

Martin nodded, squeezed her hand and left.

She stared after him.

She crawled into her hut. She glared at the wooden slats above her head.

'That was *nice*.'

What a word to choose. Of everything she could have said. As if he was a tour guide and she'd just had a pleasant day.

She groaned. She wanted to go back and try again, not fail, do something. He was with Sam now, probably asleep already. Too late.

'Tomorrow,' she assured herself. She would tell him tomorrow.

Tell him what? Tell him the whole sorry story of her life, probably, and maybe it was better to say nothing. Maybe it was better just to feel, if only briefly, that thing Hardwick had talked about: that here was someone who could see right into her damaged little soul, yet seemed to believe – Lord knows how – that she was all right.

She wanted to laugh. Martin, of all people. Dumb, naïve Martin. April was a realist: she knew such things did not last. But it had happened. Yes, she would allow herself that. It had happened.

She sat up. She had remembered something. She crawled towards her bag, unzipped it, and fished inside for her father's crumpled note. She tore it in half with one clean rip. She folded the two pieces and tore them again, repeating the action many times until the note was in a thousand tiny pieces. She scuttled to the opening of the hut and threw them high into the air. They floated down, snow in the jungle.

Martin walked back to Hardwick, trying to work out what it was he felt.

A mixture of things. Elation was one of them. What happened had been shocking and thrilling. Glorious. Yes: he said the word out loud. Glorious.

He had gone to find her because he had been worried about her. He had seen her nakedness, seen her distress, and both had caught at his heart. There was something brave about her thin body, although he couldn't explain what it was. Her tears were brave too: he understood what it cost her to cry in front of him. When he'd held her, he'd wanted to cry too.

He broke into a grin. He was impatient for the next morning. He wanted to speak to her again, look at her, kiss her. He wanted to laugh out loud. Sam was sleeping, so he smiled instead.

All this was the bubbly top note of his feelings. Underneath was something sadder. April's grief had shocked him. He had comforted her, he knew: the harder he'd held her, the more he'd felt her body relax. But he hadn't understood the strange strength of her emotion, nor the meaning of her distress.

Martin frowned, frustrated with himself and his too familiar inadequacies. He wanted to understand. It was not enough to blunder and hope for the best. This time it was important. This time he wanted to get it right.

He jumped up. He couldn't sit still: he had to walk, get some movement in his limbs. He thrust his hand into his pockets and danced in a small rapid circle. Then, knowing he wouldn't sleep just yet, walked to where Hardwick was still sitting.

Hardwick made no sign of having noticed him. Martin hesitated, caught off guard by his appearance: the man was terribly thin, and his hair, unruly always, was wild and matted. When had this happened? Why hadn't he noticed it before?

Martin cleared his throat. 'Are you all right?'

'What?' Hardwick looked up. His eyes, though directed at Martin, were cloudy and unfocused.

Martin shuffled. 'Oh. Nothing.' He sat down, embarrassed. 'It must be late.'

'Yes, it must.'

'It was interesting, wasn't it? Van's story?'

'It was.'

Martin pressed on. 'He must be pretty courageous. To go through all that.'

'Yes.' Hardwick's voice registered a flicker of interest. 'Or Stoic, at least.'

Martin asked, wishing to draw him on, 'Meaning?'

Hardwick smiled, a small, reflective smile that Martin couldn't fathom. He intoned: '*I must die. If forthwith, I die; and if a little later, I will take lunch now — since the hour for lunch has come — and afterwards I will die at the appointed time.*'

273

Martin stared at him. 'You what?'

'Epictetus,' answered Hardwick. 'A Stoic philosopher. He believed that one could become impervious to one's fate through the exercise of will alone. Must have been a dreadful pain, if you ask me.'

Martin guffawed. He was light-headed, fizzing with his recent memory of April. He pictured her, and more laughter spilled out of him. Of course, it was natural – he embraced it – that Hardwick should make him laugh like this, should deflate his anxiety with some dry observation. He wiped his eyes.

He said, 'For a minute there I was worried about you.'

'About me?' Hardwick seemed surprised, touched. 'Goodness, don't trouble yourself about me. There are – other things –'

Martin smiled. He thrust out his hand. 'Sleep well, mate. Don't let the bed bugs bite.'

Hardwick nodded gravely. He said, 'I shall try.'

Hardwick shambled back to his hut. He tried to sleep, but – despite Martin's instruction – he could not. It was the infernal heat, he supposed. After all this time he was still not used to it, and his ineffectual attempts to move some of the air around by flapping his hand only left him hotter than before.

It wasn't only the heat. His mind would not be still. It was crammed with Van's story, stuffed with the countless impressions he had accumulated on the journey. The experiences of the last months were richer than all the thin fare of preceding years put together. Used to a meagre diet of experience – the routine of teaching, the habit of Felicity – this richness was hard to digest.

He was sick, too, of being helpless. His impotence offended him. The one true act of his life – the text message to Lorraine flung out into the void – had gone unanswered.

And now he was here, in this place where misery thickened the air, and all he could do was listen and watch as he slurped the food these people gave him. Shameful. That was the true Hardwick: well intentioned perhaps, fiddling away at the puzzles history set him. Faced with more pressing questions, he had nothing at all to say.

He had thought, once, when he was a young man and on fire with a love of knowledge, that he would die for truth. More recently he had told himself that he would die for Felicity. Were these just words?

Too many questions. No answers. He turned and struggled, trying to mould his back to the hard floor.

Sam's mouth moved while he slept. He was dreaming. A frown fluttered like a feather over his forehead. The dream troubled him.

He dreamt of a faraway place, a place rich with memories but elusive nevertheless. A dream place. A house. He saw the stairs, a door, a room. His bed. Yes, his house. He saw Jen, smiling, her teeth white. She was bending over him, and her rich red hair brushed his face. He reached out his hand. He was sad when he should be happy. He wanted his daddy, that was what it was. No, it wasn't that: he liked it here in his own neat bed. He wanted not to be hot. He wanted so many things. It hurt to want so many different things, because although they each seemed quite simple he could never fit them together, and however much he forced them it was obvious, really, that something was wrong.

That was it.

He wanted to go home.

6

Corporal Paysonge made his move against the camp early, just as a fringe of light began to filter through the air.

An unseen blow juddered Martin awake. He tried to sit up but another blow threw him against the side of the hut. Sam landed against him like starfish, and although Martin saw the boy scream, a third explosion drowned out the sound, so there was only the circle of Sam's mouth and a strange thunderous stillness.

When the noise died Martin crawled to edge of the hut and looked out.

All around him men were diving for cover. He saw why. The edge of the forest had caught fire: trees were going up like torches, sending out billows of smoke across the camp. Martin's eyes watered. Through the haze, he saw April crouching on the ground, protecting her heavy black bag as if it were a child. Around her men ran with bare backs exposed to the sky. The skinny boy Martin remembered from the football game was clutching his leg. Blood seeped through his fingers.

Martin looked for Van but couldn't make him out.

He was about to dive back into the hut when a sudden lull arrested him. He crawled back to the opening, his heart thumping, and squinted for the cause.

Smoke cleared. Through the pall he saw the lanky figure of Hardwick standing graceful and alone in the middle of the camp. Hardwick looked dazed, as if he had no idea where he was. He was so incongruous a figure – dignified and perplexed – that the men in the camp, and whoever was firing on them, seemed momentarily spellbound by the sight.

Martin opened his mouth to shout.

Hardwick stirred. He lifted his head.

He began to walk, slowly and with purpose, directly towards the source of the fire.

To be truly heroic is to master your fear, so Hardwick had always believed. He believed, also, that this was not something he would ever be able to do.

In his final moments he was proved right, though only in part. He did not overcome his fear. It coursed through his unsteady limbs, clutched at his hollow chest. He was weak with fear; with each step, he believed he must fall.

He was right only in part, because although his brain screamed at him to stop, he knew without question that he must go on.

He walked because he hoped that their shadowy attackers might share the shock that he himself felt at his recklessness. Even if the shock lasted only a few moments, it might be enough to give his friends a chance to escape.

So he hoped. And his hope seemed justified. All eyes were fixed on him, and nobody moved as he walked slowly forwards, his head erect and his white hair flying. Birds and insects fell silent. The wind dropped.

The jungle was beautiful. He lifted his head, steadied his breathing, and walked.

His thoughts began to dart, haphazard as mayflies in an Oxford meadow. He saw Felicity, then Lorraine, then the little nightclub singer from Van's story. Their faces swam together, merged, became one. He brushed them away.

Elation rose in him. It was an odd thing, this prickling sensation, this lightness in his blood. He had a name for it.

Happiness.

Corporal Paysonge kept the outlandish figure in his sights, even though he, like his men, had no inclination to shoot. His heart was beating hard. This was, of course, one of the foreigners he'd been pursuing for so long. He should have no compunction, really, to end his life.

He felt stirrings of fear, as most people will when confronted with something alien to them. He did not, though, find the requisite hatred. The man was old. Though he was trying to walk steadily, Paysonge could sense his terror. And there was his flying hair, and his great height: was this not the image of the *Pha Nom,* the Big Man, whom the *Khia* insisted would arrive one day to save them? If so, then to fire would be useless anyway: the *Pha Nom* was impervious to bullets. Paysonge knew, without asking, that his men were thinking the same thing.

The figure stumbled and slowly righted itself, and Paysonge was certain: this was no legendary saviour. He was an old and frightened man, doing his best – and how extraordinary that he was attempting it – to draw their fire.

Paysonge's finger loosened on the trigger of his gun. He turned to his men impulsively, deciding to give the order not to shoot.

As he turned, he heard a crack. His heart sunk like lead.

Martin was the first to react. Like the others, at first he had simply gaped as Hardwick, tall and vulnerable, walked towards the guns. His first thought was that Hardwick had gone mad, his wits unbalanced at last by the heat. When it dawned on him what the man was doing, his mouth fell. Hardwick seemed to him then, as he had seemed to Paysonge, something extra-human, not the polite, vague man he knew. He remembered the cave, and how April had called Hardwick the god of that place. He wondered, for a brief moment, if Hardwick had become more than he appeared.

Hardwick stumbled a little and was a man again, and Martin felt something else.

Love.

He knew that he must act quickly. Holding Sam in his arms he ran towards April, still hunched over her black bag. He urged her up and they ran together out of the camp.

He heard the crack of the bullet that killed Hardwick, saw, in his minds eye, the gangly figure crumple inwards at the chest and fall. But he did not turn to look.

April stumbled onwards, her head down, panting. Martin's grip on her arm was painful. The jungle swallowed them.

She looked back and saw no one. They were not being pursued. Her relief at this was soon replaced by another fear: she had no idea where they were going, and without food or water their survival skills were minimal. She smelt sulphur in the air. Behind her, the trees were burning.

She turned to Martin. She was about to shout at him to stop when she heard other breath panting, more feet running. A moment later she saw a flash of brown skin. Soon Van's hand was on her shoulder. With a nod, the old man indicated that he would guide them.

April moved on. The undergrowth was tangled. She pushed through it, fighting for each step. She could feel thorns prickling her, and sticky sap smeared her arms. She ached with the weight of the dollars in her black bag. Van was choosing his route carefully, taking unexpected turns and doubling back on himself. Their progress was horribly slow.

No one spoke.

She didn't want to think about Hardwick, or what he had done for them.

The sun rose high. Martin was grateful for the shade the trees offered; whenever they reached a gap in the leafy canopy, heat crashed down on him. As it was, humidity was a sticky soup they had to wade through. He slowed, and looked at April. Her face was set in a grimace, but she held herself upright and walked steadily, clutching her bag to her chest just as Martin clutched Sam.

Blankness overtook him.

Midday came and went. The sun rose to its ferocious full height and began to descend. After a time, Martin's mind drifted. Van and April were there but separate, outside of the bubble into which his reality had contracted. It was only Sam that he was connected to, through the weight in his arms and the tug at his heart.

As the sun set they reached the river, and the bridge that Van's father had built. Van stopped.

'Here,' he whispered. 'This is where you cross.'

Martin sank to the ground. He stared at the two soldiers in the middle of the bridge. He began to shake.

'It's impossible, isn't it?' he whispered. 'They'll shoot us on sight.'

Van cocked his head. 'Then you must go back to the jungle.' His tone was flat.

Martin sighed. 'No. We can't do that, it's obvious. You brought us this far. Thank you.'

Van nodded. 'You trust me now.' It was a statement rather than a question.

'Yes. We trust you,' Martin said.

'Then you must try.'

April asked, her eyes narrowed, 'Have you tried?'

Van laughed. 'No. I have not tried. But I am Van. You are April. You can try.'

Martin looked down at Sam. 'What do you think?' he asked. 'Shall we try?'

Sam nodded. Of course they should try.

April looked at them, the stocky man and the small boy, both resolute in their different ways. She shook her head, knowing she was more of a coward than both of them. She turned to Van, and thrust her black bag into his arms.

She said, 'I think you know what this is. I thought you would take it from me on the first night. But you didn't. You could have, and you didn't. I don't know why.' She paused. Something stuck in her throat. She said, hurriedly, 'Anyway. It doesn't belong to me. I want you to take it.'

Van took the bag. 'Thank you.' He smiled. 'If he could, my friend would thank you too. Mo would thank you.'

April nodded.

She turned back to Martin, and took Sam's free hand. She smiled at them both.

'Well. What are we waiting for?'

The three of them stepped, hand in hand, onto the bridge.